For the inspirational Jenny Brown,
my wise and generous agent

Scotland

FYVIE
CASTLE

ABERDEEN

LOCH LEVEN
CASTLE

STIRLING
CASTLE

DUNFERMLINE
PALACE

EDINBURGH

HOLYROOD
PALACE

DALKEITH
PALACE

TO
FRANCE

"A rich atmospheric novel, giving voice to the women of Scotland's past." *Ailish Sinclair*

"All the ingredients of a thrilling read – royal jewels, a secret compartment, family intrigue, ghostly superstition and a treacherous husband." *Sara Sheridan*

"Brilliantly evokes the lives of the women around Mary Queen of Scots ... Beautifully written. I loved it." *Elisabeth Gifford*

Praise for Sue Lawrence's previous writing:

"From the Jacobite intrigues of eighteenth-century Edinburgh to Scotland's dark and sea-battered islands ... eye-popping incident. An amazing story." *Sally Magnusson*

"Swept me along breathlessly ... The cruelty and complexity of eighteenth-century Scottish society is richly represented. And what a story to uncover!" *Dr Annie Gray*

"An imaginative telling of an extraordinary true story ... against a wild landscape in unforgiving times." *Sarah Maine*

"A fascinating historical novel ... utterly compelling ... a book we'd highly recommend." *Undiscovered Scotland*

"A haunting, moving story." *Kirsty Wark*

"Enthralling. It's a cracking story beautifully told." *Lorraine Kelly*

"Sue Lawrence is a rock star." *Guardian*

"Plenty of intrigue, there is much to enjoy here ... smart twists ... particularly strong descriptions ... her characters are all distinct individuals." *Louise Fairbairn, Scotland on Sunday*

"Excellent ... Intriguing ... Full of fear and danger [and] page-turning ... many twists and turns." *Historical Novels Review*

"Lawrence's parallel plotlines advance in lock-step with each other over alternate chapters ... until they're entwined to great effect towards the end." *Sunday Herald*

"A gripping tale." *Daily Record*

"Fascinating ... Lawrence's skill of storytelling allows for the tension to really build throughout." *Scottish Field*

"The intertwined stories ... will keep you in suspense until the very end ... Enthralling and beautifully written." *Brisbanista*

Also by Sue Lawrence:

The Unreliable Death of Lady Grange
Down to the Sea
The Last Train
Fields of Blue Flax

The
Green
Lady

SUE LAWRENCE

CONTRABAND

Published by Contraband,
an imprint of Saraband,
3 Clairmont Gardens
Glasgow, G3 7LW
www.saraband.net

ISBN: 9781913393328

1 2 3 4 5 6 7 8 9

Printed and bound in Great Britain by Clays Ltd, Elcograf S.p.A.

Prologue

He turned the heavy iron key in the lock and pushed at the knotted oak door. The elderly nun swept past him, then turned to hear him whisper, "I'm sure the master would only permit one short prayer with her, My Lady."

A haughty raise of the chin. "And I am sure your master, my nephew, need not know the minutes, or indeed hours, my devotions might take." She motioned to the door. "I will send for you when I am ready to leave."

The short, unkempt man opened his mouth to speak again but she dismissed him with a flick of her hand. He withdrew, and the towering figure in grey, with her white cloth wimple wound around her head and neck, stepped away from the door and into the cramped room. She shivered in the damp cold and looked up at the unglazed window opening, the only source of light. The door creaked shut behind her and she crunched her way over debris and twigs towards the bed. A putrid smell hung in the air.

She wondered if she was too late; the body was lying so silent, pale and still. But then there was a wheezing cough and a shuddering of emaciated shoulders as the blankets shifted. She sat down gently on the filthy covers.

"Lilias, my dear." She took a bony hand in hers. "I cannot ask if you are well, for it is obvious you are not. The sight of you saddens me greatly."

The eyes blinked open slowly and she tried to lift her head, to no avail. The nun stretched out both arms and pulled the skeletal figure up with gentle hands, cradling her like a child.

"Oh Marie, it is you," the woman in the bed whispered. "You've come to help me. God be praised." She ran her tongue around her cracked, chapped lips. "After my last confinement ended in yet another girl, Alexander sent me away from her – and all my little ones – to this cold, wretched place. To die."

"Your husband sent me a letter telling me you'd been suffering from digestive complications for the past few months and couldn't keep food down, that you were near the end. I took the decision to come and see you, so I arrived by boat this morning. Without his knowledge."

She shook her head. "No, Marie. He was lying." She panted, as if struggling to breathe. "He is so set upon a male child, he is determined to marry another; I mentioned her to you, I think, in my last letters, before I was brought here." She turned her watery grey eyes up towards the nun. "He is starving me to death."

Part One

Chapter One

1615

Marie Seton

As I lie on my bed, not far from death, I have asked Sister Agnes to bring me over my journals and my letters, which I have not looked at for so many years. I feel ready to reflect on my long life before I begin my journey into the next. I had just received news that Alexander Seton, now Lord Chancellor of Scotland, is to begin preparations for the royal visit from London to Scotland next year. The plan is for King James and Queen Anne to tour the country, from Dunbar to Aberdeen, presumably at great expense. The King never travels without hundreds of servants and horses and probably the entire Court and its attendant trappings. But my nephew Alexander has never been one to let the mere matter of money get in the way of his great schemes.

I believe he was generously rewarded for his guardianship of Prince Charles who, in his first few years while his parents were in London, was brought up by Alexander at his properties in Scotland, including Fyvie Castle. As well as receiving an annual income, my nephew was also made Earl of Dunfermline. And now that the young prince's elder brother Henry is dead, Charles will be the next king of England and Scotland. How Alexander will be rubbing his hands in glee that he brought up the future King Charles I of Great Britain.

But, as I lie here thinking about my life and my relationship with Alexander Seton and also with his first wife, Lilias, I wonder what would happen if his royal patrons knew what he actually was. Then perhaps he would not be lauded as one of the greatest men in Scotland, one of the finest legal minds and among the

5

most gifted patrons of the arts. If only I had the King's ear, as I had his mother's ear during all my many years in her service. His mother is now more often spoken of as Mary, Queen of Scots, even though she was not only Queen of Scotland but also Queen of France, and her name, like mine, was Marie, not Mary.

I sigh as I think back to those times, when I was one of her four Maries, at first her childhood companions and friends in France, then later, at Court in Scotland, her ladies-in-waiting. But whereas the other three abandoned her when their men came courting, I was the one to remain loyal and true, though I too had to leave her shortly before her death. That I regret even to this day.

I force my ancient, arthritic bones upwards in the bed so that my head can rest against the cold stone wall. I pick up my diary and flick back through the pages to those happy times when, instead of wearing this simple habit of coarse grey wool, I would dress in fine Court attire, in gowns of silk and velvet, with gold and jewels woven into the fabric and pearls plaited through my hair, and all of this even more sumptuous and lavish at special banquets and assemblies.

I have a notion to read more about life back then and, in doing so, remember the conversations I'd always meticulously recorded. I had wanted my journal to be not just a written account of what happened, but a memory of all the voices. I inserted comments and addenda along the way in later years. And now I shall listen to them all again, whisperings in my ear of old promises and of secrets and lies.

The Diary of Marie Seton
March 1565

Mary Livingstone's wedding was a splendid affair. The Queen had insisted the celebrations take place at Court, and she provided a lavish banquet of fine French dishes. The brilliant musicians ensured we could all dance until dawn, as if we were still young girls. She had paid for Mary's wedding dress too, but this was, in my opinion, far too ornate for a mere Marie. It was as if she were a royal bride. John Semphill's face when he saw his bride's gown was a picture. It was almost as extravagant as one of the Queen's own, studded with pearls and flecked with silver.

Our first names are never uttered by her, only our surnames; Mary is the name only to be used by Her Royal Majesty, she insists. And so we follow suit, obediently, though usually we call each other by our French name, Marie. As well as it meaning maid, the other definition of Marie – as a virgin – is also being eroded, as the first of us became married. I for one, however, do not intend to renounce my vow of chastity for any eager man, no matter what his standing. My brother George would not permit my marrying a man of lower status, but when the other Maries and I had discussed whether John Semphill was of high enough rank for Livingstone, they did not seem to mind. And obviously the Queen did not either, so that was that.

The dancing at the wedding was joyful and raucous and as the day grew into night and more and more candles were lit, the jewelled tassels on the cushions sparkled and the gold thread on the wall tapestries glittered. It was already looking magical and then, just as the servants were refilling our goblets, she arrived. She had evidently decided she would not show up till late – she always liked to make an entrance. If this were anyone else, I might have wondered if it was deliberate, to upstage the bride, but with the

Queen that was impossible, for she was always kind and loyal to her friends.

We Maries all bowed low, curtsying in our usual manner, with arms spread out as if in supplication. When we stood up tall again, Livingstone gushed with joy and rushed over to embrace her as if she were not just a Queen but a goddess. Then, as the music started up again and the Queen took to the dance floor, everyone gazed at her perfect face, flushed with colour, and at her beautiful purple gown trimmed with ermine, a new arrival from France. The only Marie as tall as she, I had, as usual, been the one to have had the honour to wear it in for her. I admit I did love the soft feel of the fur around my neck; it was wonderfully warm and sensuous.

Perhaps I was also the only one gazing critically at her red, lustrous hair, which would be dull and frizzy had I not attended to it some hours earlier, adding curl and bounce and sheen in the way, as she continually tells me, only I can arrange. Her crowning glory, she always says; well, wasn't that an ironic statement for a royal person? What would she do without me, she insists; yet where would I be without her, my Mistress, my friend, my Queen?

Mary Beaton sat down with a thump on the chair beside me. I smiled at my confidante and looked down at the fulsome figure bulging out of her blue gown. She leant forward to whisper in my ear.

"I can't shake him off. Can you please agree to dance with him?"

I looked around and asked who she was referring to, and she gestured over to a group of men, all white ruffs and glittering buckles and velvet doublets.

"You know, Randolph."

"Oh, the English ambassador. Well, no, he's not exactly handsome, is he?"

"He's also ancient. Same age as our parents." She glanced around. "But it's not just that: I'm convinced he is courting me to spy on our Queen."

"Really? I'm sure he wouldn't dare." I shook my head and patted her plump hand. "Let's go outside for a breath of air. I've had enough of the revelries for now."

We descended the narrow stairs in the tower and pushed open the outer door. We looked towards the high crags silhouetted under a star-filled sky and shivered as we walked. The March night was cold and there was a chill breeze in the air. Mary pointed over to the south.

"You know there are some ladies who have climbed up those cliffs?"

"Really?" I said. "Why on earth would a lady want to do that? They're so steep."

She shrugged. "To prove to their male companions that they are as good as them?"

"Ha! We know we are – we don't need to prove it!"

I chuckle as I recall saying that. There I was trying to insist that women were as able as men even though I knew then we were always physically weaker. And now I know we still have no agency, not an inkling of power – unless you are a Queen.

We stood arm in arm and I huddled close into her bosom for warmth.

I took one deep breath then shivered. "That's enough fresh air now, let's go back inside."

As we turned around, we were greeted by two figures leaving the palace. Squinting in the dark, I made out my brother and his son.

"George, is that you?"

He strode towards me and the boy ran alongside. We gathered

in the courtyard where there was a little light under the flambeau. George embraced me and his son bowed deeply as if before the Queen; he has always been a rather showy child, favouring the theatrical, which of course his royal godmother loves.

"Yes, I was trying to persuade Alexander that it was time he left for Seton Palace, but he is having none of it. Are you, my lad?" He looked down and patted the boy's head.

The lanky boy looked up at Mary Beaton and me and smiled. "Good evening, Aunt Marie. And Aunt Marie!" he sniggered as if he had just thought of the joke. Simply because he is the Queen's godson, he thinks he can get away with anything, and he likes to call all four of us his aunts, even though I am the only one officially qualified for that role.

"Is it not rather late for a ten-year-old to be out in the evening, young man?" Mary asked kindly.

He shook his head. "I'm nearly eleven. Besides, I can stay as long as I like; the Queen said so." He smirked and looked up at his father, whose devotion to his second son was rather too obvious, in my opinion; but what do I know about raising children?

I asked my brother when Alexander was due to go abroad for his education and he answered, with not a little pride, "He will leave in a few months for Rome and the College of Jesuits and then at some stage later, to Paris. It is all arranged. He should be away some ten years in all."

"Ten years! What a long time to be away from the family. And how do you feel about all this, Alexander?" I asked my nephew.

"It is God's will." He shrugged. "I shall learn as much as I can then come back to Scotland and take a wife who will bear me sons. Then I will take over from my father as Master of the Queen's Household."

I remember bursting out laughing. He was so assured for his age and had such ambition for a mere child.

"But surely that role would fall to your elder brother Robert. He is the one who will take over your father's title, after all."

The boy's eyes narrowed. "Robert might become Lord Seton after father's death, but I shall be a Lord in my own right. You wait and see, Aunt. I am already Prior of Pluscarden."

"For one so young to be honoured is nothing short of a miracle. He has such spirit, I believe he will achieve something remarkable," George said, patting his son on the shoulder and beaming with pride.

"But even if you should fulfil this dream and marry, Alexander," I said, "there is a good chance your wife may also have daughters." I smiled. "And then what?"

"That, Aunt, will never happen. Only sons can inherit, so what is the point of girls?"

I recall shivering once more, both with the cold and at the boy's steely resolve. And so I took my friend's arm and suggested we go inside.

I looked down at my nephew. "I await the next decade with interest, Alexander Seton."

And under the light of the flame, I saw in his eyes such a look of chilling defiance and determination that I knew he would stop at nothing.

Chapter Two

1615

The Diary of Marie Seton

June 1566

For the first few months of 1615, though our roles are now different after Livingstone's and then Beaton's weddings, we four Maries have been at the Queen's side as often as possible during her pregnancy. When the Court moved up from Holyrood to the security of Edinburgh Castle for her confinement, we were together constantly. In comparison to the luxurious Holyrood Palace one mile down the hill, the castle was cold and draughty. There were fewer wall hangings and tapestries at the castle, so any heat from the fireplace seemed to disappear into the bare stone walls. Also, perhaps because the castle was at the top of the hill, the windows always let in blasts of chilly air from the north. Only the Queen was allowed to wear ermine and so we Maries tried not to shiver as we all huddled around the royal bed, pulling the drapes around as we perched on the embroidered bedspread, gazing at her increasingly huge belly in wonder.

It was during these weeks that the Queen let us all know how much she values us.

After her marriage, Livingstone had been entrusted with looking after the Queen's collection of jewellery. The rest of us accepted this as a fact, though Fleming mentioned to me one day that she was the one who ought to have been given this honour, since only she was a direct cousin of the Queen. But then when we heard what would happen should the Queen die, we complied with her every wish, as we always did with our Mistress.

Well, I certainly was happy with everything, although none of the jewellery pieces we were promised then, during those happy weeks spent together around the royal bed, were as splendid as the parure the Queen gave to me some ten years later, her gratitude for my long service and friendship.

It was about a month before she gave birth that she let us all know who would receive what, should she die in childbirth, something which filled her – and of course us – with such dread. We four Maries were to have many of the splendid possessions from her jewellery collection. I turned back some pages to remind myself what we were each promised.

Mary Fleming was to receive her favoured white enamelled necklace and the set of gold beads and chains. Mary Beaton would have three enamelled chains and an emerald necklace she had always admired. Mary Livingstone was to receive a pearl belt, some chains and a gold necklace. And as for me, surely the most loyal Marie, I was to have three gold enamelled brooches and some pearls, which I'd always adored and indeed had often worn before she went out for a soiree, to warm them up. The Queen could not possibly have to endure the feel of cold jewels around her delicate white neck. We were each to have one of her special ruby rings as keepsakes, whether she lived or died.

Indeed, I have worn mine on my thumb almost always, a constant reminder of the woman I served for so long, Queen Mary. Sometimes I ponder how strange it is that for the rest of my life, I have then served her namesake, the Virgin Mary.

The bed at the castle provided for her lying-in was magnificent: fringed in embroidered black velvet, it had curtains of blue velvet, lined in scarlet taffeta. The baby's cradle was covered with embroidered Flemish cloth of cream and purple. The midwife wore a black velvet dress, created especially for the occasion, and the drapes and hangings in her lying-in chamber were hung all around with royal blue taffeta and silk. We four Maries giggled when we first saw the luxurious extravagance of the bed as we imagined what John Knox might say about the bright gaudy colours and textiles and how inappropriate they were for bringing a royal prince into the world.

The day her son arrived was momentous. She began her labour on the eighteenth of June and during those many hours of excruciating pain, all four of us, her Maries and best friends, told her repeatedly we wished the pangs of labour could be cast upon us. Let us endure the pain, we whispered, willing the agony upon ourselves. If only this were possible; anything to alleviate her distress and discomfort. But of course this was not to be.

What a terrible ordeal mothers must go through. The agony they have to endure is unbelievable. As I continued to cross myself, along with the other Maries, terrified at the prospect of catastrophe, of the fact she might not survive the trauma and pain, I assured myself once again that I'll never put myself through this. The only one constant in my life, should the Queen die, would be God. I will never take any man into my life to cause this agony.

Finally, she gave birth on the nineteenth of June to a healthy and chubby baby boy whom she immediately called James, after her father, grandfather and indeed all her royal forebears. While the midwife was cleaning up the child, we helped wash and change the Queen. Dear God, what a lot of blood there was everywhere. Afterwards, she held the prince and gazed at his face, smiling dotingly as presumably only mothers can do, for the baby truly is not bonny. He has tufts of black hair all over his bald head and his nose, even for a tiny infant, is long and pointed, not snubbed and pretty like the Queen's. She sighed with a contented air, then announced that he was in need of feeding – surely this was the cause of his sudden bawling – and could the wet nurse come at once.

Later that evening, Lady Reres was still sitting in the corner, a soft, woollen stole enveloping both her massive breasts and the tiny, swaddled child. She had continued to feed the hungry child almost without a break as we all cooed over the baby and cosseted his mother, until we were all startled by a sudden boom as the full artillery was fired from the castle. The young prince did not stir one jot from the milky breast as we Maries rushed to the window and looked out to see the many bonfires blazing brightly on the surrounding hills.

"You should see all the fires, Your Majesty. All over your kingdom they are celebrating," cried Mary Beaton, jumping up and down as she always does when she is excited. Really, she can be so childish. "You have brought such joy to everyone!" She gurgled with delight.

The Queen lifted her weary head from the pillow and propped herself onto an elbow as she tried to peer over towards the window.

"Perhaps not to my cousin Elizabeth in London," she muttered. And I could not help but notice a sardonic smile on her lips.

Then she slumped back onto the bed and shut her eyes, exhausted and in need of a long, restorative sleep.

Chapter Three

1615

The Diary of Marie Seton
May 1568

I stood at the window watching the tiny boat glide across the loch. I held my breath as long as possible, not daring to move till I saw it reach the shore. There, a man – presumably my brother – helped her out and over the reeds onto a waiting horse. Only then, when I saw her sit upright in the saddle and ride off beside him, did I allow myself to sigh with relief.

But now what would become of me? My heart was thumping as I sat down on the chair and nodded, smiling with relief, to the serving woman at the door. Like me, she had been waiting, wondering if the plan was going to work. She would have to unbar the door shortly and they would soon find that the tall figure standing at the window dressed in regal finery was not in fact the Queen, but a mere lady-in-waiting, impersonating her, as she made her escape. What punishment would be fit for a traitor such as I?

I remember the feeling of dread and apprehension as I waited to be discovered. And when I was, after the initial fury, they locked me in the room while they went after her. They took their time deciding what to do with me. And during those anxious days, I had never felt so lonely – nor so proud – for I was the one who had enabled Queen Mary to escape from the prison of Loch Leven Castle. And though solitude became my companion later in life during my many years at the convent, it was at Loch Leven Castle that I found it was isolation that irked. It was the first prison I had been in, although it wasn't an actual prison; we were not kept in the dungeon with bars on the windows. But it was the first of many castles I ended up staying in with the Queen during her captivity. I flicked back through the pages.

October 1567

Loch Leven Castle in Fife is reasonably comfortable, certainly less draughty than Edinburgh Castle, but it is the freedom to come and go that is lacking. The Queen does not allow talk of the word "imprisonment", but there is no other term.

Apart from a small area of garden outside, where we are permitted to take a turn in the fresh air once a day, we are stranded on a tiny island in the middle of a loch some thirty miles from home. The Queen yearns not only for the opulence of the Court, but also for the simple things she enjoys such as hunting and riding. One day, she said she even missed her regular spats with John Knox.

Also, it is so quiet. Gone is the bustle of courtiers and the shuffle of servants. We have always been accustomed to our full quota of Maries, yet now I am alone, the only one lady-in-waiting to the Queen. Where there had been dozens and dozens of attendants to answer her every beck and call, now there is only a handful.

During the months we've been confined to a castle in the middle of Loch Leven, I have come to find company in loneliness. Yes, she wants me to sit beside her as we sew and stitch, and yet in those first few weeks, she remained silent, especially after the tragedy of her miscarriage. She hardly spoke after that. And because I know her so well, I knew that after it was all over and she began to feel physically stronger I should not mention it ever again.

But even when she decided to get out of bed and wanted to get dressed again, attending to some official business now and then, it was obvious her heart was broken. She was perhaps thinking of Bothwell or of her dead husband Darnley, but most of all, she was clearly thinking about her child. The little prince was being well cared for at Stirling Castle, but he should be with his mother. We were even nearer Stirling from Loch Leven than Edinburgh, and she said this somehow made her feel the loss even more.

Well versed as I am in her often volatile moods, I knew better than to engage her in conversation; and so I simply kept my peace and waited until she felt able to return to discourse. As well as missing her baby, she also feels her country has abandoned her. France is no longer her home and now Scotland, where we've lived for six long and happy years, seems to be forsaking her. The Lords are determined to get rid of her and now there is the young prince, they have a new sovereign. They could divest themselves of this troublesome woman.

Gone is the fun and gaiety we had enjoyed at Holyrood Palace: the masked balls, sumptuous dinners and dancing, the latter much to the annoyance of Old Johnnie Knox. She hated it when we Maries call him that. But, after all, he was ancient – fifty-four – when he married poor Margaret Stewart, who was only just seventeen. When the Queen railed against the betrothal, the nobles around her suggested she pick her battles elsewhere, that John Knox was already too powerful. And Margaret's father, Lord Ochiltree, had always had it in for his regal cousin. I would not put it past him to take up arms against the Queen. He is a traitor, so unlike my loyal family. The Setons are always there for her and she knows it. She treasures all of us and has clung to us faithfully over the years, as we have to her.

The Queen and I spent eleven long months at Loch Leven castle and everyday life, sadly, was dull. I recall we had dinners instead of banquets and, though the food was acceptable, it was nothing compared to the elegant creations cooked by the French chefs in Edinburgh. I read on and smiled at the memory of one dinner.

Yesterday, we had goat meat for dinner, which so horrified the queen she flung the ashet from her table onto the floor.

"Je suis votre reine, pas une paysanne des champs!"

Where are her fine gilded quails, her capons with rosemary, and her favourite goose roasted with prunes from Bordeaux? The cook at the island castle only seems to own two spices – cloves and cinnamon – and these overpower everything with their brashness. We miss the delicate flavours of saffron, mace and ginger. Even the claret is not fresh and too often is doctored and served highly spiced and overly sweet.

At Holyrood, after the Queen had chosen the choicest morsels for her own plate, we four Maries ate and the courtiers were served, then finally the assembled servants, from tailors, milliners, grooms and cupbearers down to the table servers. But here at Loch Leven, the attendants are far fewer and so I note that they all eat in great quantity – if not in quality.

I skimmed forward through the diary, recalling that it did not take the Queen many weeks after her miscarriage to forego the silence and to begin her daily whisperings. I of course was the recipient of her muted conversation, and because there were undoubtedly spies in every chamber, I had to lean in close to hear. I can still recall inhaling the heady aroma of the damask rosewater she rubbed lavishly all over her white neck every morning. It gave me the same feeling of intimacy I enjoyed when I attended to the Queen's hair, brushing out her auburn locks then rubbing in the cinnamon oil I'd had Joan, the kitchen maid, produce. I'll never forget her, the only servant there with any sort of brain; the first one I'd asked used a whole forpet of cinnamon in the oil and it was so strong the Queen nearly fainted and felt nauseous all day. When Joan eventually produced the oil according to my own receipt, it worked as well as the one I'd used at Holyrood. It helped me untangle and shape her beautiful hair, then thread through the pearls and ribbons she wore every day, whether at Court or in this new state of imprisonment.

March 1568

After many weeks of silence, she has begun to converse in agitated whisperings. And though "escape" is the one word she never utters, the notion of it hangs in the air between us. She has been staring at me strangely for some time, as if measuring my height, and so when she told me in those hushed tones that I could easily impersonate her, since I was as tall as her, at last I understood why. And as she revealed her plan, I knew what I had to do when the time was right: I was to pretend to be her, dressed as a Queen in all her finery, with furs, velvet and jewels, while I stood at the window of our first-floor chamber, for anyone to see.

And all the while, down below, dressed as an ordinary country-woman, she would escape across the loch to safety in a little boat rowed by young Willie, the page. He is such a good and faithful servant, a kind lad who is much loved by the Queen.

My brother George, Lord Seton, would be on the far shore await-ing the arrival of the boat, and he'd help her up onto her horse. Then, together with his men, they would head south to Niddry Castle to assemble their loyal troops.

Thankfully, that May morning when I'd pretended to be the Queen at the window, they managed to evade capture, but not for long. It all ended badly at the battle of Langside where those treacherous Lords, including of course John Knox's father-in-law Lord Ochiltree, defeated her and managed to scatter her loyal forces far and wide.

I recall so well those ten anxious days' waiting, imprisoned in that room in the castle, while my keepers decided my fate. Then one morning, the door was unlocked and the Earl himself walked in. He told me I was a treacherous and disloyal servant of Scotland, and I steeled myself for words of hanging – or worse – but then he announced that I was of no importance and so could leave Loch Leven Castle unpunished. I left in a daze that afternoon and joined her at Langside where the ill-fated battle had just begun.

It was a relief to be once more at her side, even though our long years together as prisoners were starting over again, this time not in the comfort and familiarity of Scotland, but in England, where, under the keen eye of her English cousin, our lives were to change forever.

Chapter Four

1615

The Diary of Marie Seton
April 1575

There is no more magnificent gift from the Queen than my parure, given to me this afternoon. She has been a prisoner now for some seven years, first at Carlisle Castle then at Bolton Castle, Wingfield Manor and now here at Sheffield Castle, but most often at dank, dingy Tutbury Castle. There, the Queen and I spent many days, weeks, months and indeed years, huddling to try to keep warm as we bent over our embroidery, often with Bess of Hardwick, wife of the Queen's keeper, the Earl of Shrewsbury.

Today will be etched in my memory forever. The Queen had one of her maids call me from my chamber to visit her and she bade me sit beside her. After my customary deep curtsy, I looked up at her and saw her broad smile. She had a glint in her eye, one I have come to know well.

"Seton," she said, "of all my Maries, you have been the most dedicated, the most faithful and the most loyal. You have worn in my dresses and my shoes and warmed up my pearls and gold necklaces. You have tended my hair, so that, even though it's now thinning and dull, you manage to make it shiny and lustrous. And most of all, you, out of all my Maries, have remained devoted."

She took the velvet case from her lap and handed it to me. "This is a small token of my appreciation, dear friend." She beamed then leant towards me as I opened the case.

I could not help myself gasp as I lifted the necklace, earrings and brooch up towards the candlelight where the gems twinkled and shone. The gold was fashioned into exquisite scrolls and snake links, with large and smaller pearls, rubies and delicate circles of tiny emeralds surrounding the pearls in both the necklace and the earrings. I do not think I have ever seen such intricate work, even in the Queen's own jewels. I could not speak, I was so overcome by the beauty of them.

"The gold came from Crawford Muir in the south-west of my realm. During my father's reign, the gold mined there was used to start producing the pieces in the Scottish regalia. The gold is the finest in the world."

She took the necklace from me and held it up to the candlelight where it twinkled and gleamed, then laid it on my open palm.

"You shall wear the parure to remember me, Marie, when I am gone."

"Madam, I shall wear it now to remember your kindness."

And I gestured over to a maid to help clasp the necklace round my neck.

"And so perhaps all thoughts of your going to Aunt Renee's convent might be banished for a while." She smiled and I realised only then that this was more than a gift of friendship, this was affirmation that I should stay with her, if necessary, to the end. I took up the brooch and held it up once more to the light where it shone and sparkled.

I slipped off the seat and knelt before her, offering my hand, which she kissed. I am bound to her forever now, I thought as I touched the bejewelled gold chain around my neck.

I remember thinking that though this was not exactly a manifestation of serfdom or slavery, there was no doubt that she had always been and would always be my Mistress. Even as I look round the austerity of my small cell here in Reims, devoid of luxury or indeed of any embellishment at all, I feel proud to have served a Queen for most of my long, blessed life.

October 1584

After what seems like an interminably long sixteen years serving the Queen in captivity and in various levels of damp discomfort and cold confinement, when my bones have ached from morning till night and my heart is tight with sorrow, I know I have to start thinking of myself, of my own well-being. And the only way ahead therefore is for me to retire from her service, something that would have been unthinkable ten years ago, but now is becoming an imperative.

George has written to say he is to travel to France next spring on a mission for the Queen and has suggested I travel with him to ensure my health, which has been failing, does not suffer any longer.

In the Seton family, it is a tradition that the unmarried middle-aged women retire to a convent for their last years. I know I will never marry, so surely now is the time to devote myself to God rather than to my Queen? After many discussions with the Queen, she has eventually agreed it would be better for my health that I leave her, and I have accepted the invitation that I received so many years ago, when I was still a young woman. At last, I will join the Abbey of Saint Pierre in Reims, whose Abbess is the Queen's aunt, Renee de Guise.

During those years of indecision when she came to rely more and more on me, her only Marie, I often could not sleep for worrying. But then early one morning as I lay in the dark before the hope of light that the dawn brings, I asked myself a question: if she were me, would she continue in service, to the detriment of her health? Or would she grasp this opportunity and for once think of herself? I knew immediately the answer. Once my decision had been taken, I felt neither fear nor trepidation, and of course she acquiesced, with *tears and sighs, but also with fortitude; this is, after all, her battle with her cousin, Elizabeth, not mine.*

But first, before I exchange one form of incarceration for another, I need to live, for just a short period, in freedom. Since George is not leaving for France till the month of March in 1585, I agreed that I would first recuperate with my family. It's been decided that I would travel, after a short stay at Seton Palace with George, to Fyvie Castle in Aberdeenshire, which his son Alexander has just bought from Andrew Meldrum of Drumoak. My nephew wants to show it to me before I leave for France, and I too am excited to see what is soon to become another Seton family home.

I shut my eyes tight as I remember writing these words and the excitement I felt in my new venture, including a visit to my nephew's new property. I believed it could be the last time I would set foot in Scotland. As it turned out, of course, it was not, and I had to return another sixteen years later to attempt to put right the wrongs my brother's son had visited upon his own dear wife.

It was during those few months of freedom residing up at Fyvie that I first met Lilias Drummond. She was not even fifteen, yet already betrothed to my shrewd, ambitious nephew, Alexander Seton. There was such an immediate connection between Lilias and me, even with the age difference; I was already forty-three years old. And by the end of my stay there in the wilds of Aberdeenshire, I had decided without any doubt that it was she who would be the recipient of my beautiful parure once I had gone. Those sparkling rubies, emeralds and pearls would be so beautiful around her fair neck.

Such spontaneity was not in my nature, but I felt somehow that God had guided me to this decision. Alexander may have been the Queen's godson, but to me, Lilias was more than a goddaughter could ever have been; she was the daughter I never had.

Chapter Five

1585

Lilias

Mama swept into my chamber, looked me up and down, then sighed.

"Why are you wearing that green gown, Lilias? I thought your sisters told you to wear the blue one, it becomes your fair hair more. It is not just a baptism we are attending. You are about to meet your future husband for the first time. Everyone will be looking at you."

"You know I hate to be centre of attention, Mama. And I don't see why he isn't marrying one of my sisters. He is ancient and I am not even fifteen."

"You will be fifteen in a month and your fiancé is only thirty. And he has never been married before, so you have the most perfect match. It's unusual for a gentleman of his age and standing. Besides, your younger sisters are not yet of age. And though it's unfortunate that Catherine's fiancé has just died, we will find another suitable union for her and..."

"If you and Papa would stop choosing fiancés who are twice our age, this might not happen,."

She flicked her hand at my interruption and continued. "But as for you, dear child, your father and I have been working on the alliance for some time now, since the days we were close neighbours of the Setons in East Lothian."

I adjusted the lace at my neck and looked at my mother. I knew what she going to say next. I'd heard it all before.

"And now we live up here in the north, it is even more perfect that Alexander has just bought Fyvie Castle. You will be Lady Fyvie after the wedding and live in that most beautiful place. It's the talk of Aberdeenshire, you know. He has transformed the castle from dour Scots to classic French in style. It was so clever of him to employ an architect from France. The results are quite stunning. They say it is like a château on the Loire."

"So I've heard," I muttered, while pulling an errant strand of hair behind my ear.

"Here, let me do that. Can your maid never manage to fix your hair neatly as I continually ask her to?" Mama yanked my locks up and I winced as she pushed the clasp in tight.

She headed for the door. "We leave presently, Lilias. Please do your best, we have invested a lot in this espousal. Be charming. Smile. Pay attention to the baby with the other ladies. That will make your future husband even more interested in you."

"You know I love babies. In fact, I'd far rather stay here with my own baby brother. But you won't allow that, I suppose?" I smiled, anticipating her response.

"On no account. Sweetheart, your father and I are delighted with your betrothal. It's not as if you are our first daughter, with the pick of beaux. Now, shoulders back. Remember you hail from the illustrious family of Lord Drummond of Drummond Castle!"

With that, she flounced out. I love Mama, truly I do, but sometimes she puts outside appearances, rank and nobility above everything else. And now she had eight children to consider, she hardly had much time for us individually. But we always felt cherished. We all craved her attention as she was both warm and affectionate, but Papa expected her to tend to him too. So we children have always been far down her list of priorities – and, for the six of us girls, even more so.

I bent down in front of the glass to check my hair; it would just have to do. I picked up my shawl from the bed and followed Mama down the stairs to the front door to prepare for the journey to Fyvie Castle.

I will never forget my first sight of Fyvie. Whereas Drummond Castle is an ancient dark fortress built in cold grey stone purely for defence and certainly not beauty, the stonework of Fyvie Castle seemed to be bathed in a hazy pink, rosy hue, against the brilliant blue January sky. There was a magical air about it, and as we trotted up the slope towards the entrance, I marvelled at how elegant it looked, not at all what I was used to.

Mama stole a glance at me and smiled. "You see what I said, Lilias. Isn't this castle something else? It's the French, you see, they have such style."

I had to admit she was right.

Grooms rushed out to help us down from our horses, which were then taken through the open portcullis, clip-clopping through the pend over the stone cobbles into the courtyard beyond. I walked forward and looked up at the stone arch high above the dark oak of the open entrance door. Underneath this triumphal arch were three windows and each had a coat of arms beneath, presumably belonging to the families who had previously owned the castle. I then looked to either side of the entrance way where there were two tiny narrow windows.

"These are the two guardrooms, Lilias. Fyvie would have required considerable fortification in the past."

Looking at the heavy portcullis and solid door studded with iron bolts, it certainly seemed secure to me.

"I think I told you it was also a royal residence in the past. Princess Matilda, daughter of Robert the Bruce, lived here. And though our own dear Queen has not visited – and sadly is unlikely to do so now – the Setons are perhaps her most loyal Lords. She depended upon them so much after those treacherous noblemen abandoned her. And your husband-to-be is of course her godson."

Mama beamed, delighted at our impending royal connection. "As I said, this castle has a long and glorious history."

I nodded. My sister Jean was fascinated by all Mama's tales of grandeur, and indeed had she been my age instead of only twelve, I would have insisted she marry this Alexander. I did not care for any of this, certainly not marrying someone so old.

"Mama, remind me again about the baptism. Why is it here and not at Rothes?"

She pointed over her right shoulder at a red sandstone building with a belfry, adjoining a stone wall that surrounded a beautiful garden.

"The chapel here is small but splendid. Any noble family nearby would be happy to have their child christened here. But in this case, James Leslie, the Master of Rothes, and his wife Margaret wanted the baby christened here while their chapel is being renovated. It's too cold in January with an open roof for a newborn, even well wrapped up. They are old friends of Fyvie. Their connection to the castle goes back a long way; their family is of good stock. In fact, if the Master was not married to his own wife, I would have been delighted for one of my girls to marry him." She tilted her head to one side and smiled. "I hear she is always poorly, so who knows what may transpire."

"Mama! You must not say such things!"

She leant in close as we were about to enter the castle. "But do remember the other reason we are here is not the baby or its parents; it is for you to meet your future family and to stay awhile. I hope they will, as suggested, extend the invitation for you to reside here for a few weeks. That is why we have packed an extensive wardrobe."

She turned to check the luggage was being unloaded as she had requested.

"I believe Alexander's aunt Marie Seton is here at the moment.

You will enjoy her company. She is not only a striking woman –
the same height as our Queen – but a formidable character. She
is leaving in a few weeks for France to take the veil at the convent
run by the Queen's aunt. She is a woman dedicated to service –
first of all, for all those years, to her Queen, and now to God."

I wrapped my shawl tight around my shoulders as we stood in
front of the dark entrance before stepping over the threshold on
the tiptoe of expectation.

Chapter Six
1980
Maggie

I got off the bus at Priory Cottages and waved at the driver.

"Thanks again for all your help," I shouted as he climbed back up the steps and into his seat. Happy to assist when I'd boarded in Aberdeen asking if I could get off at the top of the road near Fyvie Castle, he'd just swung my weighty bag down the steps for me. He deposited it at my feet with a wink.

"What's in here then? A dead body?"

I grinned as I watched the Elgin bus pull away and hitched up my rucksack onto my back, then grabbed the handles of the heavy duffel bag to pull it along on its base. It was far too heavy to carry. I'd stuffed so many books into it, it was bulging.

Soon I realised that the base would collapse if I pulled it for the next mile on this bumpy road riddled with potholes and stones, so I hauled the handles up and swung it over one shoulder, cursing the fact all the books were hardback. When Mum had asked how on earth I'd manage – "You'll never be able to pull that heavy bag for a long walk!" – I'd laughed.

"Mum, I'm still only nineteen, not ninety. I'll be fine, stop fretting."

But as my shoulder began to ache, I realised that as usual Mum was right. This was not easy.

She'd shaken her head and muttered again about how ridiculous it was Dad had never let her learn to drive and I raised my eyebrows as usual about the word "let". Under normal circumstances, Dad would obviously have driven me here himself, taking pride in my new job, but now I'd no choice but to get the train to Aberdeen then the number thirty-five bus to Elgin. When I thought of Dad, I still always felt choked, tearful, but what was done was done and there was no changing what had happened.

When Mum and I had pored over the Aberdeenshire map to locate the castle, she'd pointed out Old Meldrum just down the road from Fyvie.

"That's where my Granny Owen came from. Her maiden name was Forbes, which I'm pretty sure is a local name." She chuckled. "She used to roll her 'r's so much, it was comical. When she said Meldrum, I got a fit of the giggles."

Since Mum never talked about her family, I was fascinated, but as usual she changed the subject when I probed about this granny. I took a deep breath and continued along the narrow road, pausing now and then to shift the weight by swinging the bag over to the other shoulder.

The word Owen in my head, I then smiled as the lines of one of the poems I'd studied for my Higher English came to mind, since my back was hunched and stooping with the weight. I muttered the words to myself as I trudged along. *"Bent double, like old beggars under sacks/ Knock-kneed, coughing like hags..."*

And then I spent the next five minutes trying to remember the rest of the verse.

Soon I came to the entrance gates to the castle, two tall, elegant stone pillars with a wide iron gate in between. This was closed, but beside the right-hand pillar was a sloping wall with an ornate gate inside. I tried the handle and thankfully it pushed open. Presumably the main gates were only open during visiting hours. I continued shuffling along the road, looking up at the tall trees on the verges. Among the oak and sycamore, there was a beautiful copper beech on the left. Mum's love of trees used to annoy me on family walks, but I now realised, as an adult, how useful it was.

There was a small loch on the right and I needed a break so

slumped down on the verge, under a beech tree, dumping my bag on the grass. I pulled out Mum's thermos flask from my rucksack, wishing it had cold water in it and not hot tea, but it quenched my thirst a little anyway. I looked over the water where some ducks and moorhens were bobbing about. Behind them was a little stone boathouse with a wooden door painted green.

I looked up to where some sparrows were flitting about in the branches of the tall trees above me, chirruping and twittering. The whole scene was a bucolic idyll, this beautiful countryside and the blue sky with a few feathery cirrus clouds forming high above the low, puffy cumulus. I sighed as I remembered the only reason I knew the names for all the clouds was because of Len, and so tried to think of something else, hoping that this would all fade in my memory.

History was my love, not clouds and weather. I shoved my thermos back into my bag, lugged my heavy duffel bag up onto my shoulder again, and continued along the road, waiting for my first glimpse of the castle. The more I thought about what I was about to embark on, the more apprehensive I became. This was not jittery excitement about the possibility of new adventures, it was in fact a cold feeling of foreboding, almost a fear of what lay ahead in this, my first summer spent completely on my own.

But, as Mum had told me as she drew me into a tight hug at the station that morning, I could do anything I wanted. I deserved to be happy now, she'd whispered, and everything would work out fine. That was so like Mum: though she too had been unbelievably sad about what had happened, her first thoughts were only ever about me. She'd swept my wayward hair off my forehead and told me to look to the future. Given my past, surely that was the only possible way.

I had just left the loch behind when I passed a row of trees on the left and let out a gasp. I flung down my bag and took in the sight up the slope before me. There it was, the pink sandstone castle with turrets and the crow-stepped gables I'd read so much about. It really was the fairytale castle I had seen in the photos. I smiled, picked up my bag and continued walking along the drive. My cumbersome luggage felt somehow lighter and my spirits lifted as I approached the dark oak entrance door. Everything was going to be fine.

Chapter Seven

1585

Lilias

The chapel was freezing, even with a roof on. I huddled into Mama and looked towards the front where the priest stood by the tiny altar. He nodded to someone in the first row and a gentleman stood up, then a tall, stately older lady beside him, holding the baby. I strained my neck to try to see the baby's face, but she was tightly wrapped in her shawl. Mama nudged me and whispered. "That is not Margaret Leslie carrying the baby. It's Marie Seton, your betrothed's aunt. I wonder where the mother is."

We did not have to wait any longer to find out. The priest then began the sacrament by telling us how very sadly the baby's mother had died just a few days earlier, and though her funeral had just taken place, the Master of Rothes still wanted his little daughter to be baptised as planned, in case she too was taken to join her mother.

Well, I know it's a fact that many women die in childbirth, but the priest's announcement came as rather a shock. Not that I had met the lady, but it seemed rather sad. Though as I looked around, I was not aware of anyone in this freezing chapel looking mournful in the least. In fact, as the tiny baby began to bawl and yell and a servant came running to the front to relieve Marie Seton of the wriggling creature, people were smiling, as if the death of a mother meant so little. I shivered in the glacial air and knelt down on the cold stone floor, on the priest's command.

After the ceremony, as we entered the castle, I asked Mama whether I ought to offer the father my condolences, but she shook her head. "That would not be appropriate. That was last week. Today is about the new birth, not death."

She peered at the impressive shields and swords hanging on the walls as we climbed up some magnificent wide stone steps to the Great Hall, then turned to whisper, "You go over and speak to the ladies, make a fuss of the baby. I am off to speak to the Master of Rothes about Catherine."

"Who?"

"Your elder sister, Catherine, of course. It is perfect timing."

"Mama," I hissed, "his wife is barely cold in the ground."

She gave me one of her looks.

"Go! Pay attention to the baby. And of course your future husband." She turned around, then murmured over her shoulder, "And Lilias, do not forget to curtsy deeply before Marie Seton." With that, she turned and headed for the baby's father while I forced myself to smile as I walked towards the gaggle of ladies cooing around the crib.

I did as Mama had said and waited till Marie Seton had acknowledged I was standing beside her then inclined my head, bobbed a little, and smiled. It did not feel right to bow low; she had served the Queen but she was not royal.

"You must be Lilias," she said, smiling. She looked me up and down, then took both my hands in hers. "I knew Alexander would make a perfect match. He has always chosen well, in every single thing in his life."

I was about to say that neither he nor I had much to do with the matchmaking but I held my tongue.

"What a charming colour that green is on you, Lilias. It so becomes you with your fair hair. I always notice ladies' hair." She smiled conspiratorially. "I coiffed Her Majesty's beautiful hair, you know."

"Really? I have never seen her in person of course, but have seen a portrait. She is beautiful. And so tall." And then I blushed, for Marie Seton was surely just as tall.

"Come, let us remove ourselves from this throng of admiring ladies. I can tell you all about how I did her hair." She looked down towards the crib. "I never do quite understand the attraction of tiny babies, do you?"

"I admit I rather like them." I peered down towards the baby whose tiny body was swaddled in so many shawls; even in this cold hall, she must be hot. "But she's sleeping now, so I won't pick her up. Is Grizel a family name?"

"Yes, the infant's grandmother was Grizel, Countess of Rothes. I believe she died giving birth to the baby's father, the gentleman your mother is speaking to over there. Strange, isn't it, how things come round full circle."

She leant towards me and I noticed her wrinkles and the flecks of grey in her hair. I realised that she must be in her early forties.

"In case you were wondering, I am not a godparent. Indeed, I hardly know the Rothes family, but Alexander thought it appropriate for me to carry the baby in church. He has some odd ideas, as you will surely come to know."

She led me over to two chairs by a little table and a servant pulled back hers.

"Now, tell me about yourself, Lilias. I believe you are fifteen years of age?"

"Actually, not till next month, February fifteenth." I looked up at Marie, the lines around her dark eyes crinkling as she smiled.

"What a delightful scent of roses," she said, leaning towards me and sniffing the air.

I laughed. My sisters and I had taken to drying roses last summer when it had been so hot and our days were spent languidly in the castle gardens while mother prepared to give birth. "It's the rosewater my sisters and I made last year."

"You must tell me what roses you use. In the past, I made rosewater from damask roses for the Queen, before..."

There was a noise of boots clacking together and we looked up to see a man, perhaps about thirty years old, standing before us. He had an angular face made even narrower by a long, pointed beard, which was red, whereas the hair on his scalp was more a dull brown. I realised I was staring at this inconsistency when he addressed me; and then I knew who he was and I blushed.

"Aunt Marie, I have not yet had the pleasure of being introduced to my betrothed."

And with that, he inclined his head and swept his arm out in an exaggerated manner. "I am Alexander Seton, as I believe you must know." He smiled, almost a cheeky grin, and looked at his aunt for an introduction.

"Alexander, may I introduce Miss Lilias Drummond. She is to stay here at Fyvie with us awhile, I believe."

I took in his whole body, which was bony and slender, and attempted a smile to cover my shyness.

"I am pleased to meet you, sir. I had heard of Fyvie Castle but had never imagined it would be this beautiful."

He nodded. "It's quite something, is it not? Perhaps I can take you for a tour of the castle and gardens in the next few days. For now, I shall leave you to gossip with my aunt, but I look forward to talking to you more over supper, once the infant has gone."

He leaned over and addressed us both. "Though why all this fuss has been made over a baby girl, I don't know." He chuckled and turned on his heels, and I looked at his aunt who shook her head.

"Do not worry about my nephew. Forgive me for saying this, I share this with you as a doting aunt: Alexander is rather full of himself, as if he has not yet sloughed away his teenage swagger." She smiled. "But he always was indulged rather, first by his father and also by the Queen. Even as a boy, he could be dismissive about girls, insisting their only purpose was to grow up and produce sons."

Lilias

I frowned.

"Ridiculous. But then, one day when I asked him why he only wanted sons, he looked directly at me and said, 'Aunt Marie, I am the fourth son of a first son. I may not inherit the title of Lord Seton, but I will do everything I can to become something even higher in rank. Only male heirs will help me achieve that.' I keep hoping he will change."

She sighed and took my hand in her veined one.

"And you, my dear Lilias, seem like just the girl to help with that."

Chapter Eight

1585

Lilias

After the baptism, I noticed Mama talking for a long time to the Master of Rothes and indeed there was laughter as well as Mama's well-rehearsed looks of compassion and sympathy.

As he was leaving that afternoon with the baby and his older children, she said, "I look forward to welcoming you to Drummond Castle, whenever I am back. That should be in the next day or two."

I stared at her in astonishment; I realised she'd gone ahead and proposed to this recently widowed gentleman that he marry my older sister, Catherine.

As we waved them away, I turned on Mama. "His wife's only just died. Is it not rather soon?"

Mama tickled my chin in that way she did and smiled. "It's never too soon, my child. Your sister is already nearly seventeen, which is almost too old for a first-time bride. Now, let's go to our chamber. You can wear my pearl necklace at supper. The pearls will go well with that green. I think the gown is really rather plain, without brocade or embroidery around the neckline, but I was talking to Marie Seton and she told me how much she admired the dress. I think she is already fond of you." Mama gave me a kiss on the cheek. "Keep that friendship alive, Lilias. When the Queen is released, you may be asked to become a lady-in-waiting in her place; you know Marie Seton is going soon to France, don't you?"

"Do you actually think the Queen will be let go, Mama? Papa says her cousin the English queen wants rid of her. Once and for all."

Mama shivered. "Do not say such things, Lilias Drummond. Our Queen will return to the throne, just you wait and see."

She flounced off upstairs and I ran to catch her up.

At supper, I was seated beside Alexander while Mama sat near enough to ensure I gave him full attention. I tried to be good company for my future husband who, I now saw by the flickering candlelight, was in fact not as bad looking as I had first thought; indeed he was rather handsome. He was telling me his plans for the continuing renovation of the castle. Most of the outside work and glazing were complete, as was much of the interior decoration. But his focus was also on converting the grounds into gardens that would rival the Loire châteaux, with elegant terraces surrounded by balustrades.

His eyes lit up as he explained that there were already knot gardens in front of the castle's south entrance, but he planned to enhance these with stone statues and arbours with entwined branches. I was entranced as he became more animated, sharing with me what obviously was his passion. He was even hoping to have peacocks in the enclosed gardens. Fortunately, Mama had briefed me on some of this – even on the oddity of a peacock surviving a winter in Aberdeenshire – and so I hoped I conversed with him in an interesting manner. He was such a worldly-wise man, having travelled so much in Europe. In comparison, I knew nothing, yet I found myself enthralled by him and knew I was willing to learn. I kept looking over to Mama, but she was so busy speaking to Marie Seton that she didn't notice how hard I was trying.

After supper, as Alexander led me away from the table, Marie Seton came towards us and took my arm.

"Alexander, if you don't mind, I have something to show your betrothed."

He inclined his head and turned towards the door.

"Let us go over to the window seat," she said. "I have something I want you to see."

We sat on the cushions under the window and I pulled my shawl around me as a bitter draught swirled in from around the panes.

"The colour of your dress reminded me of something, Lilias, and I remembered what it was when I was in my chamber. And I wanted to show you."

She tilted her head and put her hand behind her ear lobe so that I could see her earring. It was the most wonderful piece of jewellery I had ever seen. They were droplets of pearls with two rubies at the base. Surrounding the two large pearls were circles of emeralds, which twinkled and glittered by the candlelight. I was mesmerised.

"Do you like them, Lilias?"

I beamed. "I have never seen anything as beautiful, Lady Seton."

"Since you are about to marry my nephew, you must call me Marie – or Aunt Marie, if you must."

I was dazzled by the earrings and kept staring at them.

"Do you see why I wanted to show you them? The emeralds are the same colour as your dress. They would look wonderful on you. And there is also a brooch – though that does not have emeralds – and the most exquisite necklace you have ever seen. It has the pearls – large and small – and also many rubies and these same circles of emeralds."

She leant back. "Where do you think I got such beautiful things?"

I shook my head, feigning ignorance. Surely there was only one person who could own such jewels.

"They were a gift from the Queen. Not many people know, of course. Well, why would I tell any of the other Maries – that's what she called us, her ladies-in-waiting – they'd only be jealous." She laughed. "The Queen gave me all three pieces in the parure as thanks for my service over so many years."

Her smile faded and she looked wistful.

"I should of course still be with her, by her side. Sometimes I think I was wrong to have left her. But it is with her blessing that I go – in only a few weeks – to the convent in France to pass the rest of my days. My health was truly suffering in those dank, musty castles in England. Fyvie Castle can be a little chilly, but is certainly not nearly as damp. Your future husband has done some marvellous renovations."

She took a deep breath. "I feel so much better up here in Aberdeenshire, being able to walk outside in the fresh air at leisure, and I am sure I'll feel as healthy in France."

I nodded. I could not think what to say and I was beginning to feel so sleepy after the long journey earlier that morning.

"Is there anything you would like as a wedding gift, Lilias? Do please think about this and let me know. You will be married shortly after I leave for the convent and so I'd like to discuss this now before I go."

She grabbed my hand. "I feel so lucky to have some time left here at Fyvie with you though, my dear. We can get to know each other better. Let us take a walk in the grounds together tomorrow."

She stood up, arching her back and wincing. "I often have such pains down my back and in my joints."

I could not help thinking that convent life would also be beset with icy draughts and cold floors, but what did I know about both the weather of northern France and the comfort of a French convent?

"Good night, Aunt Marie," I said as we parted on the stairs. "I look forward to your company tomorrow." And I watched as she swept past me, those fabulous emeralds sparkling and glittering in the candlelight.

Chapter Nine

1585

Lilias

The next morning – and for several days afterwards – there was no walk in the grounds. On wakening, I looked outside and saw only sombre clouds of billowing snowflakes, swirling around. The ground was already white, covered with a thick blanket of snow. There were some footsteps, presumably from the grooms heading for the stables at the other side of the courtyard. My first thought was that Mama would not be able to leave today as she had hoped. She would just have to be patient, since the marriage discussions with my sister would obviously have to wait.

Instead of taking the air outside, I was invited to Marie Seton's bedchamber to join her for a light collation and some refreshments.

"Come, sit down, my dear. Try this." I sat beside her and took a sip. It was delicious wine. I had noticed that the wine and quality of the food at Fyvie were so much better than what I was used to at Drummond Castle.

"The difference between my nephew's wine and some of the offensive offerings the Queen and I have had to suffer during the past sixteen years is remarkable. Your future husband has an excellent cellar, but he did, after all, spend ten years in Europe acquainting himself with both the delights of fine wines in France and Italy and the usefulness of wine merchants."

She took a sip herself as I bit into a sweetmeat. "I cannot tell you how improved I feel in health after only a few weeks here."

As she put her glass down, I noticed a ring on her thumb. "Is that a ruby in your ring?"

"Yes, another gift from Her Majesty. Do you like it?"

"Yes, I do. I don't think I've seen such a large ruby before."

"Then you shall have it," she said pulling it off her thumb.

"No, no, it is yours," I cried. "It was from the Queen!"

She shook her head. "Remember, Lilias, I am about to take the veil. I shall have to renounce all worldly goods. No adornment such as jewellery can be worn." She smiled. "Though I will have a long think about my parure before I go."

I took it and put it on the third finger of my right hand. "Thank you, Aunt Marie, I shall treasure it."

"There, you see it fits perfectly where it ought to go. My fingers are too thin, always have been. And age does not help. Anything."

She pushed a tray of sweetmeats over towards me. I'd already had a rosewater one, which was so good. She watched me nibble on another then leant over and looked at my hair.

"Lilias, do you – or does your mother – have any long strings of pearls? I think that, given the length of your lovely hair, I could do some narrow plaits and weave the pearls in between, then coil it up, just as I used to do for the Queen."

I put my hand up to my hair. It had never occurred to me my hair was lovely.

"I'm sure she does. I shall try to look some out for the next time we meet."

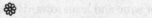

We spent many mornings together, even more once Mama had returned home. My afternoons were usually spent, certainly until the deep snow thawed, with my future husband in the Charter Room, listening to his continuing plans on the interior of the castle and his proposition for my portrait to be hung on the wall. He had commissioned a French artist, an acquaintance of the architect whose brilliant work was evident all over the exteriors of Fyvie, to come over from Paris before our marriage and paint me. I hoped that Marie Seton would still be here, for she could perhaps arrange my hair with those pearls in the way we had discussed and indeed demonstrated one morning. Mama had many attributes, but hair coiffure was not one of them. And none of our servants were skilled in attending to the fine details of a lady's toilette.

The wedding date was now set, since Mama had told Alexander she was keen for it to take place before Catherine's. I kept wondering what my sister thought about marrying a very much older man and one who already had six children, the youngest of whom was only weeks old. No doubt she would be expected to produce more children herself; was that the primary role of a wife?

This question I could never ask Mama as I know she would say yes of course, what else is a wife for? But one day, not long before my wedding and the day before she left for France, I talked to Marie about it. She raised an eyebrow.

"Do you know, Lilias, the day I witnessed the birth of Prince James at Edinburgh Castle was traumatic – obviously for the Queen, who could so easily have died, but also for all of us Maries. The other three have of course gone on to marry and produce children, but I vowed that day I would never take a husband."

There was a twitch of a smile as if a thought occurred. She took a sip of wine and leant towards me.

"I had beaux though, you know. Suitors came calling, but what with my own convictions and the fact that George would not have permitted me marrying anyone from a lower station, nothing ever happened."

Her brother George, Lord Seton, had arrived the previous week to rest before he set off with Marie to France to accompany her to the convent. It was interesting to see the difference between

Alexander and his father. Lord Seton was a kindly old gentleman who obviously adored his son, perhaps to the point of indulgence, as Marie had said. I sometimes wondered, during that time I spent at Fyvie before our wedding, if perhaps when we were married my husband might indulge me? Though the more I got to know him, the more I doubted it. Physically, he appeared more handsome with every day I saw him; and yet emotionally, he always seemed rather remote, as if thinking about something else, always in a hurry to move on to another project. Well, perhaps once we were married I would be the focus of his attention. Surely that was how it worked?

The day Marie told me about her suitors, we were walking in the grounds, strolling along the bank of the River Ythan. At last there was a hint of spring in the air, there were snowdrops all along the water's edge and there was a welcome return of bird-song. As we came to the little bridge, she stopped, took my arm and looked directly at me.

"I may appear to you as merely an old spinster, but don't forget, once I was young." She stroked a wrinkled cheek. "There was a gentleman called Andrew Beaton – no relation of Marie Beaton, by the way – who had become Master of the Queen's household during her captivity. My brother George previously held that noble post, as I'm sure you know. But he had to relinquish the role in order to undertake diplomatic missions for the Queen, mainly to France. And so we saw Andrew Beaton every day during our years in England imprisoned in those castles at Sheffield, Tutbury, Wingfield..."

She shivered, as if the memory of them brought back the chill she had suffered daily.

"Andrew began to seek out my company and, though I never thought any more about it, it was the Queen who told me one day that he had surely fallen in love with me. I didn't understand what that meant and certainly had not noticed, but the Queen was of course more versed in such things. So when I began to pay more attention to him, I realised it was true and I was in a state of turmoil when I considered the vow I'd made to myself all those years before."

"Did the Queen encourage the gentleman in pursuing you?" I asked, fascinated. How did anyone know another person loved them, unless it was their mother? That love, I realised, was unconditional.

"She did nothing to discourage him. Rather, it was I who discouraged him, not only because of my vow of chastity, but also I knew my brother would not approve." Marie sighed.

"What happened to him?"

"He died on a mission to France to try to obtain nullification of my vow. For I'd always agreed to go to the convent in France; it was simply a matter of when. That was way back in August 1577. When you were but a child." She smiled. "He managed to obtain the agreement of Renee de Guise that should I ever want to marry I could, and the vow could indeed be annulled. But sadly, it was all for nothing."

"What happened?" I touched Marie's hand; she was trembling.

"He set off from Calais and there was a terrible storm. He was drowned."

I didn't know what to say, so I just squeezed her hand and stole a glance at her face. It was unfathomable.

"I wondered afterwards if I did in fact love him; how does one know? But I suppose the main thing was the knowledge that he loved me. That I still keep in my heart."

As we walked back over the fields towards the castle in silence, I could not help but wonder if my future husband was in love with me; I don't know why, but I doubted it. Surely I could try to love him, though?

Chapter Ten

1586

Lilias

I was still becoming acquainted with marriage – and indeed with my husband – when I realised I was expecting our second child. Mama had said, when I gave birth to our first baby, Anne, only ten months after our wedding, "My darling daughter, you have fulfilled part of your wifely role." When I asked her what she meant, as I lay in bed, watching the wet nurse feed the baby in the corner, she said, "Isn't it obvious?"

"No, Mama. I have produced a healthy baby and I didn't die in childbirth. Surely that is enough?"

She smiled and stroked my cheek. "Lilias, sweetheart, it is all very well to have a beautiful daughter; I have six and am overjoyed. But I also have two sons and your father is content. So too will your husband be when he has a son."

When I realised I was to have a second child, I decided to tell my husband one morning while we waited for the servants to open the bedroom door and bring us our morning draught.

"That is good news, Lilias. Anne is not even a year old so that bodes well for your fecundity and my future children. I am convinced you will produce only sons now." He smiled and sat up, while I tried to take in his words.

"I am feeling rather nauseous, Alexander," I said, weakly.

"Oh well, that won't last long will it, my dear?" He gave me a peck on the cheek and sprang out of bed to open the curtains. "What a beautiful spring day. I shall be out hunting with Robert until the evening. Entertain the visitors well until then, be lavish and bountiful."

Our guests were his older brother Robert Seton, his wife Margaret and their children. Robert had taken over the title of Lord Seton after their father had died several months before. Their elder brother George had died when he was only twelve and so Robert, as second son, inherited. Interestingly, it was when Alexander told me the news of his father's death that I realised I did in fact know him rather well by now. For instead of looking sad or mournful, he raged and insisted he would have been better to inherit the family title since he was far more capable, even though he was already Lord Fyvie. His resentment about being born fourth seethed just below the surface.

Well, he had older brothers, what could he expect? Sometimes he was hard to fathom; at times he appeared rather sensitive, especially when telling me of the aesthetics of his beautiful gardens, and yet he seemed to place so much importance on rank. Although so did Mama, but she also stressed the significance of wifely duties, which I was still struggling with a little. But as I said to her, I was still only seventeen and was already expecting my second child. She just gave me one of her looks.

"Alexander, do you think you ought to write to Aunt Marie? Margaret said yesterday that she might not be aware there is going to be some sort of trial at Fotheringay Castle. Is that possible? Why would the Queen be on trial? She has done nothing wrong, surely."

He shook his head. "My godmother is innocent of all specious charges. Her cousin is merely jealous. But I'm sure we needn't worry, there is nothing she has the power to do."

"Queen Elizabeth would surely not execute her own cousin, would she?"

He swung round from the window, face contorted with rage. "Do not talk about things you don't understand, Lilias. Our fair Queen will emerge from these years of captivity and then all

England will be able to judge who is the stronger monarch."

I watched him stride towards his dressing room and slam the door. That was presumably part of what Mama said one had to put up with from a husband; though I cannot imagine Papa ever slamming doors or having rages. I was about to get up when I realised he still had not answered my question about Marie. Perhaps I ought to write; I would take guidance from Margaret Seton.

1587

"Sit down, Lilias, I have grave news," Alexander commanded as I entered the room, clutching my belly. Even though it was only recently confirmed, I was already big with this third pregnancy, which convinced my husband that I was carrying a fine, strapping boy.

"I have just heard from my brother. You remember the trial at Fotheringay last year?"

I nodded. He was looking very strained, indeed almost emotional.

"A deputation from London arrived there and Shrewsbury informed the Queen she had been found guilty and condemned to death."

I gasped. "Guilty of what?"

He swallowed. "Treason. The only excuse they could invent."

I was about to ask another question but noticed he was agitated, stamping about on his feet as if he stood on hot coals. I held my tongue, as I had become accustomed to doing, and soon he told me about how she was told of her death sentence only the night before she was executed. She was denied everything she asked for – her own chaplain, her own accounts and even her place of burial. She wanted to be interred in Reims, at Renee de

Guise's convent, doubtless in order that Aunt Marie could tend her grave and so that she could be laid to rest beside her mother. But no, nothing; all her requests were refused. She spent her last night alone without any company except for her servants, who were, understandably, hysterical and weeping around her.

I did not want my husband to continue, uncontrollable tears were already streaming down my face. I did not want to hear any more, but I had no choice but to listen.

"The following morning at eight o'clock, she walked into the Great Hall at Fotheringay in a manner more regal than her depraved, murderous cousin and, with great dignity and composure, accepted her death."

I wiped my tears and watched him close his eyes as if imagining the scene.

"She sent a message to her son to say she had never done anything to hinder the welfare of the kingdom of Scotland and her wish was that in time he would reign over both Scotland and England." He swallowed. "And then, with the utmost fortitude, she lay her beautiful head on the block and..." He shut his eyes. "Then they killed her."

The silence was thick in the room. I stretched out my hand to reach my husband's, but he swept it away.

"Our Queen was murdered. Murdered, Lilias!" He had an unhinged look. "Believe me, there will be a price to pay." He took a deep breath. "But in the meantime, we will rally round the prince – who is now of course King James." He crossed himself.

"Of course, God bless the King," I said, also crossing myself. "How old is he now?"

"Twenty, a mere boy."

He was distracted, fidgety. He darted away from me to look out the window and stood there for a while, breathing deeply as if trying to calm himself. His eyes narrowed as if he was trying to resolve something, but as I watched him, I said nothing; I knew better than to disturb him when he was in one of his moods. Slowly, he turned around and spoke in a low mutter. I leant towards him, straining to hear.

"He is already betrothed to Princess Anne of Denmark. We will invite him here soon. Alone or with his Danish bride."

I tried not to show surprise or indeed joy, but maintained an impassive face as my duty required. I waited and soon he continued. "So when they bear children, I swear on my unborn son's life that I will make Fyvie Castle their sanctuary. Just you wait and see, Lilias."

I did not like to point out that the new King was already Protestant and our Roman ways might not please him, but my husband was not only dogged, he was also resourceful – and exceedingly versatile. He had told me a few months before, at supper, that while he was in Rome as a teenager, he had been in a church with all the candles lit and glittering gold everywhere around the altar and the incense wafting and he suddenly asked himself if this was the right way to worship God. I was shocked – what alternative could there possibly be? – but he continued, telling me that perhaps there was value in some of the less luxurious and decidedly simpler Protestant ways.

He had mentioned that he might worship occasionally at Fyvie Church in the village, for Protestantism was all about public prayer and communion; I never imagined he actually meant it. But I remembered this now as he pledged to make the new protestant King and his future family friends of Fyvie. This could surely not happen if we continued with our Roman ways, and I knew that he would somehow achieve exactly what he set out to do, because he always did.

He turned back round and I could see his eyes blaze with determination and fire.

Chapter Eleven

The Diary of Marie Seton
February 1587

I will never forget today: the day I heard the Queen was executed. I was lying on my pallet, here at the convent of St Pierre in Reims, shivering in the February dawn, listening to the harsh, throaty calls of the *corneilles noires* in the trees outside, trying to recall the word in English for these black cawing birds. And then I remembered the name was carrion crow. Of course, how could I forget that? A crow, black and menacing in both its appearance and its ominous cry.

There was a knock at my door. How strange. No one calls at our doors, we all just rise at dawn, dress, then meet in the chapel for morning prayers.

"*Entrez!*"

I sat up as the Abbess, Renee de Guise, entered my room and sat on the wooden chair beside my bed.

I was about to speak but saw she had shut her eyes as if in prayer. I waited, trying to block out the noise from the murder of crows outside.

Eventually she spoke, in a hushed voice, as if she were about to reveal an awful secret. I was filled with a sudden dread.

"*Marie, j'ai des nouvelles graves, très graves.*" She breathed out, long and slow, as if trying to keep her composure.

I looked down at my hands as she began to speak. And I continued to stare at them, twisting my fingers round and round like a madwoman, as if trying to wring out and expel her vile account. I listened as she told me of her niece's death a fortnight earlier. She gave me few details, only that there had been a mock trial then an illegal and swift execution. She had been regal and dignified to the end, facing the horror with poise and grace.

I had not trusted myself to look at the Abbess's face as she spoke, but when I eventually wrenched my hands apart and raised my head, I glimpsed a face brimming with sorrow, an aunt trying to maintain her self-control as she recounted the murderous story. As I was still trying to understand how this could have happened, I saw her expression turn from anguish to fury.

She stood up and looked directly at me.

"*Maintenant il faut prier.*"

She told me that we must now all pray for Her Majesty's soul and for the well-being of the young prince. Then, instead of speaking of absolution and prayers of forgiveness, she finished by spitting out the words, "*Sa cousine, la reine d'Angleterre ... on ne lui pardonnera jamais.*" So there was to be no pardon granted, instead it seemed as if this holy woman was cursing Queen Elizabeth. Even with this enraged utterance, still she did not shed a single tear.

That was for me to do. She left the room, pulling the door shut, and the tears began to stream down my cheeks then all of a sudden I was shaking with sobs, bawling like a baby as my head filled with feelings of horror, of grief and of self-condemnation. For I should have been with her. Why had I not waited a mere two years longer before coming to the convent, and stayed with my Mistress when she surely needed me most? My health was nothing compared to the obligation I had abandoned, the duty I had relinquished.

I remember sitting for quite some time, considering what I should do. I wondered about going home, all the while regretting that I'd left her side. The other Maries would certainly never be blamed. I considered retreating to the Seton family home where I would surely be an embarrassment, perhaps always known as the

Marie who abandoned the Queen in her hour of need? I had no choice. I knew I had to continue my life of devotion here, come what may.

I wiped away my tears, swung my legs off the pallet and stamped my bare feet down onto the rough stone. I flung open my tiny window and the crows fluttered and flapped their wings then flew away, soaring in a great black cloud, heavenward.

I opened the drawer of my armoire and took out the ivory comb, the only vestige of my former life with Queen Mary. Everything else – all the fine gowns, the exquisite jewellery, the laces, brocades and silks – was gone from my life. I lifted it to my head and combed my greying hair, then dressed in haste. Clutching the fine comb in one hand, I took a deep breath before opening the door and striding along the cloisters walkway. I entered the chapel where I lay down on the cold stone floor and remained, prostrate with grief, the tines of the comb stabbing into the palm of my hand, until the Abbess came to lift me gently up for compline.

Part Two

Chapter Twelve

1980

Maggie

I stood at the entrance of Fyvie Castle and looked up at the turreted porch. I knew from my research that the older entryway was round to the south side, but now access was through this door here on the east. The coat of arms above was weathered but still stood proud against the worn pink sandstone. I had seen many pictures of the outside of the building and yet I had a shiver of excitement as I walked in through the great oak door.

"Come this way, Miss Hay." A stern woman of indeterminate age wearing tweeds appeared in the entrance hall and gestured to me to come in. She was unsmiling as I joined her inside and watched as she turned an enormous key in the lock behind us. She didn't offer to help with my bags, so I swung them on my shoulders and followed her further into the castle. There were suits of armour standing against every wall in this spacious hall, and heraldic shields and swords all around. I followed her over the worn flagstones to a broad staircase where she swept one arm up towards its many wide steps.

"This is Alexander Seton's magnificent wheel stair, the finest in Scotland."

She turned back round and pointed to my bags. "Leave those here and follow me into the morning room." As I climbed the worn steps, I looked up at more ornate shields with crossed swords and a beautiful stained-glass window with an ancient coat of arms embedded into the centre. I walked into the room and looked around, taking a deep breath. This room was stunning; all around the walls were portraits, some huge, presumably of ancestors of the owners of the castle.

"This was once the Great Hall, the main reception room of the castle." As I looked down at the thick carpet, I noticed my toes were becoming white with cold. Why did I think summer sandals and a light coat were a good idea for an ancient castle? Mum had told me I'd be freezing. I shivered; no wonder the woman had warm woollens on even though it was July. Inside the castle, it was chilly.

"Wait here. I shall fetch Mr David to meet you, then I'll take you on a brief tour." She looked at her watch. "The doors don't open until eleven so we should have enough time."

She swept off before I could even ask her name. All my correspondence had been with the factor, Mr Burnside; I had no idea who this Mr David was. I listened as the clicking heels faded and I looked up at the elaborately plastered ceiling, decorated with thistles and roses, perhaps created to celebrate the Union of the Crowns in 1603. I turned and looked at a tall portrait of a gentleman in full Highland regalia, in a classic setting. It had the look of an eighteenth-century portrait, but perhaps not by a Scottish artist. It was maybe Italian, I thought, and as I peered down to look at the signature, I heard a voice behind me.

"That's the Batoni portrait, painted in 1766, one of his finest." A tall, middle-aged man with silver-flecked dark hair and a ruddy complexion extended his hand.

"Miss Hay, welcome to Fyvie Castle." The handshake was limp and his palm damp.

"David Burnside," he said in a clipped voice. "Take a seat." He indicated an armchair by the fire, which was not lit.

I followed him and sat on the edge of the wide seat.

"So you wrote that you're at St Andrews University."

"Dundee."

He shrugged and continued, giving the impression he did not like to be interrupted. "And you're researching a dissertation on

Alexander Seton who used to own Fyvie. What exactly is the subject matter?"

I'd already given details of the title, sub-title and a synopsis of the contents, but I smiled and explained. "Yes, I start working on it next year, my Junior Honours year. The title's Alexander Seton, the power behind the thrones. It's basically about his influence on Mary, Queen of Scots' son, James VI, and later her grandson, Charles I."

"Yes, yes, of course, I remember now. And you want to do some research while working here at Fyvie?"

"Yes, when I saw you needed someone to help with the visitors' tours, I thought it'd be ideal as I could learn about the castle he owned for so many years." I snatched a look at him. He was gazing at my legs. I shifted in the chair and pulled my skirt tight around my bare knees. "But of course I would be doing my research only in my time off."

"I see. Well, I'm sure you'll settle in fine. This is only the second year we've had to open up to visitors. Some of the public are rather tiresome." He sighed then stood up and I sprang to my feet. "Alexander Seton must have been some man. Godson of Mary, Queen of Scots, advisor to King James VI, then guardian to Charles I. And bedded three wives and had at least ten sprogs." He chuckled. "Well, those were the legitimate ones." He started to head towards the door.

"Mrs MacPherson will take you on the tour. When are you meant to start your official duties?"

"You said Monday, so I could have the weekend to settle in and learn the ropes. I was to shadow the other guides until then."

"Jolly good." And off he strode, without even saying goodbye.

I was about to head for the stairs to try to find Mrs MacPherson when I heard the clip-clop of her sensible brogues climbing the steps, and in she walked.

"Your bags are being taken to your room in the Preston Tower. But while I have half an hour free, I'll show you round. It may help before you go on your first guided tour with Andrew after luncheon, as he'll have the visitors with him." She looked at her watch then headed towards the door at the far end. "Follow me."

I did as she said and we walked through to a smaller room with more stunning portraits on the wall. "Should I call Mr Burnside Mr David, by the way?" I wanted to get things right on day one.

"Yes, it's always been to differentiate from his cousin, Mr Charles Burnside, who is the laird and owner. You aren't likely to come across him, though, as he lives abroad. Nowadays at Fyvie, Mr David is the factor and in charge most of the time."

Calling a man Mr and his first name seemed to me rather odd, but I had no chance to speak as she was gesturing around the next room. "This is the back morning room, where we hang some of the thirteen Raeburn portraits."

I gazed at these impressive pictures hanging all round the walls, but she was already pushing open the door, so I sped after her as she walked across a landing and into a square room with two small windows letting in only a little sunlight. She flicked on a light switch and ushered me in.

"Now, this is the Charter Room. You'll hear on the guided tour about the important deeds and documents that were signed in here." She gesticulated in a bored manner to a far corner. "They say there's a secret chamber over there, but the guide will tell you more about that. Don't believe everything Andrew tells the public, though."

As I looked around the small dingy room with its dark wood panelling, all at once I was overtaken by a sudden feeling of melancholy. I have no idea where it came from, but my former feeling of light-heartedness vanished and I suddenly felt an overwhelming sadness. Perhaps it was simply because I was unsure if I did

Maggie

in fact want to spend three months of my summer holidays showing visitors around this ancient, freezing castle inhabited by cold,
unfriendly people. Or perhaps it was memories emerging from
the past.

63

Chapter Thirteen

1599

Lilias

I had just finished writing my monthly letter to Aunt Marie in France and was wondering when I might hear back from her. I'd made it a rule that, unless it was during one of my confinements or one of the children was ill, I wrote every four to six weeks if possible. I only received replies about twice a year, but I knew how much she appreciated my letters. I'd just replaced the quill in the ink when I was told the guests had arrived. My sister Catherine was coming to visit with her husband and some of his grown-up children, leaving their own two little ones at home since they were still infants. The youngest of the Master of Rothes' children with his previous wife Margaret was of course Grizel Leslie, whom I'd not seen since her baptism. That day they arrived at Fyvie was one that is forever etched in my memory.

On Alexander's insistence, I had organised a lavish reception, even though it was only my sister and her family, considerable though that was. But for some reason he wanted it all to be very grand. Because I knew him well by this stage, I presumed he had some scheme up his sleeve, as usual. Since he was about to become Lord President of the Court of Session, he would soon be away in Edinburgh even more, but he had been at Fyvie for quite a while recently. He enjoyed telling me how, having been the youngest ever lawyer in Scotland called to the bar, he was now regarded as one of the most influential and brilliant legal minds in the land. I always praised and encouraged him, which was of course what my wifely duties required.

I began to wonder about this grand reception for my sister and her family: was this so that he could arrange a betrothal between one of our daughters and one of Catherine's stepsons? Though considering the eldest of my girls was only thirteen, I hoped this was not the case. Also, I was still feeling rather weak as it was still only six months since my precious little Margaret had been born. I was exhausted with childbirth, and the threat of death seemed somehow to haunt the castle; after her sister's death two years before, I felt the weight of mourning and sadness every day for my dear little girl, taken too soon. All this seemed to pass my husband by.

We received the guests in the Great Hall, and as I greeted everyone, I could not help but notice Alexander peer over everyone's heads as if he was looking for someone. Soon he came over to where Catherine and I stood talking. In his flamboyant manner, he gave her a salutary bow.

"Dear sister-in-law, it's so good to see all your family here. But I cannot see the Master's youngest daughter, Grizel?"

"Oh, she is certainly here somewhere. Let me find her for you."

Catherine sped away while my husband stood by my side and leant in close. He sniffed the air. "I do wish you would not wear so much of that rosewater. It does not become you at all, Lilias."

I sighed, thinking yet again, what could I do that was right for my husband? All I could produce was daughters; and he was irked by my perfume that smelled of roses.

Catherine's husband, the Master of Rothes, came over to us and we made small talk until our guest leant in towards my husband.

"Is it too early to begin discussions about a possible betrothal between one of my sons and one of your daughters?"

I could not help myself. "Oh, I think it a little early, Master. Anne, our eldest, is still only thirteen and..."

"I shall be the arbiter of age and maturity, my dear," Alexander said, pinching my elbow hard. He continued the pressure and the pain increased. I lowered my head and was trying not to cry when

I heard footsteps approach. It was Catherine, leading in a young girl with the most striking blue eyes I have ever seen. She had on a dress in exactly the same colour, azure, and her thick dark hair bounced in curls off her uncovered shoulders. Alexander released his tight grip on me and moved to the side.

"This is my stepdaughter, Grizel Leslie," Catherine said, gesturing with her hand. And the young girl, only fourteen but with the confidence of someone ten years older, bowed so low, we could not help but gape at her well-developed bosom and beautiful long white neck as she rose slowly up.

"How wonderful to meet you, Grizel. You were only a baby when I last saw you," I said, trying to refrain from rubbing my elbow.

"And now, behold how you have blossomed," said Alexander, smiling.

"I believe you already met everyone here at the Rothes hunt a couple of months ago?" Catherine asked. I could not determine from my sister's voice if she took to the girl or not.

"Oh, I don't think I was there," I said.

"No, you were busy with the children," Alexander snapped. "As usual."

I turned to say something in reply but I stopped at once when I glanced at my husband. He was gazing at the young girl before him in a way that could never have been described as avuncular, even though he was well over three decades older than her. As Grizel stood there, beaming and chatting like a mature lady, his eyes blazed with fire. And it was then I realised what this day was all about: he did not want to arrange a betrothal between one of her brothers and our daughters; he wanted this young girl for himself.

Chapter Fourteen

1600

Lilias

I sat at the writing desk by the window. There had been low cloud and drizzle all day. But I was now aware of a shift in the light falling onto my paper, and I looked out towards the sky. There was a glisk, a sudden break in the clouds as the sun burst through, and for a fleeting moment I felt hope surge through the melancholy in my heart. And then, as quickly as the sun had appeared, the clouds scudded over the sun and the room was filled once more with gloom.

I sighed and took up the quill. I was writing my regular letter to Aunt Marie and always tried to sound upbeat and happy.

> *Chère Marie,*
>
> *I hope this finds you in good health. I know you said your legs and hands were still sore and you thought it was perhaps just the long cold winter. So hopefully now that it is spring, this is no longer appropriate, but I asked the advice of my cook, whose sister provides herbal remedies from her Mistress's physic garden. She recommends willow bark for swollen joints or aches. I am sure there are willows in France, hopefully within the vicinity of the convent. She says you either chew the bark or – far more pleasant I imagine – make a tisane from the crushed bark. Please let me know if you can get this, and if not I shall have one of our gardeners collect some from the willows down on the river bank and I can send it with my next letter.*

I twisted my ruby ring around on my right hand and thought of Marie who of course had no servants to call upon now, and in fact no luxuries at all; surely she was cold and alone, though I'm sure she would insist she was never lonely in her walk with God. I worried more and more about her. After the Queen was executed, she suffered so much; she told me she hated herself for leaving her Mistress, abandoning her to her fate. But as I wrote to her, what could she have done against the power of the English Queen? And of course, she had to consider her health.

Here, life is busy as ever. As you know, we have three beautiful daughters and I try not to think during every waking moment of our fourth, darling Margaret, who died so young. A mere three years living on this earth is far too short for anyone, but perhaps even more so for such a sweet child. I told you I did not wish to baptise our darling youngest girl with the same name, but Alexander insisted, saying it would be therapeutic. What does he know about healing when grief has been so profound? Dear Marie, I know you don't mind me writing some things to you that I would never utter to anyone else. Even though he is your nephew, I feel only you understand something of my situation.

I pulled up the sleeve of my gown a little and turned over my left hand where the bruising was still livid on my wrist. He had not been happy with my "disobeying" him by not attending his inauguration as Lord President at the Court of Session in Edinburgh last week. I was duty bound to appear on his arm as his loyal wife, all dressed up in finery and jewels. When I explained that I was still weak after baby Margaret's delivery and could not possibly undertake the long journey by horseback, he grabbed my wrists and pushed me up against the wall. He then showered me with abuse, telling me I had to remember what role I was meant to fulfil as a wife. He finished his angry tirade by accusing me (not for the first time) of failing him by not producing sons.

I tugged my sleeve back down and took a deep breath.

Anne and Isobel are happy, cheerful girls. I believe Anne is going to have your height, Marie, she is already tall for her age. The baby is doing well. Nurse says it will soon be time to introduce her to some solid food, though I feel that it's a little too early. But Nurse always has my husband's ear, and he will want her to be on solids soon so that he can stop having to pay the wet nurse.

The gardens have been looking beautiful in this late spring sun. Do you remember when you and I used to walk to the river, down the little hill? The gardeners have recently constructed a terrace with balustrades along the ridge so that we can enjoy the fresh air in the spring warmth from the comfort of some seating overlooking the water. Our French gardeners are truly wonderful. I imagine you have a lovely garden at the convent? You told me your chapter-room, refectory and chapel are all situated around a courtyard with tall trees. Perhaps it's also planted with some beautiful flowers and bushes?

I looked over to the window and gazed up at the sunlight, the wooden frame casting shadows on the stone floor. Perhaps later I would take some air, hopefully with Anne or Isobel if Nurse allowed me. Though I have to admit, I was feeling rather nauseous this morning. I do hope it's not another child, though the symptoms with my pregnancies are always the same. If it is, pray God I can give my husband a son.

I am not sure how much you hear news about Scotland, but did I say in the last letter that the King and Queen had a third child, also called Margaret, born only a few months ago, but we hear the poor little princess is very sickly. She was born at Dalkeith Palace, where the King and Queen often stay, as the grounds there are magnificent and ideal for His Majesty to pursue his favourite sport of falconry.

The Queen is with the baby almost constantly at the moment while she is so poorly.

Alexander has invited the King and Queen to Fyvie as you know, and this may now indeed happen, depending on the tiny princess's health, since he often meets His Majesty at Dunfermline Palace to discuss matters of state and to give him legal advice. Before her last child was born, Queen Anne had a new house added to the Palace in Dunfermline, and this is where she spent much of her time. It is meant to be quite splendid, also built in French style, not unlike Fyvie's renovations. Your nephew's greatest desire is to be involved in the royal children's lives, which to me seems rather strange since he seldom interacts with our daughters at all.

I couldn't possibly mention the fact that, when considering the royal visit to Fyvie, there was also the matter of her nephew contemplating a pursuit of the Protestant faith, in keeping with His Majesty. That would upset her so much. I put down the pen. I was so sleepy and did not feel as well as I ought to. I would call the maid to bring me some spiced wine to try to settle my stomach. Though my nagging worry was that I was about to endure another nine months of anxiety, fretting about not being able to satisfy my husband once again, and that I would produce a fifth daughter.

I shall write again soon, Aunt Marie, and in the meantime, I wish you good health, for that is surely the most important.
Your truly loving friend and niece,
Lilias

Chapter Fifteen

1600

Lilias

After it was confirmed I was expecting our fifth child, I was forbidden to ride, even though I had done so in the past four pregnancies.

"You must do everything possible, Lilias, to ensure you are delivered of a son who is hale and hearty," Alexander said over supper when I questioned why I was not permitted to go and see my mother.

"She can come here. Besides, it will not be long until she will come and stay for the confinement."

I pushed away the dish of mutton before me. I had no appetite these days nor indeed zest for life. Even being with the little ones could not lift my spirits.

"Eat what is left on your plate, Lilias. It is for your own good – and the baby's." He nudged the plate towards me. The capers tasted too vinegary and the meat too heavy. I knew I could not stomach it, but I raised my fork; I had no choice. I scooped up tiny mouthfuls, swilling it all down with gulps of claret, while he watched me, his jaw set firm, his gaze ruthless. As I force fed myself, he held sway as usual.

"Now, Lilias, I have some things to discuss."

Discuss meant he would dictate what I, his wife, would do, at his command. He opened his mouth to speak then stopped and stared at my dress as if something had occurred to him. "Why are you wearing that gown when I expressly said I do not like you in that colour? You know I've said green does not become you. It was perfectly acceptable when you were merely Lilias Drummond, but now as Lady Fyvie, it is too simple, even with that embroidery." He pointed to the brocade around the bodice of my dress.

I looked down, hardly remembering that I'd asked my maid to fetch the green dress to wear today, in some sort of pathetic act of defiance.

"Sorry, Alexander, I had forgotten."

"Well, no matter, you will be changing out of it soon. Now, you recall that I leave for Edinburgh tomorrow, but before I arrive, I am to call in to Dunfermline Palace for an audience with the King. As you know, I am his advisor on all matters pertaining to the law."

Of course I knew; why did he feel he had to keep telling me about his prominence at the Court? Was it because he felt unable to boast to his peers?

"And it has come to my attention that he is not aware that we still say Mass here at Fyvie. And so when he and Queen Anne come to visit, this will all have changed."

"But when are they coming, Alexander? I must make preparations..."

He cut me off with a raised hand. "I have told you before, Lilias. We await the news of the Queen's safe delivery of her next child at Dunfermline and then they will come up to Aberdeenshire, I hope with the children, as soon as she has recovered sufficiently."

I was about to say that could be long enough coming; the Queen usually took three months to recover after each baby, but I said nothing. And obviously no consideration had been made for my own pending confinement, which I believe would be about the same time.

"Until we know the precise date of the royal visit, we may as a family continue to say Mass; but not for much longer. I am determined that we will not display our erstwhile Roman ways when they are here. Indeed, I have decided that soon I shall engage a

Protestant minister to start leading family worship, and we will also begin occasional attendance at the church in the village. I am already in discussions with the minister about the possibility of having a Seton pew installed at the front, but the man is hardly forthcoming."

Which probably meant the minister did not fawn upon my husband as he expected.

He leant towards me and spoke softly, in a conspiratorial manner. "When His Majesty takes over the throne from the Old Hag in London – and I hear she is poorly again – I am led to believe he may wish to leave his children in our care, either here or in Dunfermline. And they must be brought up in the Protestant faith. I am hoping this will be touched upon at my audience tomorrow. Do you understand, Lilias?"

I thought back to the Seton family's strong faith. They were one of the country's most devoted and noble Catholic families. Yet, in order to remain loyal to the Crown, to ingratiate himself with the King, my husband was willing to relinquish the centuries-old Seton faith – and indeed the denomination his godmother Queen Mary adhered to until her dying day. Not for the first time, I wondered how his aunt, dear Marie Seton, would feel about it; she whose entire life was devoted to worshipping God as a Roman Catholic.

"How will the Seton family take this news, Alexander?" I glanced a look at him and wished I had held my tongue.

He scowled. "I do not care what the Setons think. I have been a devout Roman Catholic all my life and that in itself must appease them." He took a gulp of wine. "And now I feel it appropriate that we become enlightened and adapt to the times we live in. The King is a Protestant; we, his subjects, must also be. We worship the same God, after all. There is no choice and I will not contemplate any alternative. Indeed, the more I find out about the Protestant faith, the more I am drawn to it. It is uncomplicated by paraphernalia and its transparency appeals to me. As it will to you." His grey eyes narrowed as he stared at me. "I repeat, Lilias, do you understand?"

I said nothing, but simply nodded then forced a smile, as if coming round to his wonderful proposal.

"Now, of course your sister Jean has helped our cause of late, and I presume she will continue to have Queen Anne's ear for some time. She will, I hope, even be given the honour of helping to care for the new prince or princess when it arrives in a few weeks. Your sister's role with the Queen at Court and my role with the King should continue to ensure we play a part in the lives of his family."

He beamed as if everything he had just said was normal, whereas truly, it was not. Jean had been delighted when she was asked to be a lady-in-waiting to the Queen, for all she had ever wanted, since she was a child, was status and prestige; she had even renounced our Roman Catholic ways in a flash, in order to fulfil the role. My father had been devastated at the news. Jean and my husband were each as fickle as the other.

As I thought of Jean, I realised that Alexander depended on my sister greatly in this, his quest to become even more involved in the royal family. I could not help but suppress a smile, for my husband needed me for something other than to attempt to produce a son for him. I returned to my plate where I had finished all but one mouthful of the now cold, greasy mutton, which lay heavy on my stomach.

"One final thing, Lilias."

Dear Lord, what now? I was feeling queasy after being bullied into swallowing the entire plateful.

"I do not know how long I shall be away. So in case I forget to speak to you about this before their Royal Majesties come to stay, there is another matter of importance. I want to discuss the parure."

A cold shiver ran down the length of my body. I gripped my beaker of wine so tightly, I thought the glass might smash in my hand. The parure was mine, a gift to me from Marie Seton, the most beautiful necklace, brooch and earrings I had ever seen. Sometimes in my sad moments, I remove them from their velvet case and hold them up to the light of the candle to see the pearls gleam and the emeralds and rubies sparkle. Somehow these jewels bring me shreds of hope in my otherwise bridled life. The parure was absolutely nothing to do with him. I looked directly into his eyes and tried to keep calm.

"I have been thinking that, since it belonged first to the King's mother, Queen Mary, it would be appropriate for you to wear it during their visit. I know my aunt kindly gave it to us as a wedding gift, but truly that was rather too much. I think her fondness for you has overstepped the mark. Sometimes I think the parure ought to have stayed in the royal collection."

I almost spat out my wine. A wedding gift to us? What, was he going to adorn his doublet with the ruby and emerald brooch at supper? It was mine.

"I do not know in fact why I allow you to keep it in your chamber when it really ought to be in my safe place in the Charter Room. I shall address this on my return."

I was so stunned that I didn't trust myself not to say something that would make him angry again, so I quickly changed the subject.

"Have you heard from Aunt Marie recently?"

He shrugged. "No, but she writes to you, doesn't she? I admit I am rather fond of my aunt, for she has spirit, true Seton resolve. But I simply do not have time. So you may continue your correspondence with her. For now, that must suffice."

He rose to his feet and a servant rushed over to pull his chair out.

"I shall see you later."

Chapter Sixteen

1980

Maggie

I stood at the back of the crowd of visitors and craned my head to hear Andrew the guide speaking. He was about fifty and wore a kilt in a brilliant turquoise, yellow and red. When he'd come towards me to shake my hand, the reek of Old Spice hung in the air. Having listened to him in the hall and the drawing room, I wasn't convinced he was a particularly good guide as he never looked especially animated and he didn't seem to be enjoying his job. It was as if he was churning out information he had simply learned by heart.

"This is the Charter Room," he said, while grandly reaching out one arm at a time like a ballet dancer.

Everyone looked around at the dark wood panelling, the portraits hanging up high and the two small windows that gave out only the faintest of light. This room had poor lighting; it was so dingy, it was as if they didn't want people to be able to see the paintings clearly.

"In this room, many important documents and deeds were signed. And on this chair" – he pointed to a large wooden seat beside the table – "it is even believed that Mary, Queen of Scots sat to write her letters during her visit to Fyvie."

Before I could raise an objection, a stout man at the back drawled, "But I thought she never visited Fyvie."

The American was right. She never did.

"That's because it was only on record that she visited Dunnotar Castle near Stonehaven, some forty miles to the south, for court purposes. She made official visits to that castle often, whereas she would come here to relax, with just her ladies-in-waiting and a handful of courtiers."

I opened my mouth but realised I could not embarrass Andrew in front of everyone. I would speak to him afterwards.

"And here," he continued, unfazed by the American's doubts, "is the way to the secret chamber."

There was a rustle of coats and a shuffle of shoes as everyone strained to be nearest to the large wooden panel Andrew was pointing to.

"Down below, in this secret place, many of Alexander Seton's special documents and valuables were kept, including, we believe, a set of jewellery that was given to him for his wives – he had three – by Mary, Queen of Scots herself." He paused and we all stared at the wood, willing it to spring open. He smirked. "They say that down there are also the bones of one of his wives who displeased him."

There was a wave of oohs and hands went up.

"What happened?"

"Can you open it?"

"Why are the bones here?"

"It can never be opened up. Legend says that if it is, the laird will die and his wife will become blind. Two lairds have tried it; both died soon after and both wives contracted eye infections, one in fact becoming blind."

There was an intake of breath as everyone got closer to the panel.

"But now we must move along." He shuffled everyone out of the door and pointed outside. "Go past the Meldrum Stairs and through the rooms we have just seen, then wait for me midway up the Great Stairs. We shall then climb up together to the top step and look at the portrait there."

They all trudged towards the stairs and I noticed a woman

peering perilously close to one of the Raeburns. I tapped Andrew on the shoulder. He was glowering at the visitor, presumably to ensure the Raeburn was not touched, but eventually he turned around.

"I was just wondering about the Mary, Queen of Scots part of what you just said. I had no idea she visited here."

"Oh, nor do I, Maggie," he whispered. "But they all love that, especially the Americans. You must have seen their faces." He grinned and I noticed how black his teeth were.

"But the bit about the secret chamber is true, I presume?"

"Very much so. No one's opened it up fully since the seventeenth century. The curse is still with the family." He turned and bounded up the stairs, where I joined him.

"This stunning portrait," he said, pointing his finger to a tall painting of a young lady wearing a green dress, "is of Lilias Seton, née Drummond. She was the first wife of Alexander Seton who was Mary, Queen of Scots' much favoured godson."

Well, that part was true.

"The portrait is hung here, just along from the Seton Bedroom, which we shall visit next. It's not been moved for decades, centuries even, because," he bent his head down towards the eager crowd and pronounced in a loud stage whisper, "she is said to haunt the castle. So we wish to ensure she is happy and to placate her by keeping the painting here."

"Have you seen her?"

"Does the ghost only appear at night?"

"Is she an evil ghost?"

Andrew held up a palm and paused until every hand was down then said, conspiratorially, "Lilias Seton, according to some reports, displeased her husband, who some say mistreated her and eventually sent her away. I have never seen the ghost myself, but it seems to appear only at night and then all you can see is a flicker and shimmer of green."

"Ooh, so she's wearing that dress we see in the portrait?"

"Indeed she is. It was painted by an artist brought over from Paris by Alexander Seton in 1585, and as you can see, her hair is coiffed beautifully and entwined with pearls in the French manner of the time. It is said Mary Seton, Alexander's aunt, who was also lady-in-waiting to Mary, Queen of Scots, did her hair in the same way she styled the Queen's hair." He turned behind him and pointed to a stone statuette on the floor behind him. It was a beautifully carved miniature of a sixteenth century noblewoman playing a lute. She had a high collar and hair piled high on her head with strings of pearls woven through it. "This is Mary Seton, a regular visitor to Fyvie Castle. Please note the similar hairstyle."

I frowned. Was that a coincidence, or did Mary Seton in fact style Lilias Drummond's hair? How much of his tales were true? I was a history student, I wanted to establish the truth so I could give my own guided tours based on fact. I turned back to stare at the young woman in the painting, fair skinned and with a shy, innocent air about her, which was hardly surprising: she was only a teenager and about to marry a man some fifteen years older. But as I continued to stare at her, that feeling of sadness came upon me once more. What was wrong with me? I had become a more positive person recently, but there was something about her face, full of youth and naivety, that made me want to cry. And I haven't done that for ages, well, at least since last summer. I shook myself and followed the jostling crowd into the room.

Chapter 17

1600

Lilias

My mother had arrived the previous week to await the delivery of my fifth child, so I invited Catherine over from Rothes to visit. I had no idea whether she would bring any of her husband's large family. I hoped not; I wanted to converse just with her, my dear elder sister. But when I heard the sound of hooves and looked outside where a bright autumn sun dappled the golden leaves on the oak trees, I could see Catherine alight first, then the grooms helping another woman behind her dismount.

"Who is that with Catherine, Mama?"

She peered over my head. "Is that not the Leslie girl, Grizel? I have not seen her since Catherine's last confinement, but it certainly looks like a more adult version of the girl I saw then."

I heaved my enormous belly and got to my feet with a struggle, ignoring Mama's proffered hand. I had already told her that I felt better moving around, rather than marooned in a chair.

"Now, Lilias sweetheart, remember, after this visit today, you are to stay in bed. You are indecently large to be walking around like this."

I was used to people telling me what to do, so I simply nodded my acquiescence. I passed a mirror on the way to the door and stopped. Dear Lord, my face was so fat and sallow. I pinched my cheeks with my thumbs and forefingers and waited for our guests.

"Lilias, dear sister," said Catherine as she came towards me. "How are you? Why are you not sitting down?"

"I am fine, thank you. And I am actually better on my feet."

As Mama and I kissed Catherine, the girl came to stand before us. Again, the thing that struck me about her appearance was those blue eyes, pale and luminous, with long, dark lashes. She bowed deeply and I took her hand as she arose.

"Welcome to Fyvie Castle again, Grizel. How good to have you back with us. You know my mother, of course?"

She nodded gracefully and we all went to sit in the corner by the fire. I snatched a look at her sitting there with the most impeccable posture, her ivory skin so utterly perfect and her cheeks pink as rose petals. She must be fifteen by now, but what a beauty she was becoming. As the servants fussed around us with wine and dainty sweetmeats, I started to wonder what she was doing here; why would she accompany her stepmother on a visit to her vastly pregnant sister?

"Have you been keeping well, dear Lilias?"

"I am the same as I always am when expecting a child, Catherine. Not very comfortable." I smiled. "But that is not interesting to anyone else. Now, Grizel, give me the latest news please about your family. Tell me about your brothers and sisters – and yourself."

She lifted up her head and smiled so her charming dimples were visible. Her voice was sweet and childlike, the only thing that gave away the fact she was not as mature as she looked.

"As you know, I have three brothers, your Ladyship. And four sisters, but they are of little consequence as they are all older than I am and married." She paused. "And as for me, Papa says I resemble his mother, my grandmother, the Countess of Rothes, who was also my namesake, Grizel Leslie. She sadly died before I was born, but from what I hear she was a formidable lady. He says I am like her in every respect."

We all nodded and I tried to feign interest.

"Grandmama gave birth to six sons, all of whom strapping and healthy." She smiled a sweet, coy smile. "Who knows, since I am named after her, perhaps I too might have six sons, were I lucky enough to marry."

I suddenly felt very hot and started fanning my face. Mama fussed around me and the others continued small talk between themselves, but I remained silent, listening yet not hearing. All I could think of was this girl's words about bearing sons.

The door flung open and Anne and Isobel rushed in. They came over and gave Catherine a hug and stood beside Grizel as she was introduced. It was remarkable seeing Anne beside this young woman who was only a year and a half older than she was. It was as if Anne were still a child and Grizel a grown adult, both physically and in terms of character. Anne was a little taller than Grizel, but she clutched a doll to her flat chest and could not stand still for excitement. Grizel had the poise of an ice queen.

"Come with us to the nursery, Grizel, you can meet our little sister," Isobel said, grabbing her hand. I watched with, I admit shamefully, some sort of glee as my daughters took her off in the direction of the nursery. Mama went after them, perhaps feeling sorry for our guest being dragged away from the adults.

But at least it gave me the chance to talk to Catherine alone.

"Tell me about Grizel. Does your husband have any betrothal plans for her?"

"He is certainly keen to arrange something but because he indulges her so, he seems to believe it's appropriate that she has a say in the matter." She laughed. "As if our father ever gave us any choice."

"Though truly our marriage arrangements were more down to Mama than Papa, don't you think?"

"Perhaps," Catherine conceded. "Now, tell me, Lilias, how are you actually feeling?" She stared at my wan face and frowned. "You do not look your best. Why have you not taken to bed? You only have a few weeks to go, surely?"

"I am more comfortable moving around. Besides, I would hardly see the children. Nurse seldom brings the children to my chamber as she thinks it is not good for them to see their mother in bed; she has very strange ideas. And I would miss them so very much."

I suddenly felt the urge to weep. I looked away and could not help sniffing loudly. "Excuse me, Catherine, I feel a little weary."

She took my hand. "Of course you do, Lilias. This is your fifth baby and you are still grieving for the little girl you lost. Everything will be fine soon, I'm sure."

I remained silent and she continued. "How is your husband? Is he here today?"

I shook my head. "He is in Edinburgh but due back home sometime soon. I never know quite when he will arrive."

"My husband says he has the ear of the King now."

I shrugged. "Yes, it's all he has ever wanted. For the first half of his life, he was devoted to his royal godmother the Queen; and now his abiding allegiance is to the King."

Catherine looked again at my face, probing. "But he is a good husband, Lilias?"

I was silent and so she persevered. "James might be far older than me, but he is kind and gentle, which is all a wife requires, would you not say?"

I nodded then looked towards the door where Mama had entered, the three girls behind her, all returning from the nursery. As they approached, I saw that Grizel wore an expression of utter boredom and weariness on her perfectly sculpted face. Yes, this girl was in fact a woman, impatient to come of age.

Chapter 18

1600

Lilias

Alexander flung open the door to my chamber and bounded in. The first thing I noticed was the smile on his face, which was unusual. Whatever could have prompted that?

"Lilias, there is such news." He sat down by my bed and raised his chin as if about to make a proclamation.

"It's the Queen." He beamed.

"Oh, has she had her baby?"

"Not just a baby, Lilias. A prince. She has delivered a male child, their second son. Prince Charles. There is no better news in the land."

"How is the Queen? It's not long since the princess, her own little Margaret, passed away."

He shrugged. "That matters not, Lilias. The King now has a second heir, should anything happen to Prince Henry." He leant back against the chair, beaming with such overt delight, it was as if he was the little prince's father. I knew what would be coming next.

"So all we need to make this joy complete is for you to deliver a boy. How many days does the midwife say it is now?"

"It could be any day now, Alexander. Pray God you will be happy with your new child." I could not bear to utter the word "son".

He bounced up from the seat. "Indeed. And now I am going to begin preparations for my journey to Dunfermline Palace to pay respects to the new royal prince." He raised a finger. "I shall have to consider a gift. Do you have any suggestions?"

I bit my lip. "Could we ask the silversmith to fashion something special? Though there is perhaps not quite enough time to commission him if you plan to leave soon."

"Also I believe the royal family might have enough silver spoons, Lilias. Never mind, I shall put my mind to that."

He headed for the door then stopped. "Oh, what was that pie from Fyvie that I told you the King enjoyed during my visit to them at Dalkeith Palace?"

"Was it the spiced venison pie?"

He shook his head.

"Perhaps the partridge pie with ginger?"

He nodded vigorously. "That was it. Good girl. I shall have Cook make some of these today."

Good girl? I was nearly thirty years old. I sighed then realised he was about to leave so I raised my hand.

"Alexander, will you not stay for my delivery?"

"No, there is no need. Besides, as well as passing on my respects to the new royal baby, I will journey on to Edinburgh where I must continue the King's work as patron of the arts. I have artists and writers to see on behalf of His Majesty. He has been called 'a bright star of the north' by nobles at the English court. I must continue this work for him."

He looked down at my enormous belly and smiled. "But do have news sent when our son is born."

And with that he turned and strode out the door, without even a backward glance.

Another dull day stretched long before me. I was meant to waste it lying in bed with not even the joy of my three girls to cheer me up. Mama spent much of her time in the nursery with them, ignoring my requests to see them. She said she agreed with Nurse that a visit from two rowdy girls and one lively toddler would not be conducive to my taking full advantage of bed rest. But I did not want bed rest, I wanted company.

I twirled my dull, brittle hair around my finger in ringlets, wishing Aunt Marie was here to work her magic as a coiffeuse. The cinnamon oil she had made up for my hair was so beneficial the maid still makes it for me, but in pregnancy it has little effect, it's so dry. She had such a knack of making my hair look pretty. Indeed, when she did it for the portrait of me Alexander had commissioned just before our wedding, she entwined pearls through it and even my husband commented on how well it looked.

I pulled back the covers and swung my swollen ankles onto the rug. I then hobbled over towards the armoire and opened the bottom drawer. Underneath a pile of woollen and linen chemises and lace handkerchiefs was the box. I slipped it out and went over to the window where a cold blast chilled my bare feet, but I did not have the energy to retrieve the shawl from the bed to cover them. After the conversation with Alexander about my parure, I had removed it from my jewellery box and hidden it in the bottom drawer amongst my undergarments, knowing he would not dare venture there. I was sure that at some stage he would insist I hand it over to him to hide in his secret place in the Charter Room, but for now, hopefully, he had forgotten about it in his excitement over the Queen's delivery.

There was a low November sun emerging through the grey clouds to the east. I sat down on the window seat and placed the velvet box on my knees. Leaning over my huge belly, I took out the pieces, one by one. First of all were the drop earrings, heavy with pearls, the two largest encircled with tiny emeralds. I held them both up to the window where the pearls shone and the tiny rubies gleamed, while the emeralds sparkled in the light. The emerald green was exactly the same colour as the green dress I continued to wear when my husband was away from home. I had of course had similar gowns made over the years to fit my expanding figure, but the material was always the same rich green. I sometimes had the dressmaker liven it up with some brocade around the neckline. How I loved that emerald colour.

I put the earrings back down and picked up the quatrefoil brooch. In the centre there was an oval cabochon ruby in a rectangular gold setting surrounded by four claw-set natural pearls, and four enamelled red beads mounted in an intricate gold scroll work frame. I gazed at this for a while, smiling, holding it up to the window before replacing it and lifting up the necklace. Throughout the elaborate chain, several snake links in translucent dark green enamel coiled perfectly around large pearls and there were gold scrolls set with rubies. I was dazzled, not only from the glint of gems and pearls in the full sunshine, but also by the memories and emotions caught up with it. This was given to me by my dear friend Marie Seton, and ever since she had left, I had had no one nearby to confide in.

I wiped the tears from my cheeks as I stared at this most perfect and unique piece of jewellery. Here were the rubies and the same circles of tiny emeralds around the pearls as there were in the other pieces. But in the necklace, there was such intricate craftsmanship in the gold scroll work, it was as if the necklace were telling a story, the tale unfolding all around the gold strand through its ornamental coils. I sat there for some time marvelling at its beauty, feeling more calm than I had for some time.

Aunt Marie had insisted I take the parure the day before she left for France fifteen years before. She said that she had grown so very fond of me, she wanted me to have it and to think of her when I wore it. And I always did. Sitting here at Fyvie on a bleak, overcast day, I tried to think only of happy times and of our friendship. But as I put the jewels carefully away in the box, that familiar cold feeling of dread came upon me once more.

Chapter 19

1600

Lilias

The pains arrived in the middle of the night. I managed to hobble over to the door and shout for the maid to alert the midwife who had been staying with us for a few days.

"Mistress Reid, should Jeannie go and wake my mother?"

"I would prefer her presence only towards the end, My Lady. Otherwise too many women standing around doing nothing get in the way." She turned to Jeannie and gestured to the door. "Go and fetch the other maids and set the water to boil."

She had a pleasant way about her, this new midwife. The old one, Mistress Anderson, who had attended my four previous deliveries, was terrifying. I was so relieved when I heard she had injured her hip and was unable to leave her house. This younger woman seemed far less of a bully.

"Right, let's see how far on you are," she said, rolling up her sleeves.

Some four or possibly five hours later, as I was still writhing in agony, the grey dawn began to lighten the leaden sky outside.

"Jeannie, run along and fetch Lady Fyvie's mother now. It won't be long till the baby's here."

In between me thrashing about the bed in pain, I was praying. I kept asking God to please spare me from the shame of producing yet another daughter. Please God let me have a son. I was muttering to myself but Mistress Reid heard me at one stage and leant down to whisper.

"My Lady, the baby won't come easily if you are anxious. Whether it be male or female, God will smile upon his gift. What you must pray for is a healthy child."

And before I could speak, the door flung open and Mama rushed in.

"Sweetheart, how are you? Why did they not call me sooner?" She scowled at the midwife, who ignored her and nodded vigorously at me.

"Push now, push! The baby's coming!"

Some time later, I sat up in the newly made bed, my little girl's warm head against my cheek, inhaling the unmistakably intoxicating smell of a new baby. The midwife had gone to have some food and I was now alone with Mama and the baby. I kissed the downy head and looked up through the tears streaming down my cheeks.

"Mama, must we send news to Alexander immediately?"

"Of course, Lilias." She was aghast. "A message must be sent to your husband in Dunfermline today. It is for him to approve a name."

"I want to call the baby Marie, after his aunt."

Mama shrugged. "He may not want that, Lilias. He is fond of her, of course, but now perhaps she has too many connections with his royal godmother. And as we know, his only concern now is with King James and Queen Anne."

I took the handkerchief Mama handed me and tried to stop sniffling. "I think you are right. He will not want any name associated with the Seton family, as we've had for our other daughters. I have no idea what he will chose."

She leaned over to tuck the blanket around the baby's feet. "Isn't she a beautiful baby? You have done well, Lilias."

"Well? My husband only wants sons, you know that."

"There is time, sweetheart," she said, tickling my chin and smiling. "You are still only thirty. There is plenty of time to bear him sons."

I leant over to kiss the soft, peachy cheek of my little one, but even the warm, sweet smell of my baby's head could not stop that constant feeling of dismay and trepidation filling my bones.

The letter arrived well over a week later. I waited until the servant had shut the door behind her until I opened it. My hands were trembling.

> *Lilias,*
>
> *Thank you for the news that you have been safely delivered of a baby girl. After much thought, I have decided she shall be called Sophia.*

Sophia? I had never heard of this name before. It is neither a Seton name nor even Scottish.

> *It is a name from Queen Anne's own Danish family and, according to your sister Jean, one of Her Majesty's favourite names for girls. And so it is a great honour that she permits me to use it for our fifth daughter. I do not think the name Marie – or indeed Mary – suitable. As you know the King has nothing to do with his mother's old ladies-in-waiting, even though the only one still alive is the aunt of his legal advisor and confidant.*

He had to reiterate his closeness with Their Majesties to me of course.

> *I am still busy here at Dunfermline Palace with Their Majesties. The Court shall be moving soon to Dalkeith Palace for a while and at that stage, I shall return to Fyvie. Hopefully in time for Christmas.*
>
> *Alexander*

I am sure he used to write "Your Loving Husband, Alexander" at the end of a letter. And he does not even say that he is looking forward to meeting his new baby. And now as I re-scanned these few lines, I could read only disappointment and despair. If I had borne him a son, I would not have been surprised if he had called for his horse at once and galloped north to meet him. But a mere daughter? Well, why bother?

"Catherine is here to see you, Lilias," Mama said as she knocked on the door and swept in. "She is just having some refreshment and will be up shortly. Comb your hair, sweetheart, it's a mess."

It is always all about appearance with Mama. I sighed and as usual did what I was told.

Soon my sister arrived and as she hugged me, I could feel tears prick my eyes.

"Lilias, how are you? I have just seen the baby. She is beautiful – and so plump. What a joy to behold."

I nodded and tried to smile.

"I have just heard from Alexander. He wishes to name her Sophia."

"Oh." She frowned. "Well, that is a pretty name, though not commonplace. It makes her sound like a grand European princess." My sister chuckled.

We talked for a while, then, just as Mama left the chamber, she leant in. "I don't know if you are aware, but your husband has been in touch with mine, Lilias. Just three days ago."

I could barely conceal my amazement. "Obviously the Master of Rothes is more important than his wife. I have only had one letter – and it arrived today."

"Oh, yours was probably delayed. The weather has been inclement."

I twiddled with the edge of the linen sheet. "Why was he writing to your husband?"

"It was to ask about the family in general," she said, unconvincingly.

That did not sound like Alexander. Catherine glanced at my face then looked down at her hands, which were clasped together. "And he enquired about Grizel."

I clenched the sheet tight. "What about her?"

"My husband would not say exactly. I think he regretted telling me it was about Grizel and then he said it did not concern me." She shrugged. "But I think it was probably to suggest she is soon to be presented at Court and to join our sister Jean as lady-in-waiting to the Queen." She beamed. "Isn't that wonderful? My husband will be so delighted. I didn't want Mama to hear as she would not be pleased another girl might have the Queen's ear alongside Jean."

I said nothing but mulled over the likelihood of Grizel as a lady-in-waiting. And I soon realised that I did not agree with Catherine's conjecture, not at all. But I could not bear to think of alternative explanations. Even the sight of Mama walking into the room with Nurse carrying my precious baby could not raise my spirits from the depths of despond.

Chapter 20

1600

Lilias

A month later, I was sitting at the window and heard hooves down below in the courtyard. It was a cold, blustery, wet December day when no one would venture outside unless absolutely necessary. I peered out and realised it was Alexander. I leapt up and headed for the mirror then proceeded to brush my hair, sweep it up and secure it with pins. I ought to have asked the maid to do it earlier but I had so little enthusiasm for anything these days, I had asked her to leave after she laid out my dress.

Well, who would have thought my husband would arrive back today, of all days? I put on a string of pearls he had given me on our wedding day and looked again at my reflection. I still looked as if I had recently given birth, with the unmistakable bulge around my waist. But at least my hair was better, less brittle than it had been throughout my pregnancy.

I went downstairs where a servant told me Alexander had gone at once to the Charter Room. And so I was about to follow him in there when I stopped. Should I go and fetch the baby and take her in to him, rather than him having to climb all the stairs up to the nursery? But I realised I was not as sure-footed on those narrow winding stairs, having been confined to my chamber for so long. I could not risk falling with the baby. I still felt he blamed me for little Margaret's accident, even though everyone knew it was nothing to do with me and she was so ill anyway.

I knocked at the door of the Charter Room.

"Enter!"

I stepped into the cold, dark room and inclined my head.

"Welcome home, Alexander. I hope your journey was not too bad?"

He shrugged and continued to sit at his desk, looking down at papers.

"Would you like to come with me to the nursery to see Sophia? She is a beautiful baby."

He sighed and looked up at me. "Lilias, all babies are the same. I shall go and see her presently."

I continued to stand there, waiting for him to say something, anything, to me, his wife whom he had not seen for two months.

"Is there anything else, Lilias?"

"No, I don't think so." I thought madly for something else to say that would not displease him. "Is there anything special I should ask Cook to produce for supper?"

"Not in particular. I have dined so well at Court, I should prefer simple fare. I am not sure I could face another gilded roast peacock anytime soon. I shall see you at supper. Ask Nurse to prepare the children for my visit."

He buried his head in his papers once more and I shambled out of the room, endeavouring to be as quiet as possible.

We sat at supper before a simple dish of pheasant pottage with prunes and verjuice in almost complete silence. I knew him well enough by now to wait until he had had his fill, then we would speak. I kept snatching glances at him, trying to gauge his mood. I noticed for the first time that his red beard was now flecked with white, as were his eyebrows, and yet his thick head of hair was still brown all over, with not even a glimpse of grey. He ate and drank and hardly acknowledged my presence until eventually he laid down his fork and looked up at me. I could tell his smile was forced.

"Lilias, I have decided we shall go on a journey together to Fife after New Year's Day. I have a little project in mind."

A journey? Together! Well, this was unusual. "That sounds wonderful, Alexander. Shall we take the older girls?"

He frowned. "Of course not, the weather is not suitable in January for any excursion with children."

"Anne is fourteen now, Alexander, and quite grown up since you last saw her."

"She was not exactly acting like an adult when I saw her in the nursery this afternoon. She is still very excitable, like a child, and always fidgeting. So no, it shall just be us. With some servants, of course."

"Where shall we stay, Alexander?"

"William Douglas, the Earl of Morton, was at Court recently and I discussed with him the possibility of leasing Loch Leven Castle from him for a while. He now also owns nearby Aberdour Castle, which is much bigger and grander – and does not require a rowing boat to reach it."

"It sounds charming, Alexander," I said, smiling, and for once my smile was not fake. "Have you visited the castle?"

"Yes." He swirled the remnants of wine around his glass and stared at it. "It has been a safe fortress for a couple of centuries now, but there have been renovations in the past few years. Nothing as grand as Fyvie, of course."

I nodded as was my duty.

"There is the Tower House, which is strong and secure and where the earls used to bring their extended families during the plague years. Then about fifty years ago another tower was added, called the Glassin Tower. It sits above the postern gate, a fine lookout towards the loch's shore."

He leant over to take my hand and I tried not to flinch, unaware of what might happen next, but then he began to stroke along my fingers and the back of my hand in the most tender manner. He had not touched me in so long, I didn't know what to do, so I glanced up at him, trying to read his expression. I was sure it was not lust. How could it be; look how fat I still was after the baby. But was it pity?

I thought I could risk a question. "Are we to be guests of the Douglas family?"

He looked at me and smiled. "Yes. Won't that be a nice distraction for you after the baby."

"Oh, did you see her, Alexander? Is she not so pretty?" I could not help but gush.

"She is a baby, Lilias. A girl. The most we can ask for is that she will hopefully grow up hale and hearty. And when she comes of age, marry well."

He tipped the remaining claret down his throat. "We shall start to think soon about our trip south. I only hope that the weather is better than today. I fear Loch Leven Castle is not only rather difficult to reach, it is also, I believe, rather bleak. We shall need warm clothes."

I was churning over in my mind why, therefore, we should want to visit this place in the middle of winter, when I suddenly realised why it sounded familiar.

"Was that not where Aunt Marie was imprisoned with the Queen?"

Slowly he swivelled around to look directly at me, his grey eyes steely. "I cannot say I recall, Lilias. But no, I think not." He pushed back his chair and a servant rushed over to help him up.

"And now, I bid you good night."

Chapter 21

1601

Lilias

Chère Tante Marie,

Today is unusually mild for the second of January. But there is a gale howling all around, uprooting some of the smaller trees and bushes. The crows, which usually perch on the tall oaks to the east, are fluttering about menacingly as if they cannot settle. I used to hate their harsh caws, but I have come so used to their noise outside my chamber, I am almost fond now of their coarse, scratchy calls. If I did not hear them, I might wonder what had gone awry.

I hope your sore legs and hands continue to improve. It is astonishing what traditional remedies can do. It seems as if, though the willow bark is not a cure, it might have helped alleviate the pain. In your last letter, you wrote that you were overjoyed to hear the news of the new royal prince, Queen Mary's grandson, a welcome second heir to the throne. King James is not perhaps the monarch his mother was (you yourself said she was feisty and spirited, if sometimes a little highly strung), but I believe he uses his education well and indeed is a loyal patron of the arts. My husband also says he sometimes has an almost overrated opinion of himself but then again, he is the King; and I must say, Alexander is really not one to judge. He says His Majesty can also be a little impulsive, but so, I believe, was his mother?

While I mention Queen Mary, can you remind me please, Marie, where she was imprisoned first of all, in Scotland, with you by her side of course? I know you told me about your time in England, at Carlisle, Bolton and some other castles until Tutbury where I think you said you took the decision to leave for Fyvie and then France. But we never talked of your time soon after King James's father Lord

Darnley was killed, when you and the Queen were on some island castle. I wasn't even born when you were there and so I am, as usual, probably wrong, but was it Loch Leven in Fife?

My husband is taking me on a journey in a day or two and I have to say I am rather delighted about it. He has also been far more pleasant to me lately and not as critical of my every move, as I have described to you before. So, we leave tomorrow for Loch Leven Castle in Fife, which will be a long journey, but it should be enjoyable when we arrive. We are to be guests of William Douglas, the Earl of Morton. I know little of this family, but I believe they also have a connection with Aberdour Castle. Alexander has promised to tell me more of the Douglases on our journey. I imagine that he is looking forward to comparing the splendour of Fyvie to Loch Leven Castle.

The children are all well and they bring me such joy. The new baby, Sophia, continues to be a happy and chubby little thing. Though, typically, the few occasions when Alexander visits the nursery she seems to be lying in her crib, kicking her legs in frustration and bawling. But that is possibly because she is awaiting her next meal; for one so tiny, she really is rather greedy.

Marie, this letter is briefer than usual, for I must go now and instruct my maid what to pack for me for the trip; if I do not, she will put in my bags clothes suitable only for the summer heat. Jeannie is loyal and cheerful, but has little common sense, though I admit I'm sad she's not permitted to accompany me on the trip. I am going to pack your parure in my personal baggage too as I think this visit will be a wonderful opportunity, given the distinguished company, to exhibit its beauty.

And so I leave you now and look forward to telling you in my next letter about our visit to Loch Leven Castle. I do hope you continue to stay fit.

Your truly loving friend and niece,
Lilias

"Jeannie, can you try to tie plaits in my hair then entwine some pearls through them?"

I was keen to have my hair set now, on the morning we left Fyvie, so that they might remain in place for our arrival at Loch Leven Castle.

She bobbed and went to pick out a long string of pearls from the jewellery box. "Will these do, My Lady?"

I nodded and sat on the chair in front of the mirror while she plaited then interwove the pearls, before re-plaiting the braids. It was never quite as neat as when Aunt Marie did it, and indeed she always pulled my hair so tight I invariably got a headache, but the end result was passable; and a tighter plait would hopefully last three days.

"Tell me what gowns you have packed."

"The pink, the lavender and the yellow brocade one. Oh, and I'll add in the green dress as it so becomes you."

"I don't think it will fit yet, after the baby; it always was a tighter fit." I prodded at my still plump waistline and sighed. I could not believe Alexander had not scolded me more for my shape; he had been extremely critical after I struggled to regain my shape after the other babies. But I suppose he hardly looked at me these days.

"You look beautiful in that colour, My Lady," she said, folding it and placing it at the top of the bag.

I made a mental note to remove the green dress once she had left.

"That is fine, thank you, Jeannie." I turned this way and that, admiring my pearl-entwined hair in the mirror. She really was becoming more adept at hair. It was a shame Alexander had chosen none of my own servants to accompany us, but hopefully one of those in attendance might prove capable of dressing my hair.

I patted her on the arm.

"Thank you, Jeannie. Have the luggage fetched, please. Now I need some time with the children, then we hope to be gone by dawn."

She curtsied and exited, and I took a look round my chamber in case I had missed anything, then followed out the door, heading for the nursery.

On the way I called in to kiss Anne and Isobel goodbye, tucking their blankets around them and whispering that I would see them soon. In the nursery, Margaret was already up and being fed by Nurse who glowered at me as usual. I crept over to the crib and bent over little Sophia to kiss her, then went to wrap my arms around Margaret who beamed up at me. Her face was smeared with grey sludge. She thrust a doll at me.

"Kiss Doll goodbye, Mama."

And I did, then gave her a kiss on her soft cheek before heading for the door.

"It won't be too long until I see the children again, Mistress Black. Look after them well in our absence, please."

"I always do, My Lady," Nurse muttered and continued to coax Margaret with her porridge.

Chapter 22

1601

Lilias

Alexander held my hand as he guided me into the little rowing boat on the shores of Loch Leven. I sat down on the damp bench, exhausted after three days' travel. I was looking forward to putting on some clean dry clothes and warming up by the fire. I looked over the early morning mist rising from the water towards the castle. Something did not look quite right.

"Why can we not see any light or smoke coming from the castle, Alexander?"

"It's too far away and besides, it's too early; it is not long after dawn. They perhaps do not require candles yet."

"But surely the kitchen would require fires? And how can the Countess dress if not by candlelight?"

He smiled at me in a strange manner then patted my arm. "I must speak to the ferryman here, Lilias." He gestured to the man holding on to the mooring rope. "I shall be with you presently." He nodded at the boatman and the young lad at the oars, then the boat left the reeds, the boy rowing fast.

"Wait! My husband has yet to board!" I cried. I did not like large bodies of water at the best of times, and so being alone in a boat without Alexander made me nervous.

"I said I shall be with you soon, Lilias," he shouted from the shore. "I must deal with the servants and the luggage."

"Oh, I see," I said, wrapping my shawl around my shoulders and looking straight ahead at the castle, some mile or so over the black water. Though in truth I did not really see. Presumably the boat would be met by the Earl and Countess; how would it look when I had to explain that my husband would be along later? I shook my head and a feeling of foreboding swept across me as I stared at the tall grey castle on the tiny green-fringed island, looming clearly out of the mist. I sat rigid and still, terrified that if I moved even one inch the boat would capsize.

When the boat moored on the grassy bank, there was no arrival party nor indeed anyone there apart from a shifty-looking servant who kept sniffing and wiping his nose on his sleeve.

"Here, give me your hand, My Lady," he said, grabbing me and pulling me out of the boat onto the grass. I turned around towards the shore but could not see Alexander, nor indeed another boat.

"When shall my husband join me here?" I asked, looking up at the bleak castle walls.

He shrugged and pointed to a short doorway in the thick wall. He pushed the door open then turned immediately right to climb the stairs. I had no choice but to follow him, climbing up to the second floor at the top of the ramparts.

He twisted around and yanked a weighty ring of iron keys from his belt. He selected a key and pushed it into the heavy wooden door in front of us.

"Is this part of the castle the main dwelling or simply where we are to sleep?"

He gave me a strange look but said nothing. Then he gave me a little nudge towards the door so he was standing right beside me; he did not smell good. He pointed down over the walls towards a large courtyard.

"Over there is the Tower House, that's the Great Hall and beyond there's the outer courtyard with gardens. But here," he gestured inside the door, "is the Glassin Tower. And this is where you'll be staying."

"Why is everything in darkness?"

Not answering my question, he shoved me inside, as if I were an animal, and as I stood stock still at the entrance, I saw him lock the key from inside. My heart was beating fast; there was something not right. I did not understand what was happening.

"What are you doing? Where's my husband? Where is the Earl and his Lady?"

He ignored me and went over to the fireplace where a fire was burning. He poked it with an iron poker then tossed on another log. "There's water in the pitcher there. I will be back with your bag later."

He unlocked the door and slipped out, and I heard the key turn from outside.

I moved over to the bed and sat down. I felt weak and confused. Surely there was some mistake. What was I doing here all alone? Why was Alexander not here? And why was I locked in? I looked around this dingy room: there was a bed and a stool and a small table with the water jug. Apart from that, nothing. There was no armoire to hang my clothes, nor any mirror.

I rushed towards the tiny unglazed window, which was high up in the thick stone wall. I pushed a stool under it, stepped up then peered out so that I could see the loch all around and the shore. The mist had now cleared and there was a faint January light, so I could now see the reeds where we had left earlier. I was able to make out the other little rowing boat, loaded with, I thought, luggage – but when I looked all around for the servants and my husband, I realised there was no one there.

Chapter 23

1601

Marie Seton

I had just returned to my room after compline and was going to get ready for bed when I thought, once again, of Lilias. I'd been suffering with feelings of apprehension since receiving her last letter, telling me, with such excitement, of their trip south from Aberdeenshire to Fife and to Loch Leven Castle. Now, nearly three months later, I had still heard nothing. Thoughts had been swirling around in my head about why on earth my nephew would take his wife to an island castle that had been used as a prison in the past. And presumably the William Douglas she mentioned had been the same who had agreed to the Queen's imprisonment. I could not forget that a kinsman of William Douglas had been executed for his part in the murder of Lord Darnley, my Queen's first husband and father of King James.

Lilias had asked me whether Loch Leven Castle was where I stayed with the imprisoned Queen. Before I could reply that yes indeed it was, she had presumably gone. It was strange that her husband hadn't told her that was where the Queen and I had spent eleven months some thirty-four years ago, the first of her many years as a prisoner. And now there was nothing but silence from Fyvie.

The situation worried me greatly. It made me think back to the time I spent there with the Queen. It was often hard to bear, being marooned on a tiny island in the middle of a deep loch, miles away from Edinburgh. I remember William Douglas's mother Margaret did everything she could to make our time there unpleasant; she had never forgiven the Queen for usurping her son's claim to the throne, since she had borne Mary's father James V an illegitimate son whom she of course had called James.

The irony about Loch Leven Castle was that on the Queen's first visit, in 1563, they had feted her and treated her in true regal manner during her meeting with John Knox, which William Douglas had so carefully organised. But only four years later, she was held there in captivity, and under such diminished circumstances, with poor food, a reduced wardrobe and so few distractions.

We were kept at first in a small place called Glassin Tower, which was the first tower that could be seen when alighting from the boat at the shore. It had three floors, each containing a tiny, cramped room. We stayed in the middle floor, the first floor, which had a slightly bigger window than the top floor and so was a little brighter. After some weeks there, we were then moved to the larger Tower Hall across the castle courtyard, for greater security presumably.

But it was in the Glassin Tower that the Queen lost the twins, Bothwell's babies. What a sad day that was. I was the only one who knew she had been expecting again and so when the pains arrived, I tried to find help, but it ended up such a tragedy as there was nothing anyone could do and there was no physician to hand. The other hardship was that we still never knew where they buried them. The Queen kept asking to see their graves but that request, among so many others, was never fulfilled.

I looked out the window at the tall tree, already in bud in this unusually mild spring, and checked to see if the crows were there, but they were not. Perhaps they were making their presence felt nearby, somewhere else in Reims, cawing as usual with lusty voice. I shook my head, trying to shift that memory of the day the Queen lost the babies; there had been so much blood, we could hardly scrub away all of the red stains. We never spoke of that day again, and remembering it now caused me heartache once again.

I went to the desk and dipped my quill in the ink. I knew I had no choice but to write to Alexander. He would surely feel obliged to reply to me, his only remaining aunt, and tell me why I had not heard from Lilias. I would not, however, mention the fact I had been told they were to visit Loch Leven Castle; I would simply enquire after her health.

Perhaps she had become ill and been unable to write her monthly letter to me. Perhaps one of her children was unwell. I thought back to when her little Margaret was ill then so sadly died and she had been heartbroken. Perhaps she had too many tears to write to me if a second tragedy had befallen another of the children. I am sure there will be some explanation. My nephew must surely furnish me with this. And soon.

Chapter 24

1980

Maggie

My room was on the third floor in the Preston Tower at Fyvie Castle and was rather cramped, with only one small, high window, but at least it was far away from the noise of the visitors who would be pouring in at the weekends. I unpacked my clothes, cursing the fact I'd only brought one jumper with me. What was I thinking? This was Aberdeenshire in the summer. Well, perhaps I could try to hitch a lift into a nearby town at some stage on a day off, if I got desperate.

Mrs MacPherson had told me that, though the bathroom was on the second floor, down the narrow stairs, I was the only one using it. Indeed, I was the only resident in the Preston Tower. Andrew, like the other regular guide, Silvia, whom I'd yet to meet, stayed locally so I was the only one, apart from the family, who lived in. They were in the Leith Tower, at the other side of the castle from my room. I was relieved as I'd become less sociable during my two years at university, with all that had gone on, and the thought of having to take all my meals with someone like Andrew didn't fill me with joy. But he seemed to be the type of person who did whatever he liked, including telling the eager visitors mistruths.

Since my first proper shift was on Monday, I planned to study all the information about the castle over the weekend and prepare what I was going to say then. When one of the visitors had asked Andrew how old the Dunfermline passage was, I realised I had no idea. He told them that until the Gordons took over Fyvie in 1733 and did their own renovations, there had been no

108

corridors as such, simply interconnecting doors. There was still so much to find out, but right now I was going to do some work on my dissertation. I got out all the books I'd been allowed to keep on extended loans during the summer from the university library. I'd brought far too many, but there'd be little else to do in my spare time.

When I'd told Doctor Birkett the subject of the dissertation, she'd been interested as, even though her period was mid-sixteenth century, specialising in Mary, Queen of Scots, she knew little about Alexander Seton's private life, just the fact that his family was one of the most loyal to the Queen. I'm certain she hadn't known his wife was now a ghost. I smiled when I thought of that; what a ludicrous story to tell the poor visitors.

I opened my first book, which was on the Seton family, and began to read. Alexander's father George had been the Queen's Master of Household at Holyrood and also provost of Edinburgh, and his aunt was Mary or Marie Seton who was one of the famous Four Marys who attended the Queen. She was the only one who didn't marry and indeed she ended up at a convent in Reims in northern France where the Abbess was the sister of the Queen's mother, Mary of Guise. All that was common knowledge. But soon I reached the pages about Alexander's wives.

First, he married Lilias Drummond in 1585 and they had five children, all girls, one of whom died in infancy. So many children died as babies and so many of the mothers never survived childbirth, so this would not have been unusual. I began to cross-refer to notes on Lilias Drummond from another book I'd taken photocopies of from the library. I thought back to what Andrew had said when we were in the Seton Bedroom about Lilias now being known as the Green Lady and haunting the place. By that stage, though, I'd taken some things he'd said with a pinch of salt, so I wanted to discover the truth about her. I'd been struck by her portrait: she looked innocent, almost naive, and certainly not as assured as the second wife, whose portrait we saw later. They were all engaged or married so young and to much older men. But then, I was hardly one to talk.

I took a deep breath and continued flicking through my notebooks until I came to some interesting newspaper clippings from a couple of years before, which Doctor Birkett had found in archives for me when I'd secured this job at the castle. In 1972, a radio production team had visited Fyvie to record a live show about haunted castles and a strange thing occurred. The team from BBC Scotland in Aberdeen had turned up in the morning to set up before recording the programme at lunchtime, and when the presenter had arrived in the taxi from the airport they told her they'd been having problems with the microphones when they were doing their sound checks. When she insisted they mike her up and just start anyway as she had an evening flight back to London, the sound man said they'd try but they couldn't be sure it would work.

According to one of the tabloid cuttings, she told the crew that was nonsense. So-called "acquaintances" of the presenter Oonagh Donnelly were quoted as saying she was not known for her patience; indeed she was renowned for her off-hand, abrupt manner.

The crew had changed the batteries and it looked as if the sound was recording, but then it didn't play back, even though it had been fine in the studios earlier. The presenter was eager to try anyway and suggested they use more than one tape.

Resigned, the sound man miked her up, they did a test – the usual "What did you have for breakfast" – and he played it back. It worked and she gave him a smug look and insisted they crack on. This was a live show, after all, they had no time to waste. So they recorded the programme.

And then something astonishing happened. Some twenty minutes into the live transmission, there was an interruption over the recording and a ghostly voice whispered the words, "He killed me". The words were breathy and husky, but it was definitely the voice of a woman. Oonagh and the crew were totally unaware of the voice until they played back the recording later. Many listeners had written in to ask what it meant or why had the BBC inserted spooky-sounding words over Oonagh's voice in the middle of the show.

There were no logical answers, apart from specious excuses of white noise – or perhaps some audio had broken through from a tape that had been used before. What they did not reveal at that point was the fact that research was ongoing about the extremely rare phenomena called EVP, Electric Voice Phenomena, which some believed were voices of the dead – "spirit voices" – heard in recordings.

The public had presumed the words had been inserted to give atmosphere to the programme. The production team insisted they had not. And as for Oonagh, she was apparently so unnerved when she listened to the programme later that she retired from radio presenting soon after. I shut the notebook, thinking that I must try to contact this Oonagh via the BBC as soon as I could.

I went to switch on the light at the door and noticed there was an inside lock, which I pulled to. I picked up my handbag and riffled inside to find the tiny torch Mum had insisted I bring along with me. Thankfully, it was there. Even as I thought about her setting it down for me on the kitchen table with my sandwiches for the train, I smiled. Mum had always had my back covered, even more so in the past year.

I did not believe in ghosts, what nonsense. The radio recording had obviously played something that had been recorded over on the tape. Whether or not I would give the visitors the spiel about the Green Lady in my guided tour I'd yet to decide. For now, I needed to go to bed. I opened the window a little to let in the chill air and saw the crows circle and swoop around the tall oak trees in the gloaming.

Part Three

Chapter 25

1601

Lilias

I have no idea how long I lay on that bed, at first sobbing like a baby, then rigid with fear. I had never, in my entire life, been alone like this. At home when I was growing up, as well as Mama and Papa and my siblings, there were always servants around. At Fyvie, there were the children, occasionally my husband, and a castle full of maids and pages, grooms and cooks. I was perplexed. Why had Alexander brought me here and where was he?

I wrapped the thin blanket around me as the cold January air filled the small room. I looked up at the one tiny unglazed window where I just made out the grey sky and some clouds shifting and changing shape. I could hear nothing, not even birds. Perhaps there were no trees nearby. I must have drifted in and out of sleep, trying to recall in my dreams where I was, before remembering once more, as tears flowed down my cheeks, that I was in a castle, on an island. All alone.

Eventually I sat up, shivering. The fire had gone out and so I dragged myself up to poke at it. I looked around and saw that a candle still burned on the little table. I tried to use it to light the fire, but as I pushed the wick towards the wood the flame went out and I cried once more. I sat down on the chair, head in my hands, in front of the cold fireplace, and wondered what had I done to deserve this.

Then suddenly I heard a noise, a faint sound. Footsteps on the stairs? I didn't move as the key turned in the lock and the door swung open. That unclean man from earlier stood there, clutching my portmanteau. He elbowed the door shut behind him and came towards me, dropping it down on the floor. Since I felt there was something deeply sinister about him, I looked him up and down, trying to ascertain if he was armed. Seeing nothing apart from that huge heavy ring of keys dangling on his belt, I rose and held my head high. I would not be intimidated by this unkempt servant. And yet, I also felt I should perhaps be cautious.

"Thank you for delivering my luggage. I wonder if you could inform me why I am here? And when my husband is to arrive?"

He headed for the fire and knelt down. I noticed his ragged breeches and scuffed boots.

"Also, if you don't mind me asking, I presume the Earl and Countess are in residence? For I wonder when I might meet with them? There has obviously been some mistake as to my being here, in this cold, stark room." I attempted a smile as he picked up the poker and brandished it in his right hand. "Might I also ask when I shall be served some refreshments? I am more than a little hungry."

He continued to make up the fire, ignoring me all the while. He lit it then turned towards me. He screwed up his eyes and stared directly at me. It was disconcerting.

"Here's the rules. I will be in once a day to tend to the fire and bring fresh water." He struggled from his knees to his feet, wincing as if his joints hurt, and headed for the door where he picked up a pitcher of water.

"Apart from you and me, there's no one else here." He deposited the jug on the table and lifted the old one.

Then he turned and headed for the door.

"Wait! Please," I cried. "I don't understand. Where are the Earl and Countess? Where is my husband?"

He shrugged. "His Lordship and Her Ladyship haven't been here for months. They live in Aberdour Castle now." He sniffed and wiped his nose on his sleeve. "As for Lord Fyvie, well, all I know is what I've been told. To keep you here with a fire and water. I don't know when he'll be back."

How was this possible? I came towards him and the aroma of unwashed skin and stale clothes hit me. I lifted my shawl to my face, trying to cover my nose. "Did my husband say how long I am to be here?"

"No, he paid me my money and that was that. I'm a caretaker and I'm doing my job. Now I'll be off. Got plenty to do even though there's no folk here."

I was so stunned I could not even speak. I simply watched him trudge towards the door, open it and clang it shut behind him. The next sound I heard was the key turning in the lock and his footsteps disappearing down the stairs.

When I eventually stirred myself from my stupor, I staggered over to the portmanteau. When had that arrived on the island? Had Alexander come over to the castle after me and had I not seen him nor heard the oars in the water? Perhaps when I looked out earlier, the little boat had been hidden from sight on the island shore underneath my window? I dragged the bag over to the bed and sat down, shoulders drooping, and released the clasps.

There were my gowns, all packed by my loyal Jeannie. I pulled them out one after the other. There was the green one, which I had forgotten to remove after she'd insisted on packing it. When I thought of Jeannie, I was glad at least she was back home safely, with the new baby and my beautiful girls. Then I suddenly remembered about the group of servants from Fyvie we had in our company as we rode down here to Fife. Where were they? Surely that horrible man had been lying or was mistaken and they would all arrive soon, as would my husband with an apology and some sort of explanation; there had obviously been a mix up, a complication perhaps. I fervently hoped that, after I'd got into the boat, Alexander and the servants had not been ambushed by vagabonds.

I laid out the green dress on the bed; that would not fit me, I was still far too fat for the tight waist. I pulled out the next two. Both the pink one and the lavender one were perhaps too lightweight for the winter; what was Jeannie thinking of? But the final one, the yellow brocade, was ideal as it was heavy and suitable for the cold. I spread them all out on the bed and delved into the bottom of the bag.

I rummaged around, poking my fingers into the corners and leaning over to see inside. There was nothing else here. The other things I had packed – the writing paper, quill and ink, my needlework and my rosewater – were gone. And then, as the faint light glinted on the ruby ring on the third finger of my right hand, I realised what was also missing: my parure. As I scrabbled around again inside the bag, I knew that someone must have sorted through my luggage and removed all my things apart from my gowns. Who would do that? They had stolen my most precious jewels, given to me by my husband's aunt. They were my pride and joy, my dazzling royal jewellery; and now they had disappeared.

I could not even begin to consider who had taken them or why. So when a sudden thought came to me, I had to push it far away to the back of my mind, for it was truly too horrific to contemplate. Surely I was not about to spend the rest of my days here in isolation, with hunger and cold, away from my little ones and the rest of my family. I kept trying to think of something else, some reason for this mistake, of why I was here and how I could possibly resolve this dire situation.

But my mind kept rushing back to that first thought and the realisation that Alexander might have deliberately brought me here, to abandon me, forever. Because I could not give him sons, I was to be put away somewhere far away so that he could marry another. And I knew who that other was.

Chapter 26

1601

Lilias

The next morning, I awoke to a murky light. I pulled the gowns I'd lain over the thin blanket towards my shoulders as I shivered in the morning chill and looked up towards the window.

Was there any way I could climb up there and somehow get out before that vile dishevelled man returned? In my many wakeful moments through the long, dark night I raged and cried in the realisation that this was not a mistake; this was deliberate. I was meant to be abandoned here, as punishment for bearing only daughters. And I know Alexander also suspected that when little Margaret had been so ill, I was to blame for the unfortunate accident on the stairs, whereas I was not. But in his eyes it was all my fault; I had failed my husband and the Seton family for only providing him with daughters and so the name would not continue. I was a disgrace and had to be locked away.

I began pondering what would happen to me. Would I become mad, like my father's Aunt Marjorie? She had lived at Drummond Castle with us when I was little, in a room high in the tower. Sometimes we children had been forced up the winding stairs to visit her and at first it was fine, for she was in bed constantly and looked just a little frightening to our childish eyes. But after some time she refused to sleep in her bed and insisted on spending her final months on the floor under a tent, a form of pavilion that the servants had to construct from sheets for her. At first, we children thought this amusing but when she also refused to bathe and the smell in the room became increasingly foul, we all stopped going and Mama did not force us. She died in that room one day in the winter, head poking out from her tent, lying on a deerskin on the floor, all alone.

I shivered as I remembered her and tried to think what I could do. Was that vile man hired by my husband or the Douglases? Surely not the latter, though presumably they had no reason to come over to Loch Leven Castle during the winter months if they were living in the comfort of Aberdour Castle. So he was undoubtedly employed by Alexander to keep me locked in here, with the minimal comforts of water and a fire.

I flung off the gowns from the bed and strode over to stand beneath the window. I dragged over the chair and stepped up onto it. Even on tiptoes, I could only just rest my chin on the ledge, and the window was so narrow even a child would have difficulty getting through it. I looked out over the loch where a low mist hovered. There was a sudden noise, a flutter and flapping and I could see a swan take off from somewhere below me and fly over the loch towards the shore. I watched as she glided just above the mist, flying low over the water towards the reeds where she landed, so gracefully. As I strained my eyes to see whether she had a nest there on the shore, I thought of the freedom this beautiful white bird had, to fly from an island in the middle of the water towards the safety of the lochside and presumably to her little ones. And I wept.

Some time later I picked up the poker, having decided that I could threaten my keeper so that he'd have to let me out and I could get in the boat and row to the shore. I had no idea how to row, but surely it was not hard. Then I could walk until I came across a house and ask for help. I had changed into my yellow brocade dress as that was warm, in case I had a long walk.

The fire was out and I had drunk all the water; I was thirsty and more hungry than I had ever been in my life. There was a pit in my stomach and my head ached a little, perhaps from lack of food or lack of sleep. I was just practising how I would swing the poker when I heard the steps.

I ran over to the door and stood behind, waiting for the key to turn in the lock. As it creaked open, I swung the poker above my head and hovered. And as his eyes darted around the room to see where I was, I froze and I realised I couldn't do it; I could not hit him. I couldn't hit anyone. I was someone who even as a child could not kill a spider or swat away a fly. So when he swivelled round and saw me there, he ducked his head, grabbed my arm, then whacked the poker to the floor. I stood there, helpless, pathetic, snivelling.

"That could have been dangerous," he said, picking up the poker and heading to the fireplace, where he knelt down and started to make up the fire, without a word.

As I watched him, it suddenly occurred to me that this was where I ought to have used the poker, when he was already on his knees, not when he was fully standing at the door. I was such a fool.

I approached him, crouching down so I was level with his eyes, in case I could somehow arouse sympathy. "Might I have some food, please? I'm so very hungry."

He ignored me and continued with the fire then got up from his knees. He picked up the poker. "If I remove this you will not be able to stoke the fire. And it'll go out soon and you'll be cold. If I leave it with you, you'll keep warm. Do you see what I'm saying?"

I bit my lip and nodded.

He scowled then went to fetch the water.

"Please," I pleaded, "please can I leave now? I should like to go home."

He put the water down and looked at me.

"You're not going anywhere. It's the Master's orders."

"Did he say why? For how long?"

He shrugged. "Right, I've got things to do. There's your fire and the water. I'll be back tomorrow." He prodded the poker towards me and snarled. "So you want me to leave this with you to keep the fire going or shall I leave it outside the door?"

"Here, please." I looked at him, trying to see if there was any compassion in his eyes. "And is there any food at all I can have? I've not eaten since yesterday morning and I'm famished."

He shook his head, scowled once more and headed for the door, which he swung open then shut with a heavy turn in the lock.

Chapter 27

1601

Lilias

I had inadvertently settled into some form of routine during those first few days, while I still had energy. I would get out of bed and go to the table where my water pitcher stood. At first, I would pour my drink into the crude beaker beside it. After a few days, however, I simply gulped it down straight from the jug. Since I had still not eaten anything, I found my thirst almost unquenchable. It was as if my body were craving sustenance of any kind, even if that came only in the form of water.

I would then attempt to clean the room using a small broom I'd found under the bed. I brushed and swept away all the debris that fell through the unglazed window. One day I sat down on my bed and actually laughed when I found something for which I could be grateful, ludicrous though my thought was. It was that thankfully it wasn't autumn, otherwise there would not only be whatever debris swirled around on the wind throughout the year, there'd also be falling autumn leaves. Although I wondered if there were any trees on the island, since I did not hear any birds.

I then made my bed up, which entailed shaking the gowns that I laid over myself to keep me warm in the cold winter nights. After, I plaited my hair over and over again, for it gave me something to do. I'd removed the pearls from the plaits and they now lay beside the water pitcher in loose coils, the memory of a former life.

It was one day – I had no idea how many days after I had been here – when I was, as usual, feeling so weak that I wondered if I could be bothered to sweep the floor, that a thought sprang into my head when I caught sight of the pearls. I sat down on the chair to conserve my energy and wait for the vile man – Kenneth, he'd said his name was – to arrive with my water and to make the fire up.

I spent much of those long days thinking. I thought about my beautiful daughters with such an ache it caused me pain in my heart. They must be worrying about me. But then I had tried to imagine what Alexander might have told them – that I had died on the journey? If so, the servants would surely not all have lied? Though, on reflection, the servants he had picked to accompany us were not what I would have called either bright or unduly loyal. I wondered if my husband had paid them off. I went through each of them in my head and came to the conclusion that none had family near Fyvie Castle. All, to my knowledge, had come from Edinburgh and East Lothian, near the family seat of Seton Palace. So I realised, as my stomach lurched, that instead of returning home with him and his lies, they might be going on, generously paid, to their families further south.

I also thought of Mama and everyone at Drummond Castle. As I remembered my sister Catherine and her husband, I could not help recalling how Alexander had looked at Grizel that day, with such ardour in his gaze. I couldn't recollect my husband ever looking at me in that lustful way. I was just so relieved that my sister had not seen his face.

To try to remove this memory, I then thought of my one dear friend, Marie. I tried to imagine her at the convent, dressed in her drab grey habit, such a change from the luxurious gowns and jewels she used to wear at Court. It would soon be time to write to her and yet I had no means. I had already asked Kenneth for some ink and paper, but he shook his head and muttered, "You'd think I was your servant. I answer to no one but my Master and he commanded me to do two things – give you water and make your fire. That is all."

When I then pleaded with him again for some food – anything, a hunk of stale bread, some leftover porridge – he spat on the floor with contempt, then strode to the door and slammed it behind him as he left.

The key turned in the lock and I sat bolt upright in the chair. I had to try to be charming, though I was convinced Kenneth was totally unsusceptible to charm of any kind. In he came, grizzly as usual, thumping down the water and easing himself onto his knees to tend the fire. I had wondered whether to try to rush for the door, though I could not move fast these days. And I also recalled with a sigh that he always locked it from the inside too.

I waited until he had finished with the fire.

"Kenneth," I said, forcing myself to be friendly, though, dear God, he did not deserve my kindness, "I was wondering; do you have a wife?"

He shook his head and struggled to his feet.

"Or perhaps a sister? A daughter?" I had no idea at all how old he was. "A mother?"

He could have been sixty, he could have been thirty. He was so filthy and unkempt and had one of those ugly faces that would have looked scarily disquieting as a young man and chillingly macabre as an older man.

He swivelled around, eyes dull with disdain.

I held up the pearls and once more attempted a smile. "Might she perhaps like these?"

He stared at them, I thought perhaps interested. "I was wondering if you might be able to permit me some food – anything at all, leftovers – and perhaps a walk outside, in exchange for these valuable pearls?"

I was hoping that, once outside, I could run down the steps towards the boat and jump in it before rowing to the loch's shore. I was ignoring the fact that I was becoming so weak I could hardly walk, never mind run.

After some time staring at the string of pearls, he sniffed loudly. "Not worth my job," he muttered. "Rules have to be obeyed and that's that," he said, heading for the door. He turned around as if to speak, but then obviously changed his mind and unlocked the door. As I had anticipated, he did not even have a heart.

Chapter 28

1601

Lilias

I lay dozing on the bed one afternoon some days later, drifting in and out of dreams. Sometimes I was back home at Drummond Castle, sometimes at Fyvie. In one dream I was running all around the grounds of Fyvie wearing my green dress and scattering roses wherever I went; I could almost smell the fragrant petals. I then awoke and looked down, remembering that I was now wearing the green dress constantly, since I had become so thin. Before this living nightmare I now inhabited, I would have thought it was progress that I'd squeezed my post-childbirth body into this, my favourite gown, but now it was merely admission of impending doom.

Sometimes I didn't know if I was dreaming or if I actually heard footsteps on the stairs, even though Kenneth did not unlock the door. Was he watching me through the keyhole? I shivered at the thought. Though what was there to see: a lady fading away through lack of food, of course, but also lack of humanity.

I scratched at my dry face. My skin was flaking and my constant clawing at it to relieve the itchiness was making it bleed; my nails were like birds' talons now. I used to have neat, perfect nails – and such good, clear skin, but like the rest of my body, troublesome things were happening to it and I no longer felt in control of anything. My hair too was dull and hung down, limp, without its usual bounce. I was beginning to think I was going mad; often I was so restless, I wanted to move around the tiny room, but my increasingly frail body would not permit much movement. Soon I would be like Great Aunt Marjorie, alone and delirious and sad;

not that I could be any more sad.

Even when my dreadful keeper leers at me, looks me up and down, I now feel neither repulsion, as I did earlier on, nor fear, simply an acknowledgment of my fate.

I was twisting my brittle hair round and round my finger, rocking a little in time, when I bent my head to one side and listened. What was that noise? Were those voices I could hear outside? Yes, they were. Very slowly, I turned over on the bed and forced myself onto my feet, frail and light-headed as I was in this constant state of dazed stupor, which presumably was caused by hunger. I now kept the poker beside the bed to use as a walking stick to help me walk. I hobbled over to the chair under the window, like some ancient old woman, not a young lady of thirty years old. I sat down and tilted my head to try to hear better. It was two men's voices; one I think was Kenneth's. Was it Alexander come to take me away?

I got to my feet and took a slug of water. I must get up on the chair to try to look out. I held onto the chair back and dragged my legs up then shifted my negligible weight to position my feet on the seat. I grasped the window ledge, feeling lightheaded, and rested my chin there, both as support and also to listen better. I could see nothing, as presumably the conversation was taking place at the postern gate, where I had come to all those days or, more likely, weeks ago. Since it was directly underneath the tower I was in, but three floors down, I could not see anything apart from the sun sparkling on the loch and the shadows of the reeds on the distant shore. But I could now hear quite clearly.

"I don't see why you won't let me come ashore, Kenneth," an unknown voice said. This man, though not a gentleman, was far less gruff in his speech than my barbaric guard.

"I've told you before, Willie, I can't."

"But the Countess wanted me to collect something from her

chambers. When they left for Aberdour last autumn, she had forgotten to take all her things."

There was a pause and I strained to hear.

"I won't be long, I promise I'll be in and out. It's just a tapestry
she wants, from her bed chamber in the Tower House."

"The castle now belongs to Lord Fyvie, as you know, not to the
Earl of Morton. So I can't allow you to come in."

There was another silence while I watched a swan waddle into
the water and drift away, head high in the air as if ignoring these
irritating humans.

"So now will you let me in, Kenneth? There's a lot of money
here in this pouch."

Another pause then the familiar, rough voice replied. "Well, if
you must. Yes, I'll take that. But you must go straight to the bedchamber. In fact, I'll come with you. Now hurry up. Throw me the
rope, we'll tie up the boat."

Then I heard footsteps, fading into the distance as, doubtless,
the two men crossed the inner courtyard towards the Tower
House.

So there was another man inside the castle. My heart raced as
I considered what I could do. It was obvious that he had bribed
Kenneth with money – clearly far more than I could offer by
means of my pearls.

I climbed down, unsteady, and sat down with a thump on the
chair. What could I do to attract attention? I looked around and
thought I could make use of the poker and the pearls. I listened at
the doorway, then, when I thought I heard footsteps coming back
across the courtyard, I began to whack it against the wooden door
with as much strength as I could. But I was so weak and feeble, it
made hardly any noise at all. When I once again heard the voices
down below, I knew the other man, Willie, was climbing back into
his boat. So once again I hoisted myself up onto the chair, a little

at a time, cautiously, taking in short shallow breaths as I pushed my puny body upwards. I laid my chin on the window ledge then clenched my string of pearls up in my fist.

"Well, farewell, Kenneth. I shan't be seeing you again, I don't imagine. Enjoy your solitude."

"Aye, I always do, Willie."

"You won't change your mind and come and see your old mother?"

"No, I'm too busy here. She'll be fine, always has been."

"She can't live forever, Kenneth."

"She's lived till now and she doesn't need to see me."

"Well, I shall tell her you are well and were asking for her."

Then there was a splash as if the oar was in the water and the man was starting to row. I strained to look out and suddenly I could see the boat with a grey-haired man rowing. I yelled as loud as I could. "Help! Help!" I cried again and again, before thrusting my pearls up through the window, swinging them with as much strength as I could muster as I shouted and shouted as loud as my faint voice would allow.

But the man was facing the other way and the wind clearly did not carry my feeble voice, for he did not turn around as he rowed across the water. Then, about halfway across the loch when my voice had given up on me completely, I thought he glanced backwards so I tried to yell once more but my voice was husky and weak. I thrust my hand through the narrow opening and tried one last time to swing the pearls, which would hopefully glint in the afternoon sunlight.

But I watched him turn back around and continue to row to the shore. My last vestige of hope disappeared as he reached the reeds then dragged his boat onto the shore and tied it up.

As I clambered down from the chair, disconsolate and hoarse, I did not even have the energy to go to the bed. I just collapsed onto the floor and lay there, on the cold stone slab, sobbing silently as tears flowed down my cheeks. This had been my last hope. I had been given one attempt and I had failed again. Like everything else in life, I was a failure. I curled up into a ball and prayed to God that I would die.

Chapter 29

1980

Maggie

During my first few guided tours, I'd tried to avoid mentioning the rumours of ghostly sightings at Fyvie Castle. But the minute I stood the visitors around the portrait of Lilias Drummond in her green dress, someone would always say, in an eager voice, "So, is this the famous Green Lady who haunts the castle?"

I realised I had no choice but to bring it into my tour and indeed, having chatted to Silvia over lunch one day, I recognised this was the highlight of the tour for many.

"It's incredible, Maggie," she said, putting down her soup spoon, "This is my second year doing the summer tours here, ever since Mr David was forced to open Fyvie to visitors to save it from bankruptcy last year. And it's the question that's most often asked."

I finished my soup and sat back in the chair. "But has anyone in the family actually seen her at night? My lot this morning wanted actual evidence. One said there's something about roses too. What's that?"

Silvia dabbed her mouth with her napkin. She was a rather fastidious person, fussy about her appearance, always pushing her old-fashioned spectacles up her nose. She had an air of vulnerability about her. I think she was about my age and at college doing shorthand and typing. She wanted to be a secretary and was hoping Mr David might give her a job once she had her exam results.

"Some people have said that when she goes into the Seton Bedroom, there's not only a ghostly presence shimmering in green, but there's also a smell of roses. I've no idea why but I tell my groups it's because she liked to pick roses from the garden the summer before she died."

"But do they not ask for evidence?"

She shrugged. "You could ask Mr David I suppose, but I just tell them she's haunted the Seton Bedroom ever since her husband took a second wife who was really young – and then a third one too. All three wives were only about fifteen when they married and by the time number three came along, he was nearly forty years older than her." She grimaced. "Can you imagine!"

I swallowed. Yes, I could imagine, but I wasn't going to bring up Len to Silvia, who obviously enjoyed a gossip.

"Do you have a boyfriend, Maggie?"

"No," I said, perhaps rather too brusquely. I had become such a recluse over the past year, I was unused to doing small talk. I really had to relax a bit in other people's company. "Sorry, Silvia, that sounded rude. No, I don't have a boyfriend at university, I just don't have time, I'm so busy studying." I forced a smile. "I really want to do well in my Honours years so I can carry on in academia, hopefully do a PhD, but a lot depends on my dissertation."

"You're so clever, Maggie. I'd have loved to have gone to university, but I only just made it into secretarial college."

"But you enjoy it, don't you?"

"Yes, I suppose so."

And I realised I then had to ask about her love life, to deflect from mine. "So what about you? Any boyfriends on the scene?"

Her eyes lit up and she leant in towards me. "I met someone just last weekend at the Young Farmers disco. He's got my number so I'm hoping he'll call me."

"Couldn't you phone him? Did you not get his number?"

She looked aghast. "I couldn't do that, it wouldn't be right. That's what my big sister tells me, anyway." She looked up at the clock. "Help, I've got to go, I've got a two o'clock tour. See you tomorrow."

I watched her run towards the door just as it was opening. She ducked out of the way as Mr David came in.

He walked towards me and sat down. There was something shifty about him. I couldn't quite decide what it was, but I definitely could not take to him. Silvia had told me his cousin, Mr Charles the owner, who lives with his wife in Tuscany, is much more friendly, a real gentleman.

"Miss Hay. Mrs MacPherson tells me you are doing well with the tours and that the feedback she is getting from the visitors is good."

"Thank you. I probably over-prepare everything." I tried to sound light-hearted.

"Over-preparation is better than laziness." He leant forward. "Is there anything you need from me or anyone in the family? My cousin Charles's wife will be returning from Tuscany for a short stay. You will no doubt meet her."

I was about to shake my head, then stopped as a thought occurred. "Actually, the question about Lilias Drummond, the Green Lady, always comes up. Do you know anyone who has witnessed the ghost? Anything I can add to my story about her?"

He sighed. "I'm sure you're aware by now she has become one of our biggest attractions in a way. Her portrait used to hang – a long, long time ago – in the Preston Tower where your room is, but we decided to move it to prime position at the top of the Great Stair so the tours can see her up close."

He paused. "My aunt, Charles's mother, said she was once in the Seton Bedroom late one evening – God knows why – and suddenly felt icy cold and was convinced there was a flash of green coming through the closed door and heading towards the window. But Aunt Ethel was in the early stages of her dementia then so who knows if that was true."

He stood up. "Now, I must get back to work."

And off he strode, again without a goodbye, leaving me wondering what his work actually was.

But I had a blissful afternoon free and I intended to continue researching poor Lilias Drummond. I had just begun reading about her time as a prisoner at Loch Leven Castle and I feared the worst.

Chapter 30

1601

Marie Seton

Chère Tante Marie,

I was pleased to receive your letter and you must accept my apologies for not having written sooner. There is so much to do up here at Fyvie and as you are aware, I am very often at Court. The King requires my counsel on many matters pertaining to the law.

I hope this finds you well. Over the years, I have kept abreast of how you are keeping, through your regular communications with my wife. And I was pleased to read that your aches and pains seem to be less severe these days. As you no doubt know, Mama continues in reasonable health, having recovered from her recent fall and despite the fact she is now in her seventieth year. Her mind is not as agile as it was, according to my sister Margaret who is near enough to see her regularly.

I presume that means he never bothers to see his mother himself. Even as a child he always was fickle, choosing the people in his life who would help him along the way. A mere woman – unless she were Queen Mary, or a wife to give him heirs – could not fulfil that role.

But, dear aunt, to matters less genial. The reason I have not written before is because we have all been worrying so much about Lilias. Since shortly after New Year's Day, she has been ill and is now confined to bed. It all began with mild digestive problems, then, because she could not keep any food down, she began to become increasingly weak. Now she sleeps much of the time and the physician has advised me that her vital organs are failing.

I stopped reading. I did not understand. They were to travel to Loch Leven on the third or fourth of January. Surely she was not suddenly struck down when they were there? She had a strong constitution, she enjoyed her food and ate heartily. How could a digestive ailment suddenly strike one so healthy?

It is with great sadness that I must convey the news that she may not have much longer on this earth, but instead she may go to join our dear departed daughter Margaret. I have not wanted to tell you before, as we of course always believed there would be some improvement, some remedy that would restore her to health. But now it seems there is nothing that can be done. The doctors say it could be only a few weeks.

I leant back against the chair and stared at the letter. None of this was feasible, nothing made sense.

I am so sorry, dear aunt, to have to write with such sad news. And my next letter, I fear, will be even sadder.

Please do not let this news distress you, however, for we all know how loved she has been in her thirty healthy years by us all.

Until I write again, chère tante, please keep well

Your loving nephew,

Alexander

I shook my head. How was it possible she had been at Fyvie Castle suffering from some fatal digestive problem since I had her last letter? I presume that meant she never in fact travelled to Fife? But why had she not written to me earlier on, when perhaps she began to feel unwell but was not yet incapacitated?

A harsh caw right outside my window shook me from my rev-erie. This did not make sense, none of it did. But whatever was happening, I knew what I now had to do. I would go at once to see the Abbess and ask permission to take leave and travel back to Scotland immediately; it seemed as if I had little time. As I thought about the long journey ahead, I knew what I also had to do. Instead of travelling directly north to Fyvie, I would stop first at Loch Leven Castle.

I pushed the chair back and got to my feet. Usually my bones ached, but, in a minuscule way, some of the pains were assuaged. Perhaps God was about to make me stronger for the journey ahead. I stood up straight, crossed myself, then inclined my head to listen. The noise from the carrion crows outside had changed. Instead of their usual harsh squawk, there was now a shift in timbre to a sinister rattling cry, a sure sign that there were predators about.

Chapter 31

1601

Marie Seton

"Is that you, Willie Douglas?" I said to the elderly man who opened the door to the little cottage on the shore.

He broke into a smile and bowed deeply.

"So it is you, Marie Seton. I could not believe it when I got your message."

I smiled. "I have perhaps changed somewhat in the three decades since we last met, Willie."

He gestured that I go inside. "Please, go in to the fire. I'll tell your man to go round the back, there's hay for the horses."

As he spoke to the young lad I'd employed to accompany me on this journey, I stepped inside the house belonging to the man we knew as Young Willie Douglas all those years ago. An illegitimate cousin of the Earl of Morton, he had been employed as a page at Loch Leven Castle during the Queen's captivity there from 1567 until the following year. He was the one who had befriended her by smuggling in letters and then ended up rowing the Queen across the loch to the safety of my brother's awaiting horses. Thankfully, after a few agonising days of waiting, the Earl had let me go to join Her Majesty. Willie was about ten years younger than us, and I hadn't even thought of him until I'd decided to come here, to Loch Leven, on my way back to Fyvie.

He came back inside and sat in the chair opposite me in this simple stone cottage with one small window looking out over the loch.

"I'm just so sorry my wife's no longer with us. She would have loved to have met you. I used to bore her with stories of those months I was with you at the castle."

He went to fetch a jug of ale and poured it into two beakers. "I'm sorry this is probably not what you're used to," he said, pointing all around the small room, which had a bed in one corner opposite the fire.

"Oh, life at the convent is not grand, you know, Willie." I beamed at him. He had aged well, he was a handsome man now at, what must he be – nearly fifty years old. "I am sorry about your wife. Was her death recent?"

He nodded. "Only last year. It still hurts." He bowed his head and I felt he needed time so I looked out the tiny window across the loch. I could not see the castle from this angle so I got up and went to peer out the window and there it was, off to the right, shrouded in morning mist.

"You said you wanted to get over to the castle, Marie," he said as I returned to my seat. "That won't be easy, I'm afraid."

"I thought you might be able to borrow a boat?"

"Oh, I have a boat, Marie. It's tied up on the shore down there." He gestured outside. "That's not the problem; it's the keeper on the island. He won't allow anyone into the castle. I had to bribe him to even go and get something the Countess wanted."

"Countess?"

"The Countess of Morton. The family lives now at Aberdour Castle but she realised she'd left something at Loch Leven Castle after they all moved out last autumn."

"Why won't he permit visitors?"

"Says his Master won't allow it."

"And who, pray, is his Master?"

"Lord Fyvie." He raised his hands in the air. "But of course, he's your brother's son, isn't he?"

"Exactly. So I am sure we can persuade him to let me in."

He bit his lip. "Might I ask why you want to go there, Marie?"

"I feel I know you well enough to tell you, Willie, what the purpose is of me leaving my convent and coming all this way. So, strictly *entre nous*..."

I proceeded to tell Willie about my concerns for Lilias. As I ended my story, he sat back against his chair and took a deep breath. "Well, that's some tale, Marie. But that of course might explain why he was so reluctant to let me step ashore – and when I did, he never left my side."

He scratched his head. "That day I went over, I was rowing back across the loch when I looked back around and was sure I saw something at the top window of the new tower – the Glassin Tower. It was white, maybe shining a bit, sparkling in the light. But then I thought it was maybe just a reflection from the water as it was a sunny day. Now I think about it, I wonder if that's where she is and if she was trying to attract my attention."

"So can you take me?"

"Of course I can, but Kenneth's not an easy man. He's a second cousin of my late wife and she said that when he was a boy, everyone thought he was just a little simple. Until he started killing things – birds, animals – just for fun, not to eat. He was always sly, always a loner, not a pleasant man at all, sad really. Perhaps that's why he was given the role of Lady Fyvie's keeper." He frowned. "I hope she's all right."

I sighed. "It's my sad conclusion that she is not, Willie. How soon can we go?"

He stood up. "We can go now if you're ready. But I have to warn you: getting him to let you on the island isn't going to be easy."

He looked down, shuffling his feet and said, "Do you have any money spare? That might be the only thing that sways him. I'm sorry to say I haven't any."

My shoulders sagged. I had barely enough for this journey. "Don't worry, Willie, I'll find a way."

We must have looked a strange sight in that small boat: one tall, elderly nun dressed in grey habit and white wimple sitting opposite a stout, middle-aged man rowing, and in the middle of us stood a massive, shaggy, grey dog. Willie had insisted he get his deerhound from the kennel as, though the huge dog was tame and gentle, and indeed he kept licking Willie's hand affectionately, he might be useful in trying to persuade the keeper to let us come ashore.

As we approached the castle and I could clearly make out the shape of the tower as the tall ramparts came into view, I felt such a pang of nostalgia. Was it really over thirty years ago that the Queen and I stayed here for eleven months and endured so much trauma? There was not only her miscarriage, but that was also where she heard she had lost the Crown, having been forced to abdicate in favour of the baby prince. We were still young then, but our carefree days of luxury and fun ceased when we arrived there.

"Is that the Glassin Tower?" I asked, pointing to the newer tower we were heading towards.

"Aye, it's where Her Majesty stayed for the first few weeks, d'you remember? Then they moved her over to the Tower House for safety." He glanced over his shoulder as he slowed down his rowing strokes. "Any sign of anyone on the shore yet?"

I shook my head and he continued to steer the boat skilfully towards the short wooden pier beneath the tower.

He jumped out and offered me a hand to climb out of the boat and onto the grass. As he secured the rope to a post, I looked up at the high walls and the tower. So many years later, our arrival here was still fresh in my mind. And though she was a captive, the Queen was allowed out once a day to walk over the inner courtyard towards the garden round the back and of course I accompanied her. I felt a pang of sadness as I thought of her, dead now for over thirteen years; it was unbelievable.

I was standing on the grass looking around to the left to try to recall which was the way into the garden, when a coarse voice bellowed, "What d'you think you're doing landing here, Willie Douglas!"

A short, angry man, of indeterminate age, rushed towards us from the postern gate.

"I told you last time you came. No one's allowed here." He stared at me, scowling.

Willie stepped forward, the hound by his side, so that he was between me and the man.

"I've brought a special lady over. She is your Master's aunt, Lady Marie Seton, and has a request."

Normally I would have insisted Willie should not elevate my rank – I was Sister Marie now – but nothing here was normal. The man, presumably Kenneth, took one step forward and the hound growled, low and threatening.

"Now, Kenneth, will you try to be civil in front of this holy lady and listen to what she has to say." He nodded at me to speak and I cleared my throat.

"My nephew Alexander Seton's wife is, I believe, here in this castle and in need of prayers. I have come to pray with her." I stopped there; I had to establish she was in fact there.

He looked from me to Willie as if choosing carefully what to say. "Did the Master give you permission to visit her?"

So she was here.

"As a prioress, I need no permission to conduct prayers and devotions. If someone wants me to pray with and for them, it is my duty. And I do not answer to my nephew, but only to God."

The dog pointed his nose straight at the man and the low growl continued. It was obvious Kenneth was scared of him.

"Well, how do I know you are who you say you are?"

"Kenneth! You would doubt a lady who has taken the veil?"

The hideous man narrowed his eyes. "I don't get paid much for this job. Might there be any financial..."

I stepped forward so I was directly before him. "No, there will be no financial recompense. This is a mission, sanctified by the Almighty. You will show me to Lady Fyvie's chamber. At once."

We stood staring at each other, unblinking, while the hound's growls grew louder. I could see out of the corner of my eye that he had lowered his head as if preparing to pounce.

Kenneth cowered back. "Well, I suppose you can have a short time with her, though there's little point. She's..."

"She's what?"

"You'll see," he said, gesturing to the door in the wall. I walked over the grass and turned to hear him say to Willie. "You and the dog can stay right here by the boat." He let me through the door and I stepped onto the narrow stairway to the right, then heard the outside door slam behind us.

Chapter 32

1601

Marie Seton

He turned the heavy iron key in the lock and pushed at the knotted oak door. I swept past him then turned to hear him mutter, "I'm sure the master would only permit one short prayer with her, My Lady."

I raised my chin and towered over the diminutive figure. "And I am sure your master, my nephew, need not know the minutes or indeed hours my devotions might take." I motioned to the door. "I will send for you when I am ready to leave."

I shivered in the damp cold and looked up at the unglazed window opening, the only source of light. The door creaked shut behind me and I crunched my way over debris and twigs towards the bed. A putrid smell hung in the air.

As I approached the bed, I wondered if I was too late, for the body in it was lying so silent and still. But then there was a wheezing cough and a shuddering of angular shoulders as the blankets shifted. I sat down gently on the filthy covers beside her, fighting away my tears. It was distressing to see my friend so ailing. There was a fetid smell all around as if she had not been washed in weeks; but also something worse – an air of rotting and decay.

"Lilias, my dear." I took a bony hand in mine. "I cannot ask if you are well, for it is obvious you are not. The sight of you saddens me greatly." Her cheeks were sunken, her skin flaking and sore and her body, even through the thin blanket, emaciated.

The eyes blinked open slowly and she tried to lift her head, to no avail. I pulled the skeletal figure up as gently as I could, shifted myself further onto the bed and cradled her in my arms.

"Oh Marie. It's you," she whispered.

It was difficult to make out what she was saying, her speech was slurred and her voice so quiet. I leant down to hear her better.

"You've come to help me. God be praised." She ran her tongue around her cracked, chapped lips. "After my last confinement ended in yet another girl, Alexander sent me away from her – and all my little ones – to this cold, wretched place. To die."

This made no sense, she was rambling, clearly delirious. "Lilias, your husband sent me a letter, telling me you'd been suffering from digestive complications for the past few months and couldn't keep food down. He said you were near the end. I took the decision to come and see you and so I arrived by boat this morning. Without his knowledge."

She shook her head weakly. "No, Marie. He was lying." She panted, as if struggling to breathe. "He is so set upon a male child, he is determined to marry another; I mentioned her to you, I think, in my last letters, before I was brought here." Lilias turned her watery grey eyes up towards me and spoke in short bursts, her breath now laboured. "He is starving me to death."

I could not take this in. Surely she was hallucinating and was suffering from delirium; she was so weak, she was obviously disoriented, confused. I knew my nephew was merciless and single-minded, but was he capable of leaving his wife to die, like this, alone? Surely not. I gazed back down at her and I murmured some prayers, while stroking her rough, hollow cheeks. She had closed her eyes again, obviously too exhausted to stay awake.

"I am going to go and get some milk and bread from the keeper and come straight back and try to get you to eat something." I began to lay her back down on the bed and she tried to shake her head. I bent down to whisper in her ear. "Is that all right, Lilias?"

She struggled to speak once more. "He won't give you any. I told you, he's starving me. For Alexander."

Then she shut her eyes and seemed to fall into a deep sleep and her breathing grew shallow.

I blessed her then strode to the door and flung it open. I walked down the narrow stairs past one wooden door on the first floor, where I realised the Queen and I had slept, and to another on the ground floor. I knocked on the door then entered and there, in front of a raging fire, was the vile man. He leapt to his feet, glowering at me. From the corner of my eye, I could see a rat scurry for cover across the floor.

"I need some bread and a cup of warm milk to try to bring this poor girl back to life. Why is she so thin? Why have you not been feeding her?"

He looked at me again and I realised this odious man was scared of me, perhaps because of the authority he saw in my nun's habit or perhaps even my height. He ran, like a child being scolded by his mother, over to the table and poured some milk from a pitcher into a pan, which he began to warm over the flames. He pointed to a grey bannock on the table. I began to break some up into crumbs between my fingers over a bowl. Everything was filthy, but there was little time to waste.

He turned from the fire. "She would not eat and my Master said not to force her, that she was imprisoned here for a reason and if she chose to die, so be it."

I threw the bannock down. "What? Why did my nephew say she was to be kept here, to die?"

He peered into the pan then brought the milk over to the table where I poured it over the crumbs, preferring to stir with my finger than with his filthy spoon.

"I repeat. What, pray, was this reason?"

"You must know."

"Enlighten me."

"Well, that she'd killed one baby and that my Master was fearful for the safety of the others."

I stood gaping at this idiot. "And you believed that?" This man was no better than an animal, a low beast. "This gentle, kind and lovely woman has been transformed into a starved skeleton, all because you believed this fabrication?"

He looked down and shuffled his feet.

"And I presume for your trouble and your secrecy, you have been paid admirably?"

"Perhaps a little, My Lady."

I shook my head. "I cannot believe this has been happening." I picked up the bowl. "Go and tell Willie to come upstairs to the top floor at once."

The hideous creature darted to the door.

"And you!" I called after him. "Do not go far, we may need you later."

I swept past him and headed for the narrow stairway, trying to climb the steps as fast as my old body would permit.

I opened the door to her room, went over to the bed, put down the bowl and pulled her up towards me again. But there was a change in her. She was still warm, but lifeless; I knew she had gone. Her mouth was open and no breath came from her.

I laid her back gently onto the bed, pulled the filthy blanket up over the green dress that in her youth had showed off her beautiful, shiny hair so well. Now her hair was so fine and her scalp was visible, but I tried to comb it through, with my fingers, then swept it up behind her head so that it looked a little neater. I lifted up both her arms and crossed them over her chest.

It was then I noticed my ruby ring on her thumb and felt a pang of sorrow; she had worn it all those years, a memory of our friendship. I hoped it had given her pleasure to wear during her short life. Her fingers had obviously become too thin and she had at some stage moved it to her thumb so it would not slip off. I put my fingers around it and slid it off gently and put it on my thumb. The gold was still warm and I felt tears begin to flow down my cheeks as I stared down at her body in repose. I pressed my hands together, shut my eyes and began to pray for her soul. Please God let her find peace at last.

"Mon Dieu, qu'elle repose enfin en paix."

Chapter 33

1601

Marie Seton

Willie rushed into the room while I was on my knees, praying, and stood quietly at the end of the bed.

"Is she still...?"

I looked up at his anguished face and shook my head. "I was too late. And now we must think what to do."

He was silent for a while, then, as I got to my feet, I saw him look up towards the window.

"Marie, it's getting late. It'll be dark soon and the wind's getting up. The loch's not a safe place to be on my wee boat at night. I wonder if we should maybe get back over to my cottage just now and come back first thing in the morning with, well, some sort of coffin?"

I had no idea what time it was, but could see his logic. I looked down again at poor Lilias, who now, at last, looked peaceful. I crossed myself.

"Kenneth's waiting at the bottom of the stairs. He didn't want to come anywhere near the boat with the dog still in it. I said we'd be leaving soon."

I nodded and followed him towards the door. "Are there lodgings nearby where my man and I can stay?" I was trying not to worry too much about money. My meagre funds were fast running out and I still had to pay the lad for the horses and find the money for the boat back over to France.

"Not at all, Marie. You can stay at my cottage. I'll go to my sister's up the hill, it's not far. I'll be back at dawn to see what we can find in the way of wood. I should have something suitable round the back, I can look in the morning light."

We walked down the stairs to where Kenneth was skulking.

I stood directly in front of him and he stared up at me, shifty.

"We will be back in the morning. Do not go anywhere near her, do you hear me?" His eyes grew wide with fright. "Is she...?"

I lifted my head high and sighed. I had no desire to converse any further with this wretch.

I went through the postern gate and saw that it was already getting dark. The sun had gone and there were ominous black clouds building up in the sky. I strode towards the boat, where the dog sat up on his hind legs, wagging his tail when he saw Willie emerge through the gate. I stood on the pier and waited for his master to help me into the boat.

I settled down by the dog, holding onto the sides of the vessel as it rocked in the waves. The dog licked my hand and Willie pulled the oars into position. As he started to row, I saw Kenneth standing on the pier watching us, one hand on his chin, the other jiggling some keys attached to a heavy ring at his belt. Soon, his figure became smaller and smaller as the boat tilted and lurched and Willie heaved the oars through the water as the wind got up.

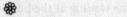

The next morning, I awoke to the sound of the wind howling around the cottage. I could hear banging as if something was being thrown around in the wind in the small courtyard at the back. I said my prayers in haste then went outside to see the dog lying on the ground beside Willie who was dragging some wooden planks out of a small shed. The shed door was swinging back and forth in the gale. The dog jumped up and began to wag his tail.

The strong gusts of wind made it difficult for him to hear me shouting, but soon he turned around. "Oh, you're up, Marie," he cried over the wind. "How did you sleep?"

"Fine," I said, telling an untruth, for I had tossed and turned in the narrow bed all night, trying to expunge the memory of Lilias's dead body from my mind.

"I'm just getting the wood out. It shouldn't take me long to put a box together. Your lad's going to give me a hand. You go inside and have something to eat." He put his hand in his pocket and pulled out a cloth. "My sister made these bannocks for you earlier. Here."

I took the warm bundle from him and went back inside.

I had just finished the delicious bread when Willie came in.

"Marie, the gale's still blowing. I think we'll have to wait till the afternoon to go over. Especially with extra ballast in the boat, it'd be too tricky a crossing in the high wind.

"Of course," I said. "You know what's best."

He then went outside, where I could vaguely make out voices, as he shouted instructions to my servant Johnnie over the wind.

I spent the morning thinking about what to do next. Obviously, I wanted to confront my nephew about the atrocity that he had clearly condoned. But I'd looked in my purse earlier and realised I had just about enough money to pay Johnnie for the horses and to settle the fare for my return boat to France. There was no way I could contemplate a six-day round trip, with attendant costs of lodgings and food, to reach Fyvie Castle. Also, I was only permitted leave from the convent for two weeks. The Abbess was now almost eighty and exceedingly frail, so she had granted me this one trip on the proviso that it must be short; she needed me to assist her in almost everything these days. Since she saw me as family, because of my relationship with her niece, the Queen, no one else could fill in.

I kept trying to work out what I would do after we got poor Lilias's body out of that room and into the coffin, but then at the very thought of her corpse I collapsed once more into tears. To try to alleviate my sadness, I spent much of the morning also praying for her soul, and for God to give me guidance.

After perhaps a couple of hours, Willie came back in and said the coffin was ready and the wind was beginning to die down sufficiently for us to row across to the island. Johnnie and he carried the coffin towards the boat as I plodded after them, my footsteps slow and sad. The dog was howling round the back in his kennel, since Willie had said there was no room for him and the box. The two of us sat in the boat, the wooden coffin balanced precariously in the middle. I held on to it as Willie rowed across the choppy water. As we drew nearer to the castle, I kept looking out for Kenneth coming through the gate, but it remained firmly shut, even when we arrived at the pier and Willie tied up the rope. He then hauled the box up onto the grass and helped me ashore.

"Well, this is strange, Marie. Kenneth's boat isn't tied up here. And he's usually straight out here when he hears the oars," he said, looking around. He walked towards the postern gate and tried the handle, but it was obviously locked.

"Where could he be, Willie?"

"I don't know. But I know a way in through the wall round the back."

"I thought the castle was completely secure? That's why the Queen was brought here."

"There's just one tiny opening that hopefully I can still get through. One of the kitchen maids and I used to squeeze out that way and go to meet under the big sycamore tree at the back of the outer courtyard. I'll see if any of the other gates are open, and if not, try to find that way in. You stay here for now. If Kenneth appears, tell him to come and find me round the back."

I nodded and stood on the grass while Willie headed off towards the left. I was weary, so I sat down on the edge of the box, my back to the castle, looking out over the loch. Thankfully the wind had died down a little and I noticed a swan was flying low over the water, coming from the far shore towards the island. I watched its graceful flight and its perfect landing on the shore just along from the pier. What a beautiful creature it was, so elegant and noble. It was such a contrast to the flapping and fighting of the cawing crows at the abbey. I was watching it waddle off over the grass just as the postern gate flung open and Willie stood there, a grave expression on his face.

"I think Kenneth's gone. There's no sign of him anywhere."

A sudden feeling of dread overcame me. "Is her room unlocked?"

"I don't know, Marie." He gestured inside. "Shall we go up together?"

We went up the narrow staircase to the top floor and found the door to her room wide open. I swallowed; this was not good.

I tiptoed over towards the bed. She was gone.

"The scoundrel's taken her body away. That's why his boat wasn't there," Willie said, his face contorted in anguish.

And once I realised the implications of what had happened, my feelings turned from anger to sorrow, for there was nothing in the world we could possibly do now.

Chapter 34

1601

Marie Seton

Dear Sister Marie,

Thank you for your letter. I am sorry you have not heard from my brother-in-law. I presumed he would have written to you, but I suppose he has been very busy at Court, and also with his impending nuptials.

I have spent the past five months wondering why my nephew has not had the good grace to inform me of his dear wife's demise. And now I read in Lilias's sister's letter that he has also omitted telling me he is about to remarry. Is that not rather indecently soon?

But first I must tell you the news you have been waiting for. My account is immeasurably sad and I must say it has taken me these few months to try to come to terms with it. For my beloved sister, Lilias, is dead.

I don't know if you knew but Alexander had taken Lilias on a journey south to Fife in early January when fortunately the weather was unseasonably fine. She was very much looking forward to it as it was not long after her fifth confinement and she was still rather fatigued. The intention was to stay with the Earl and Countess of Morton at Loch Leven Castle for a few days, during which time my brother-in-law was to attend Court nearby in Dunfermline Palace.

The first time we knew something was not right was when they did not come home after a month, but the weather had changed and we presumed it was due to that. Then two months later, Papa received a letter telling him Lilias was gravely ill and had been infirm for a while, with a terrible digestive illness that meant she could not keep any food down. Alexander said he was with her as often as possible and had employed a physician but thus far no medication was helping. He said we should prepare for perhaps worse news. Of course, Mama and I wrote to him saying that we would travel together to nurse her, or that my sister Jean who was nearer could go to her at once, but that letter went unanswered.

But also, we simply could not believe this of our robust, healthy Lilias. And to be honest, none of us worried too much as Alexander was prone to exaggeration and we all assumed she would be back at Fyvie Castle very soon, brimming with health. You can imagine the shock then when the next letter came to Papa and he and Mama had to go to Fyvie and tell her darling children that their beloved mama had died. It was heart breaking; the girls even now ask for her. Then when Alexander arrived home in the month of May he told us he had decided to bury her in Fife and not Aberdeenshire, as the Queen wished to pay her respects at the grave after the funeral. So she was laid to rest in the nearby kirkyard of St Bridget's in Dalgety Bay. None of her own family, therefore, were able to mourn at her grave.

I took a deep breath. So she had a decent burial near to Loch Leven and even had a royal person to mourn her passing. Well, that was something, I suppose. The more I had thought about the entire matter, the more I'd become convinced that Alexander could not possibly have planned her death, though I was still bewildered by the cause of the horrors I'd witnessed.

We are all trying to get on with our lives and thankfully we ladies are always busy with households to run, and the children, while the men go about their normal business of hunting and looking after the estates. But on the few occasions I have met Alexander, I have tried to snatch a look at him to see if he, like us, is still suffering. Thus far, he seems to be hiding his grief well.

And indeed the other news is that he is very soon to marry my stepdaughter, Grizel Leslie. She is nearly sixteen and therefore of marrying age. My husband, her father, is pleased at the match and the girl herself is overjoyed as she has always wanted to have a title. And now she will become Lady Fyvie.

I was going to end my letter here, dear Sister Marie, but I know that my sister confided in you, so I hope you don't mind my doing the same, for there is no one else I can speak to or write to about my misgivings. And though they do concern your nephew, I feel I must put our family's side to you.

I had begun to wonder about Alexander and his feelings about the death of his wife, my beloved sister. When we were all at Fyvie last month to celebrate his betrothal with Grizel, I heard him telling his eldest daughter, Anne, to cheer up. I was within earshot and could hear her tell him that she did not want him to marry Grizel and he turned on her and demanded, in an urgent whisper, to know the reason. When the poor girl said she did not want another mother, that she was still sad about her real mama's death, he only shook his head and walked away.

I went over to her and put my arm around her and she started to cry. She is so young to have lost her beloved mother.

I tried to comfort her, stroking her hair as I told her things would turn out fine. I said that hopefully she would end up becoming best friends with her papa's new wife as they were so close in age.

She turned her tear-stained face towards me and told me quite clearly that Grizel didn't like her, nor indeed any of them; she only liked her papa.

I told her that was nonsense and wiped her tears away as Grizel herself approached. As usual, her father had agreed to buy her a new gown, again in the same colour as her remarkable blue eyes.

Her thick dark hair was hanging loose around her bare shoulders. I had suggested to her before we left Rothes that she have her maid put her hair up or wear a small cap, but she said she had all the time in the world after her wedding to wear her hair in a fashion suitable for a wife. I should have known; she never listened to advice. You were always so talented at hairdressing, dear Sister Marie, and you will understand why I thought loose hair around her shoulders inappropriate.

I nodded. Loose hair means loose morals, Old Johnnie Knox would have said.

Anne was silent so I decided to speak to them both. "Grizel, I was very much hoping you and Anne will be friends when you marry her father. You are so close in age."

Because I had lived with this rather conceited girl for so many years, I could read the expression that first spread across her face, even though she had then covered it with one of her charming smiles.

"Well, if that is my husband's desire," she said, looking down at poor Anne, "then of course." She held out her hand as a Queen would to a subject. Anne had no choice but to take it and they stood there holding hands, Anne self-conscious, Grizel revelling in the power she would soon wield.

Mon Dieu, Catherine was not disguising how she feels about this girl.

You will detect from my choice of words that I am not overly keen on the choice of second wife for my brother-in-law; sadly this is true and I must say I was surprised to hear my opinion of her confirmed by her father. For later that day, once we were home and my husband and I were alone, I asked him what he thought of Grizel's future husband's character.

"*Most noble, wonderful, committed,*" he had said, looking up from his supper, before enquiring why I was interested.

I told him there was no particular reason, it was just that men often saw a different side when conversing with other men. Then I added that presumably he had no worries about Alexander being a good spouse for Grizel?

He took a while to respond then I am sure he smirked as he told me he thought Alexander had met his match. When I asked James what he meant, he said, "You know how my daughter can be head-strong and, if I may suggest, a little self-centred?"

I was dumbfounded, dear Marie, at this response. It really was a revelation, for it was the first time James had ever criticised his favourite daughter. And he continued. "So I believe that Alexander may be able to tame her a little, while indulging her fancies. And of course, he will make her Lady Fyvie; Grizel would never be one to turn down a title at her young age."

He smiled then put his head down and I knew that was a sign there was no more discussion on the subject and now I should let him finish his supper.

I will leave this letter here, but I do hope all this news does not leave you too sad. I am only sorry you had to hear so long after my dear sister died. I shall write again soon, if I may.

Your friend,
Catherine Leslie

Chapter 35

1980

Maggie

I had just started my tour one rainy day in early July when a hand went up. I had been giving them a brief introduction in the entrance hall before the tour began and was explaining how Fyvie had been held by the crown until 1370 and then by the Lindsay family then the Prestons, the Meldrums and, at the end of the sixteenth century, the Setons. As usual, I had mentioned the fact that George Meldrum of Fyvie had married Mary Fleming, one of Mary, Queen of Scots' Four Marys, and was about to tell them about the castle's connection to Mary Seton when a small stout woman's hand shot up. I nodded at her.

"Are we going to see the bed Mary, Queen of Scots slept in?"

"Well, there are actually no records of her visiting Fyvie Castle, sorry. But her godson was Alexander Seton, who I've just mentioned bought the castle from the Meldrums and..."

"But the man who did the tour last year showed us her actual bed, which was amazing, but I didn't have my camera so I've come all the way back this year from York with this." She pointed at the massive camera swung around her neck.

That must have been Andrew as last year there was only Silvia and him doing the tours. Everyone was looking at me. Should I denounce my colleague as a liar or go with the flow?

"Perhaps last year there was a bed in one of the rooms in the Preston Tower, which is no longer open to the public." I was stalling.

"No, it was in the Seton Tower, which you said we were visiting." She stood her ground while the others in the group fidgeted.

"Well, I'm sorry but this morning's tour won't be showing you Mary, Queen of Scots' bed. Perhaps the 2pm tour will if you want to sign on for that one instead." This was Andrew's tour today. I felt hot all over even though as usual it was freezing inside the castle.

Before the woman had a chance to speak again, I started heading for the stairs, hoping she might stay put. "And now we are going to see the beautiful portrait of Lilias Drummond, Alexander Seton's first wife. Please follow me."

I managed to slip away at the end of the tour before the woman could pounce on me again but afterwards, I headed straight for the small dining room at the back of our kitchen. There was Andrew, sitting with a mug of tea in his hand regaling Silvia with some story in his usual blustering fashion.

"Andrew," I said, "Could I have a word?"

"Of course, come and join us, Maggie. I was just telling Silvia about the preview of a film I saw at the cinema last night in Aberdeen."

I sat down, glancing at Silvia who was even paler than usual.

"You all right, Silvia?"

"Yes, Andrew was going into the gory details of *The Shining* and I hate any spooky stuff. I just don't know how he'd want to watch it."

"It looks excellent. And I thought I could bring things from it into our tours maybe. It's all about a haunted hotel, really scary in parts and..."

"This is what I wanted to talk about, Andrew, making up things just to liven up our tours." I relayed what the woman had said that morning.

"Oh well, yes sometimes I do tell them the Queen slept in the bed in the Seton Bedroom where the Green Lady visits."

I shook my head. "But that's not based on fact. She never visited the castle."

He shrugged. "They love it. Looks like the woman came all the way from Yorkshire to Aberdeenshire just to take a photograph. That must say something."

I was aware Silvia was glancing from one of us to the other, fear in her eyes. She was clearly not one to enjoy witnessing an argument.

"It says to me that your idea of a guided tour of a historic castle is different from mine." I stormed over to the soup pot and started ladling out my lunch.

I had contemplated speaking to Mr David about it, but when I asked Mrs MacPherson if he was around, she told me he was away visiting family on Orkney for a few days.

"Have Mr Charles and his wife never lived at the castle then?"

She gave me a cold stare. "They both reside in Italy, it is good for Mr Charles's health. But Mrs Burnside returns to Fyvie every few months, just to check on things."

I wanted to ask what kind of things but had the feeling the conversation was over.

I spent the afternoon engrossed in my books and notes, thinking no more of the morning's incident. I had come upon some information about Loch Leven Castle, where I'd assumed the only connection with Alexander Seton was that his godmother and his aunt, Mary Seton, were imprisoned there for eleven months in 1567 and 1568. But as I delved deeper, there was more. It seemed that Mary Seton had returned there in 1601 and had been in contact with Willie Douglas, the page who had been instrumental in ensuring the Queen's escape from the castle. Mary Seton must have been nearly sixty by then – elderly in those days – so it would have been an arduous journey.

I looked up from my notes to the high window and saw, thankfully, that the rain had stopped and the clouds were breaking. I shivered in my thin cardigan. I really must try to get to a shop and buy a warmer jumper at some stage.

It looked like Mary Seton had travelled from her convent in northern France to Scotland, to see Lilias Drummond just before she died. But why on earth was Lilias at Loch Leven Castle and how was Willie Douglas involved? I couldn't find out any more in my books, so I began looking into Lilias's place of burial. And what I discovered was a surprise: she was buried at Dalgety Bay in Fife. Why would she be laid to rest in Fife, where there were no family connections, and not here at Fyvie?

Well, that was not going to sit well with all the Green Lady theories as surely ghosts only haunt somewhere near their place of burial? Silvia had told me she mentions in her tours that the secret chamber below the Charter Room may contain Lilias's bones as she was never actually given a proper burial. But between Silvia's naivety and Andrew's blatantly misleading lies, I began to wonder if there was perhaps a glimmer of truth somewhere.

As a history student, I wanted to find out. Since Mr David was away, perhaps I could try to take a look at the old books and files I'd seen in those numbered filing cabinets in the Charter Room after Mrs MacPherson had gone home one day. Surely there was no harm in trying to find out the truth?

Part Four

Chapter 36

1601

Grizel

I had hardly slept all night, I was so excited about my wedding today. We had arrived at Fyvie a couple of days ago and all the preparations were now in place, from the food and the drink to the music and of course the ceremony. I sat down at the glass and stared into it; I did not think I had those puffy bags under my eyes yesterday. I was sure I didn't look as fresh as a bride should be. But, as I flicked my hair from side to side, I knew that Alexander would still be more than happy with the way I looked. He had not even seen the new gown that Papa had bought for me. Catherine of course baulked at how much the silk cost, but I was, after all, his youngest daughter and his last to marry.

Jeannie was just fastening up my new gown, when in swept Catherine, looking dull as always, in a grey dress that would look more appropriate on a nun.

"How are you feeling, Grizel?"

"I am fine, thank you, Catherine."

I had refused from the age of eight to call her Mama even though Papa had tried to insist that, like my siblings, I address her in that way.

"What are you planning to do with your hair?"

"Jeannie is going to put it up, loosely, not in tight coils, and intertwine with pearls."

"Lovely," she said, peering down at the dressing table. "And jewels? What have you decided to wear around your neck?"

"I have everything ready." And I looked up at her with what I hoped was a charming smile. "You'll see later."

"Jeannie, leave us for a moment, will you?" She gestured to the door and the maid went out, pulling the door behind her.

She sat down beside me and took my hand. "Grizel, do you know what to expect on your wedding night?"

I glared at her. What age did she think I was?

"Yes. My elder sister has told me." Her face was a picture; she looked so relieved she did not have to continue her explanation. "In fact, I am looking forward to it immensely," I added, beaming.

"I see," she said, looking rather bewildered. "Well, you know you can come to me if there is anything to discuss? And certainly when you think you might be with child?"

I nodded. "Thank you, Catherine. I know you are never far away." I tried to sound sincere. She was as bad as her sister who had been so sweet and full of loyalty and compassion, it had almost been too sickly. Lilias always seemed to say the right thing and undoubtedly loved Alexander. But she could not always do the right thing by him. Whereas I would produce a son for him. I knew this in my bones.

"I shall see you in the chapel later."

She gave a nod then headed out of my room, leaving the door open for Jeannie, who bounded in rather too quickly. She had obviously been listening at the door. She gathered up my thick dark locks and, without saying a word, began to interweave the pearls.

The day passed in a daze. It was such a happy occasion with everyone overjoyed. The feasting and dancing went on until late and I knew that I had never felt happier. The servants addressed me as Lady Fyvie and even Catherine told me I looked lovely. And before Alexander even said the words "You look beautiful" I could feel from his gaze that he was mesmerised by my appearance. I must say that, having never really taken much notice of how he looked, since he was so old, I found him rather handsome today, in his elegant attire and neatly chiselled ginger beard that was flecked in a fetching way with grey. Of course, he was thirty years older than me, but at least that meant he was mature and experienced. I only wanted to make him happy, but included in that, presumably, was a good relationship with his children. I know it was bad of me but I was always irritated by his daughters, especially the eldest who was only a year and a half younger than me but acted like a child. Still, I had decided I must try to be sweet to her and not only win her over but her younger sisters too.

It had annoyed me greatly when my stepmother had insisted that, shortly before the marriage ceremony, I should say to my new stepdaughters something along the lines of "I can never replace your mother Lilias, but I hope we shall be friends and that you can come to me if you need any maternal or indeed sisterly support." But say it I did, and afterwards Anne sniffed, as if she was about to cry, and Isobel gave me a sullen scowl and the little one looked up at me as if she had no idea who I was. The baby just slept on. I had tried.

When it was eventually time to retire to our bed chamber after the festivities, the maids scuttled around the room, helping me out of my gown, giving each other knowing looks that I pretended not to see. Jeannie wanted to remove my jewels, but I told her that my husband might want to do that himself. She shrugged her shoulders then left me. Soon after, Alexander entered and approached where I sat at the glass.

"Grizel, I must say once again how beautiful you look." He gazed at my neck and touched my hair with a gentle hand. "Tell me, have you enjoyed wearing my wedding present to you?"

I turned to look up at him and smiled. "It is the most beautiful gift I have ever been given. I am so lucky to have you as a hus-band." How pleasant the word "husband" sounded. "You prom-ised you would tell me its history."

"And I shall. Where is the box?"

"Here," I said, unbuckling the clasp on the black velvet.

He bent down towards me and I felt his hot breath on my neck and smelt the claret on him. He unclasped the necklace at the back and held it up to the candlelight. "This is the Seton family necklace. As you can see it is exquisite, like the brooch and the earrings."

He began to remove those from my ears and then the brooch from my bosom.

"There are rubies and emeralds – and pearls to match the ones in your hair," he said, stroking my hair. "The gold is the finest in the world, from Crawford Muir in the south-west of Scotland."

He held an earring up to the light. "This parure is so perfect, it is fit for a Queen." He looked at me, expectantly.

I smiled. I was not sure how I was meant to react.

"And indeed," he said, now stroking my neck, "it was made for Queen Mary, the King's mother, my godmother. She gave it to her lady-in-waiting, Marie Seton, my aunt."

Ah, so it was the nun's parure and she obviously had to give it up when she went to the convent.

"And my aunt is so fond of me, she bequeathed it to me to give to my wife to wear."

So Lilias had worn it too. I was not sure how I felt about that, but it was hardly as if she had only died yesterday; she was buried some five months ago now.

He laid the earring down in the box and shut the lid. "What do you think?"

"I think I am very fortunate to have married such a wonderful man and to have been given the most beautiful parure."

He raised an eyebrow. Perhaps that was not grateful enough.

"Thank you," I said, "I shall treasure it."

He smiled. I was learning all the time how a wife should be, but clearly I still had much to grasp. He held out his hand to mine, led me over to the bed and pulled back the covers. As I climbed onto the bed, I sniffed the air.

"What a lovely scent of roses," I said to Alexander.

He looked at me rather strangely. "I can't smell a thing," he said and blew out the candle.

Chapter 37

1602

Grizel

I lay in bed, pulling the covers around me in an attempt to get warm. I had had to use the chamber pot again and even sitting there for two minutes had chilled me. It was a bitterly cold March night and the wind battered against the window, and the branches of the trees creaked as the storm continued to howl.

It was the second disturbed night I had endured all alone in this dark, cold room. I was not used to being by myself at night. My husband was away at Court on important matters of state and would not be back for another week. How I missed him; but he would soon return, and I could not wait to guide his hand to my belly where I could now feel the wonderful movements of our baby son – here an elbow, there a knee. It was the only thing that gave me strength as I lay there in bed, cold and scared.

I had always hated the dark and had never slept alone all my life. Invariably I had one of my sisters with me and then as they all left to get married, I had the maid sleep in the room. I had considered asking my maid here at Fyvie, Jeannie, to sleep with me tonight, but her attitude towards me was not improving at all, even after I'd had to admonish her for not treating me with the respect I deserved in my position as Lady Fyvie. I told her that day that, if she mentioned her old Mistress, Lilias, one more time, I would ensure she left my employ upstairs and went back to where she came from, downstairs in the kitchen, washing pots. I had hoped that would teach her, but although she never mentioned that woman's name again, she was still constantly surly.

I was fair with the staff, but I had a feeling that some of them, because of my age, did not respect me the way they did my husband. They revered him, bowing whenever he was near, pandering to his every desire. But I always had to ask for things; they never seemed to be able to anticipate my needs or offer their services willingly.

When I told two of the servants downstairs to remove the portrait of Lilias from the top of the Great Stair and hang it instead in one of the unused rooms in the Preston Tower, they were silent. When I repeated my request, stipulating that it was sanctioned by my husband, one of them – that sullen old man, John – said then why did we not just wait until His Lordship was back. I stamped my foot and said I wanted it done while he was away since my portrait was nearly finished and I needed them to clear the wall in readiness of hanging it for his arrival home. I could see them giving each other conspiratorial looks, but eventually, after some clearly audible mutterings, they began the process.

Only yesterday, the artist said my portrait was finally finished and I was keen for it to be on display when Alexander returns next week. When he showed me the painting, I was at first surprised, for I didn't think it looked quite like me. He had managed to achieve the likeness of my shapely figure, before my belly began to grow, of course. And my hair looked rather lovely and my eyes were the most perfect shade of blue and the gown I wore matched them well. But there was something about my expression that I did not feel was right. There was a suggestion of a sneer in the smile, so I asked him to correct that. My smile, according to my husband, is the most sweet and charming he has ever seen, and so I asked the artist to alter it for me to view again today.

If only I could get back to sleep, but it was so cold and the wind was still whirling outside, so I opened my eyes and saw only black. The fire had faded hours ago and there was no moon outside to shine through the window. I lay there, staring upwards at the canopy above the bed, which I could just make out in the gloom. I began to think of our son and what my husband might want to call him. I had mentioned James would be a good name, after my father and also of course the King. But I think he preferred Charles as that was not only the royal prince's name, but also a Seton family name.

I sniffed the air and looked around. Was that roses I smelt? I had told the maid I did not want rosewater used in my toilette as my husband said he did not like the scent. So it couldn't be that, and it was too early for roses to be in the vase upon the table. I breathed in deeply now and was sure the smell was still there. It was a honeyed, sweet aroma that now permeated the night air. I pushed myself up onto my elbow and looked all around. I wished it was not so dark. I wanted my husband with me, I really did not like being alone.

Then, in amidst the black I saw something green, a luminous shape that was the same colour as the emeralds in my parure. I slipped down under the covers and peeked out, trying to see what the green could be – a reflection of something from outside or from my glass? But there was no moonlight to reflect. The green seemed to move across the room from the window and hover at my dressing table. Too terrified now to move, I placed both hands on my belly, compelling the baby to be still. The radiant green seemed to drift around the dressing table, perhaps in the shape of a gown, perhaps in the shape of a creature. Had God sent a spirit down to castigate me for becoming Protestant when I married? Well, I hardly had any choice since that is my husband's faith.

I was frozen with fright but something in me, perhaps a maternal instinct, a desire to protect my baby, made me thrust out my hand, grasp the bell on the table and ring it and ring it and ring it again. My heart was thumping as I watched the green flicker, and soon I heard footsteps outside rushing towards my room. The door flew open and I turned to see Jeannie standing there, in her nightdress, a candle in her hand. I have never been so glad to see another human.

I sat bolt upright and looked towards the table. There was nothing there.

"Come over here, Jeannie. I need you to look around the room. I thought there was something or someone here." Saying nothing, she moved over towards the table and lowered her candle.

"I thought I put your parure back in its box last night, My Lady, and shut the clasp tight."

"You did. Why?"

"The box is open."

Shuffling to the end of the bed, I looked to where she held her candle low and I could see the gold and emeralds of the necklace gleaming in the light.

Chapter 38

1602

Marie Seton

I had received another letter from Lilias's sister Catherine and I must say it was illuminating. Not only had Alexander's wife provided him with another child, but the circumstances at Loch Leven Castle became rather suspect again. I brought the candle closer and began to read it once more.

> *Dear Sister Marie,*
>
> *I hope this finds you well. I am delighted you enjoy hearing the news from Scotland. Before I tell you about my recent trip to Fyvie to meet the new baby, I want to relay what I'd found out the day before. We were entertaining guests from Perth here at Rothes. Sir Duncan Murray and his wife Jane were staying in Laichie at her sister's but had ridden over to visit us. I had not seen them since my wedding, but Jane and I corresponded with each other now and then.*
>
> *She and I were sitting in the cosy nook in our Great Hall while my husband James and Duncan were taking a walk in the grounds. As we sipped our wine, we talked of our families and friends of old. And then Jane mentioned Lilias.*
>
> *She told me how terribly sorry she was to have heard the news of my dear sister and took me by the hand as she spoke. She told me that she'd only met her once, but was charmed by her, remembering her as such a sweet girl, which of course she was. There was nothing but good in my sister.*
>
> *It still upsets me to remember her and to think that her own family did not know she was ill until too late. I'm sure you feel the*

same, dear Marie. Mama has never been quite right since. Her mind is most definitely wandered, though Papa does as much as he can to protect her by speaking for her.

I thanked Jane and then explained how it was even more tragic to all of us that she was so far away when she died, since none of us could be with her at her time of need.

Jane said she'd no idea she was not at home when she died. She presumed she was at Fyvie.

I told her she had been in Fife, and explained that was why none of her family could make it in time to see her, when we eventually heard she was so ill. By then we could not give her support of any kind as it was all too late.

I shook my head. It was all indeed too late, I thought, remembering all too clearly the dreadful sight of her emaciated body, her bones protruding from her soiled green dress on that filthy bed, all alone.

Jane had still looked puzzled and said that presumably Lilias was buried up here, nearby in Aberdeenshire, so we could at least visit her grave.

I told her she is buried at Dalgety Bay in Fife as it was near Loch Leven and she still seemed confused and asked me why there and not near her family.

I said my brother-in-law had told us the Queen wanted to pay her respects and of course Her Majesty could not possibly have travelled all the way to Aberdeenshire. Jane seemed to be taking this information in slowly before eventually nodding, but I can assure you, dear Marie, she looked decidedly unconvinced.

I shuffled in my seat. The old suspicions returned.

So I started to explain that it was Loch Leven where Lilias and Alexander had stayed during those awful few weeks when she was ill. I asked Jane if by any chance she knew the Earl and Countess of Morton who own Loch Leven Castle, since I don't know anyone who lives anywhere near there. I have no idea about the geography of Fife.

She replied that their house was not that far away, perhaps about fifteen miles, so not too onerous on horseback. She said it was such a pity we had not gone to stay with them if we'd had the chance to visit Lilias there. She continued to frown, then told me she still did not understand. She asked why I had been talking about Loch Leven Castle, which she said had been empty for many, many months now. The Earl and Countess moved from there over to Aberdour Castle, which is their grander residence — and easier to reach of course — quite some time ago. She paused and said she would work out dates in her head.

I watched her count on her fingers before she told me they must have left in October in the year 1600. She said she remembered this precisely, as she and her husband had met their friends the Mansfields at a family baptism and they had just been to stay at Aberdour. Apparently the Mansfields are cousins of the Earl of Morton.

Something did not seem right with those dates and so I queried this with her, suggesting she must have meant October 1601, since poor Lilias died in the spring of that year. But she shook her head and insisted it was definitely the year before as she remembered Elizabeth Mansfield telling her that the Countess, Anne Douglas, had declared it to be a wonderful start to the new century. Aberdour was apparently luxurious in comparison to the rather austere castle on the loch that they had left, and she was relieved not only to be living in a more spacious castle, but also one that did not require a boat to reach it.

I took a deep breath and read on, a cold feeling seeping through my ancient bones.

This was all rather strange so I asked her who had been living at Loch Leven Castle after the Mortons moved to Aberdour and she shrugged before answering — "no one at all". But then she qualified this by saying that is what she believed and perhaps she was wrong. She suggested I ask Alexander for clarification as he of course must know. She then asked if I saw your nephew and his new wife often. Then she remembered that Grizel is my stepdaughter and she said how delighted my husband James must be to have his daughter living so near. I confess I found myself stumbling over my reply, but eventually agreed. But it was now my turn to sound unconvinced.

I now felt a chill throughout my entire body and shivered. All of what she had written was unwelcome information. Yet still none of it made sense.

The day after Jane's visit, I set off, with only a maid and a groom beside me, to Fyvie. I had wanted James to come but he dug his heels in, even when I said Grizel would surely want her father to meet her new baby. He had insisted that all babies look the same, but of course asked to be remembered fondly to the mother and child. Men can be so strange with regards to little ones.

As we rode, I kept thinking back to what Jane had said about Loch Leven Castle and how I should phrase it when I asked Alexander about it. But I did not see how I could, unless I mentioned what Jane had actually said.

It was still troubling me as we approached Fyvie and the horses' hooves clattered to a halt on the cobblestones at the pend. I looked up at the splendour of the pale sandstone, which was almost dusky pink on this beautiful summer's day, then the groom helped me dismount. I walked through to the entrance hall with the steward, Donald, whom I knew well from the many times I had visited my sister here. As we walked towards the Great Stair, we had an interesting conversation. After the usual pleasantries, I asked after Lady Fyvie's health.

He told me he believed she was well, but added that few of the staff have seen her for she "tended to issue her commands from her room on the second floor."

So I then asked if I would have the pleasure of meeting Lord Fyvie during my visit.

To this question, he drew nearer and told me no, for Lord Fyvie had to go on essential Court business to Edinburgh the day before. I said that was a pity and that the business must be something of great importance.

I don't know if you remember Donald? He was never the most discreet of the Fyvie servants. He continued to tell me there had been talk the English Queen might not live much longer, since she is already nearly seventy, and so there are many arrangements to be made for when she dies. Ambassadors from England were due to arrive that very day and he told me the discussions would not be easy. I digested this information then asked if I could be taken straight up to see Lady Fyvie and the baby.

At the top of the stairs, he led the way through some anterooms towards the bedchamber, which of course used to be Lilias's. He knocked at the door then announced me and I entered the stiflingly hot room and went towards the bed where I could see Grizel lying, flat, not even sitting up against the pillow. It had been three weeks since the baby had been born, but perhaps she was taking her time returning to normal.

I looked at her wan face, her pallor making her blue eyes stand out even more against the white skin, and asked how she was.

She lifted a limp hand and spoke in a feeble voice, telling me she was slowly recovering from the ordeal and that it has all been rather tiring. Her labours, she insisted, were the worst a woman could ever have to suffer and that the midwife said so. I admit I caught a glimpse of the nurse standing by the bed rolling her eyes.

Even I, who only witnessed childbirth once, and that was at the bed of a queen, cannot imagine a midwife ever saying that. It seemed my nephew's new wife was prone to exaggeration or self-pity; or perhaps both.

Grizel then turned and snapped at the nurse to go and fetch the baby. "Don't just stand there," she shouted. "Go now!"

If she'd still been at Rothes, I would have remonstrated with her about how we must never speak to the servants in a rude manner. But here, she was Mistress of Fyvie and so I could not say a thing.

I told Grizel how sorry I was not to be able to see her husband and she smiled weakly and said that she too was sorry, since he was so very proud of her. She insisted there had never been a happier father anywhere in the land.

The nurse brought the baby in and, once I had taken the seat beside the bed, she handed the little swaddled bundle to me and I uttered the usual remarks one does at such times about how lovely the baby was, what a sweet little nose and such adorable tiny fingers it had. I confess I do love holding newborn babies.

Grizel pushed herself onto her elbows to come closer and whispered to me that her husband told her she had done so well, for at last he has a son. Their little Charles's arrival had given him so much joy. She added that she had fulfilled her duty as a wife. Then she sighed and leant back onto the pillow, telling me that I mustn't mind if she shut her eyes and that she was indeed listening, but she was just so very tired.

I rocked the baby while gazing at the little face, his features all screwed up tight. As I swayed from side to side, I thought, this little one has no idea how much his arrival means to his parents. Alexander will be pleased that the line of the great Seton family will continue and the inheritance here at Fyvie is ensured.

So at last, he has his boy. Alexander will be overjoyed. Hopefully now he will treat this wife with more respect than he did poor Lilias.

I told Grizel what joy this little one had brought everyone and how wonderful babies are. But when I had no response, I looked over to where she was snoring lightly, now sound asleep. It was hardly surprising as the fire was blazing and the room was far too hot. I asked the nurse if she thought it healthy for it to be quite as warm, with a newborn. She shrugged and told me it was Her Ladyship's wish. She said she sometimes has to take some of baby's clothes off as Grizel insists the fire is roaring even during the hot spell we had here in Scotland last week. I looked back down to the baby and began to fan his little red face with my hand, trying to bring some cool air onto his hot little brow.

I have written too much once more. Sister Marie, please forgive me revealing my innermost thoughts in this letter, but I feel I must tell someone my misgivings.

But now I take your leave and wish you continuing good health.
Your friend,
Catherine Leslie

Chapter 39

1602

Grizel

Nurse could be so tiresome. If I stayed too long in the nursery, I could see from her expression that she was chiding me. If I did not come to see the baby for a day or two, it was the same, always judging. Though of course when she overstepped the mark – as she did often – she was admonished. And yesterday I could hardly believe what she said when I asked why the baby was still crying after so long.

"Babies are not just small humans, you know. They need special care and attention."

"Well, it's obvious to me you're not giving my son that care he needs if he continues to bawl."

"My Lady, if you think you can do any better, then why don't you try to calm him yourself?" She handed me the wriggling bundle then stomped off towards the door. "I shall be back tomorrow. If you recall, I am due a day off to see my mother who is ill."

Off she swept, leaving me holding the mewling child. The insolence of the woman! How dare she speak to me like that; her sullen expression, just like Jeannie's, was astonishing. How could she think it was proper to address Lady Fyvie in such a manner?

I was going to have to deal with everything myself upstairs until the next day when Nurse would return. Jeannie and a kitchen maid were, of course, assisting, in particular with the foul matters that had to be attended to, and the wet nurse came upstairs when required, which was often. Dear God, how often could a baby feed? But one thing was certain: small babies were not stimulating company.

I sat there while Jeannie rocked him up and down, walking around the room so often, I began to feel dizzy. When eventually there was silence and she placed him in his crib, I sighed with relief. I peeked a look at him and he lay there, tiny fists flung behind his head as if in submission, but with a peaceful look on his face. At last.

"Stoke up the fire, Jeannie," I hissed.

"The room's already too hot, My Lady."

Did she ever just obey rather than question?

"Just do what I say. I am going down now for supper with my husband," I said, tiptoeing towards the door. "Then I shall return later to kiss him goodnight."

"I can't stay here all that time, My Lady. Cook needs Meggie here so I have to deal with the upstairs rooms and all the girls while supper is being served. You'll have to come back as soon as you've eaten. Then I can join you when I'm free."

I stared at her. "But I cannot be alone with the child. What if he needs changing?"

She shrugged and began to fold up the pile of clean clothes in front of her. Then she turned to me, sullen as usual, but with a smirk playing around her lips. She was enjoying this.

"Grizel, I have important information to impart. You must listen very carefully," Alexander said, pausing from eating to look directly at me. Sometimes he spoke to me as if I were a child, though I suppose that, compared to him, I was. I turned my head to the light so that he could see the glint of the rubies and the sheen of the pearls. He liked me to wear the earrings from my parure when I had on my crimson, pearl-encrusted gown.

"I am not sure if you are aware, but the English Queen is very old. She might die at any time now."

I nodded, though I was trying to calculate how old my husband was. He must be forty-seven, so, although not as old as her, he too was beyond middle age. Though he does not like me to ever mention the age gap between us, perhaps because I am so much younger or perhaps because he is beginning to look a little, well, ravaged around the edges.

"You will recall that I was at Court a couple of months ago to speak with the Ambassadors and of course the King himself. He is ready now, when she dies, to go to London to take up the throne there and so unite the crowns of Scotland and England."

"That is such interesting news, Alexander. And presumably the Queen will go with him?"

"Obviously, Grizel. Every man needs his wife to be at his side; and the King especially so. Sometimes you say the most stupid things."

Once more I felt the many years between us keenly.

"He will take the two older children, Prince Henry and Princess Elizabeth, to London with him as well as the Queen. But the third child, Prince Charles, is rather weak and sickly."

He paused to stab a large chunk of beef with his fork then turned to me, beaming. "And so I am to be the prince's guardian until he is stronger. He will live with us here at Fyvie and then we shall take him to London to join his family."

He chewed on the meat then took a swig of wine while awaiting my response. I knew what he had just told me was an honour, but I could not help but think there was already one child called Charles at Fyvie who needed constant attention; was that not enough?

"I see. Well, Alexander, this is a wonderful tribute to your relationship with the King. And of course we shall do whatever His Majesty wants. But might I ask how old the little prince is?"

Please God let him not be a baby like our own Charles.

"He is soon to be two, but as I said, rather delicate and so needs special care. He is not yet able to walk. But mentally, he is strong and indeed, when he has mastered even basic words, I shall begin his education, for I am not only to be his guardian, I am to be his tutor."

I was trying to take this in and consider what the implications were. "Will we have more servants to tend to his needs?"

"Obviously. The King will pay me well. And everyone will envy the trust His Majesty has invested in me to look after his precious son. Of course, he is only the second-born prince, but who knows, he may one day ascend to the throne himself. Then what an accolade, to have the distinction of having raised a future king."

I breathed deeply. "I presume we will not hear any more until the English Queen dies?"

"Precisely. I simply wanted to inform you now because I intend to start converting the Preston Tower into a nursery and rooms suitable for a prince."

My first thought was that was where I had had Lilias's portrait taken and that I must deal with that as soon as possible. But I said nothing. I merely smiled, which my husband always expected.

"Now, I must go to the Charter Room. I have many letters to write. I shall no doubt see you upstairs later." He stroked the nape of my neck lightly then stood up as the servants rushed over to pull back his chair.

It was already dark when I got back up to the nursery. The wet nurse was just leaving and she said the kitchen maid Meggie should be back soon. She had laid the baby in his crib and I peeked over. Even in the candlelight, I saw his eyes were shut and he seemed to be sleeping peacefully. Thank God. I sat there for a while, turning over in my mind the fact that, at some stage in the next few years or perhaps even months, our home would have a royal prince staying in it. It was all rather too much to take in. As I was musing over the possibility that our son Charles could end up a friend of Prince Charles and how wonderful that would be, the baby began to stir. I stopped twiddling with my earring and kept completely still, hoping he would settle himself.

I could just make out his face in the low light and saw, with horror, that he had opened his eyes. Dear God, where was the maid? I was far too exhausted to have to deal with a crying baby. He began to whimper and I kept looking at the door, wishing it would open and the maid would appear.

Then I sniffed the air. There it was again, the undeniable scent of roses all around. How was that possible? I looked about the small room but could see no flowers. Whatever could it be? The baby was now yelling and I got to my feet, ready to pick him up, when the door flung open and Meggie the maid rushed in.

"Sorry I'm late, My Lady. Cook had so many dishes to prepare, the washing up took forever. She uses so many pots and pans, and there was no one else to help me with that just now."

As if I needed such tiresome domestic detail.

"Well, you are here now. The child needs to be picked up and rocked to sleep; he's been crying." Though when I looked down into the crib, he seemed to have settled himself.

I sniffed the air. "Can you smell roses?" I whispered as Meggie tiptoed over towards the crib.

She shook her head. "No, nothing at all, My Lady."

And when I breathed in deeply again, I realised the scent of roses had vanished.

Chapter 40

1603

Marie Seton

Dear Sister Marie,

I write this letter in the midst of interesting times. I do not know how much — if any — news from England or indeed Scotland reaches the convent, so I thought I would write, in case you have not heard, that the English queen is dead and our King must go to London to take up the crown there too. He will be England's King James I and our own James VI.

Well, well, so my beloved Queen's son now rules over both countries. The little baby I saw come into this world that momentous day in Edinburgh Castle, with his sharp, pointy nose and tufts of black hair all over his bald head, is now King of both Scotland and England. What would my Queen have made of that, I wonder. I know in my heart she would have been overjoyed, no doubt about that. Though perhaps she would have also liked France to have been included in his domain.

I took up the letter to continue reading, then had a sudden thought about James. Should I write to him and offer my compliments, my homage? But I was no longer a subject and he had taken no interest in me during my lifetime's attendance on his mother, so why bother him now? I raised my head to the ceiling, as usual wincing as I felt how stiff my neck was, and sighed. Should I mention to him that Renee de Guise, his great aunt, had died last year and now I had no income at all and indeed was now almost a pauper?

But we've had no communication these past decades and so

how would that appear? Besides, I was a Seton; we do not beg. Perhaps I could instead simply write to my nephew and ask him to pass on my felicitations to his Master the King. I had often wondered about what I would write in a letter to Alexander after the horror I witnessed at Loch Leven Castle, so now might be the chance to focus my attention on corresponding with him. I had not written to anyone in Scotland since Catherine's last letter. Perhaps it is time, though to be honest, my command of English has become rather rusty. I speak only French here.

I told you in my last letter that Grizel, your nephew's new wife, was safely delivered of a baby boy. His name is Charles – just like the King's son – and he fares reasonably well, though he does seem to be prone to chills and coughs. For this reason, his mother – who is really but a child herself – always insists on having the nursery far too hot; the fires were again raging the last time I visited and it was a warm day outside.

I see Alexander seldom, for he is so often at the King's side, though that is all about to change since the Court will reconvene in London as soon as Their Majesties travel south. We hear the King has promised to return to visit Scotland every three years at least, and yet many I speak to doubt he will fulfil this promise. The King's second child, Prince Charles, is to be brought to live at Fyvie Castle under the tutelage of your nephew and his wife Grizel. As you can imagine, though this a great honour, it is proving a great deal of strain on relations at Fyvie, both with the family and also the servants.

Oh, how Alexander will be in his element, I thought as I looked around the bare cell that was now gloomy in the late afternoon light. I tried to imagine the beguiling little boy I once knew as an ambitious, ruthless middle-aged man now. Though I recall his obsession with male heirs started long before he was even betrothed. When I considered what had happened to Lilias, the word ruthless did not seem strong enough. I have thought long and hard about my visit to her since I returned to Reims and the convent. I spent the first few weeks in the chapel on my knees praying not only for her soul, but also for his. I admit, my knees have not recovered since.

The more I thought about it, the more I realised there must have been a reason why poor Lilias had been left to starve. Surely there was some sort of valid explanation. My nephew was driven and could be selfish, but a murderer he was not. I met Lilias only at the end when she was delusional and her mind had been altered by the lack of food; she was clearly hallucinating. So what actually happened at Loch Leven to end up with her dying in such a sordid and agonising manner?

I was lulled out of my reverie by a noise. I sat still and listened. It was coming from outside my cell. I got to my feet and walked slowly to the door then pulled it open a little. Sisters Janette and Albertine were talking to each other, agitated.

"What seems to be the trouble?"

They jumped apart and the younger one, Janette, bowed. *"Désolées, Mère Abbesse, mais nous avons des nouvelles."*

"Je ne suis pas Mere Abbesse." I sighed. These younger nuns had no idea how to conduct themselves. I am not the Abbess, I am simply looking after things until Renee's great niece is able to journey here from Lorraine.

Albertine stepped forward. "Sorry, Sister Marie. We have just heard the news about the English Queen and did not know whether to tell you now or after compline."

I sighed again.

"Thank you, Sisters. I have already heard. And now it will soon be time for prayers. Please go to prepare the chapel." They both turned and scuttled away.

I shook my head. The responsibility was really too much now. It was perfectly manageable when I was just a nun and Renee de Guise was Abbess, but now I was in charge, albeit temporarily, I found it all too intrusive; I never had a moment's peace. Also, even though Renee was eighty when she died, I am now over sixty and find my energy dissipated and my creaking bones less able. But I suppose it was what I had signed up for when I came to the convent all these years ago, when Renee came to treat me as her confidante and friend, rather like her niece did.

I had no idea I would end up running the convent, though thankfully not for much longer. I was still hoping the new Abbess would arrive soon. We kept hearing the weather was not conducive to travel. But it was now March, so surely she would be here soon to take over the duties of Abbess. I was not groomed to lead, but only to be led. It was my calling with Mary my Queen, and I was ready to return to that lowly status here at the convent.

There is another matter I feel the need to mention to you, Sister Marie. As you know, I spoke with some friends several months ago who know the Earl and Countess of Morton. You will recall I told you Lilias and her husband were to be their guest at Loch Leven Castle. It has been on my conscience since I met these friends, wondering if I ought to have told you what I was told during their visit. I have concluded that you might be interested to hear it has been confirmed that the Earl had sold Loch Leven Castle before Lilias even arrived there. And that he, his wife and their entire family have been living at Aberdour Castle for some time now. I still have not felt able to ask Lord Fyvie about this since, as you know, your nephew is not always the easiest man to speak to and he is seldom in residence at Fyvie when I visit. There are many things that still do not make sense.

He seems now to be happy with my stepdaughter Grizel since she has produced his long-awaited son. The last time I saw him, which was some time ago at the baby's baptism, he had had several glasses of claret for he swayed as he stood. He took my hands in his, leant towards me and told me how overjoyed he was with his baby son. He then whispered in my ear that, if only my dear sister could have provided him with a male heir, she might still be here.

When I looked askance, he then muttered something about her anxiety and stress contributing to the illness that killed her. I could of course not say that before she was married she was carefree and content. For this was clearly not what His Lordship wanted to hear.

But I mention the matter of the ownership of Loch Leven Castle to you as there is no one else I can relay my fears to. I hate the thought of my sister having been there alone or at least without her family; presumably there were servants to attend to her in her sickness.

Oh, if only there had been servants, not just that evil caretaker.

Now I must end this letter and hope that it finds you well. I don't suppose you can ever leave the convent now but if you ever do, you know you would be most welcome to stay here with us, though I imagine you would prefer to stay with your nephew at Fyvie.

Your friend,
Catherine Leslie

Chapter 41

1603

Marie Seton

The following day after morning prayers, I decided to visit the grave of Marie de Guise, Queen Mary's mother. Situated at the back of the church in the little chapel of remembrance here at the Abbey St Pierre, it's a place I often go, to sit still and contemplate as I feel it is somehow a conduit to my friend, her daughter. As I strolled around the cloisters, there was a sudden flurry of flapping wings up high in the large oak tree in the middle of the cloister garth. I looked up to see four crows leave their perches to fly towards the south, in the opposite direction of the bells that were now ringing from the cathedral.

Renee and I had discussed early on that my Queen Mary's body would be brought here to be buried beside her mother. Mary had such an affection for her aunt Renee, indeed it was almost a daughter's affection, not merely a niece's, after her own mother died. But this did not happen and she is buried at Peterborough Cathedral instead, a place she has no links with. Just thinking about this makes me sadder than I could possibly have imagined. It was on the command of the English Queen. But I wonder if, now her son is King, he will move her casket back to Edinburgh or perhaps even to Westminster Abbey where I presume Elizabeth is to be buried.

Marie de Guise's tomb is magnificent. It is marble, with a life-size bronze statue of the lady in royal robes, holding a sceptre and the rod of justice in one hand. For many seem to forget that she too was Queen of Scotland, just like her daughter, who absolutely adored her. Mary de Guise was Queen Regent after her husband

King James V died, and from all accounts she was well-liked and respected. Admittedly, not admired by everyone; John Knox of course, even before he began to lambast my Queen Mary, criticised the Regent Queen's every move, despite the fact she kept Scotland – a country she hardly knew, having been brought up in France – stable at times of potential uprisings and revolts.

I looked up to her face, carved in such delicate splendour in bronze. She seemed serene, noble and yet kindly. The bells of the cathedral had stopped and the crows had returned to the trees above. But for once they were silent and I was able to think back to when Queen Mary had been told of her mother's death. I recall that we four Maries were in attendance to her at the French court, since she was Queen of France at that time, before her first husband Francois's death. Even when King Francois died only a few months later, her grief was nothing compared to how she reacted when the Cardinal of Lorraine arrived to pass on the news of her mother. Afterwards, she railed against the French nobles who'd decided she shouldn't be informed immediately of Mary de Guise's death. When I think about it now, I agree it was shocking that it was a full ten days after she had passed away that the Cardinal arrived with the news.

Her grief was insurmountable and even though we Maries tried to console and comfort, she wanted only to take to her bed and cry and cry as her body collapsed with such sorrow. On her instructions some months later, her mother's body was brought back over to France and buried here at Reims, where she knew Renee would pray at her grave. When I thought back to that day, it gave me an inkling of how she must have felt when she was wrenched away from her own beloved son, whom she never saw again after we fled to Loch Leven.

I finished my prayers, crossed myself and struggled to my feet. Really, my knees were getting worse and worse. As I walked back around the cloisters, I thought once more of Loch Leven and Lilias. It occurred to me that I thought of Lilias the way Renee thought of her niece, with such familial affection. My feelings for Lilias had been almost motherly.

I decided that I would write to my nephew and probe a little about her time in that awful place. Surely there must be some explanation. Of course, it was too late, she was gone, and this Grizel had delivered a boy and so Alexander would be happy – if that were an emotion he was ever capable of expressing. But what if the child died – Catherine wrote that he was prone to coughs and chills – and Grizel could only produce girls. Then what would happen to this new wife? Might she suddenly disappear too?

I entered my cell and sat down at my desk. I picked up my quill, dipped it in the ink and began to write.

Chapter 42

1980

Maggie

I'd been walking in the grounds of Fyvie Castle, first along the river Ythan and then back along the side of the loch to reach the castle. Even after a month here, the sight of it suddenly looming up behind the trees never ceased to impress. It was so majestic in both size and style. Also, it was not at all obvious that bits had been added on over the centuries. I walked over the muddy ground and up the slope to the south-east of the castle, to the ruins of a small chapel in what used to be called the inner garden. This had been a symmetrical knot garden with shrubs and low hedgerows, created by Alexander Seton to impress his distinguished guests as it was visible from the relatively large windows of the main rooms on the first floor. I stepped over the remains of the walls of the chapel and stared down at the weathered flagstones on the ground. I realised there were inscriptions on the stone and peered down to read.

I knew Alexander Seton wasn't buried here, but at Dalgety Bay in Fife, and I'd discovered that Lilias's grave was also there, though I still couldn't find out why she'd been at Loch Leven Castle. I presumed his second and third wives were also buried in the family vault in Fife.

The inscriptions included crests, letters and some Latin numbers. I decided I'd come back with my notebook and take notes and sketches, look more closely. One stone had an M and an S on it – but the date was impossible to read. Did the letters stand for Margaret Seton? The distinctive crescent of the Seton family crest was visible beside the engraving, so it was definitely one of the Seton family. But Alexander had two daughters named Margaret, one who had died in infancy, and of course his third wife was my namesake, Margaret Hay, later Seton. When I'd discovered the fact we shared a name, I felt rather spooked, but then I began to think that perhaps she was not just the only wife to outlive him (by decades) but also hopefully the one wife to get the better of him, as I already had the feeling he didn't treat the first two well; he came across as ruthlessly ambitious.

Also, though he was an almost acceptable fifteen years older than Lilias, he was thirty years older than Grizel and then thirty-seven years older than his third and final wife, Margaret. Even given my own situation, that age gap was indecent. Especially as the wives were all fifteen or sixteen when they married. I shivered: what a horrific thought.

I had been thinking of Len rather a lot. Though I had known him all my life – he was Dad's best friend after all – we only properly got together after Allison died. I remember so clearly being at her funeral and everyone saying such sweet things to the grieving widower. I'd just had my Higher results and knew I had got into university, so I was just seventeen; he was forty-two. When I think about that now – rationally – it seems ridiculous. But I was in love and thought it was reciprocated.

I thought back to the Hogmanay party the year before she'd died and the moment he kissed me at midnight, when Allison was in hospital. I was so infatuated, I didn't even care if Mum or Dad saw us lingering far too long in each other's arms. From that moment on, I wanted more. Yes, he was twenty-five years older than me, but that did not matter. Then we started seeing each other casually at the tennis courts where he would tell Dad he was coaching me for great things. There was always a special bond between us, even in those innocent early days.

When I spent that summer before university as a chamber maid in Oban, I remembered my friend Ann's face when he arrived in his flashy car. I hadn't said anything about Len being much older and she looked at first confused and then utterly shocked as he stepped out of the car and rushed over to kiss me; but not as shocked as Mum and Dad, when they found out.

I sighed and headed back to the castle for my 2pm tour. I had not yet had an opportunity to get into the Charter Room before Mr David returned at the weekend and so I was desperate to get this last tour over with. Would I be able to find a key for those glass cabinets and old wooden filing drawers?

I had found out that Lilias only bore daughters – five – of whom one, the first Margaret, died in infancy. I was still to determine what she died of, but there were so many infant deaths in those days. And then the second wife, Grizel, had first a son, Charles, then later a daughter whom they named Lilias, which seemed rather odd to me. When I read that his third wife Margaret had a son and then a daughter, I chuckled. Surely he would not want to name this baby girl after his previous wife, but yes, I discovered her name was Grizel. Alexander Seton perhaps felt he needed to salve his conscience for the way he had treated his first two wives by naming the first daughter of his next wife after the last. By this stage of my research, I was sure I did not like him one jot, but I had to admire his gall.

Part Five

Part Five

Chapter 43

1604

Grizel

"We will be leaving in a fortnight's time, Grizel, to journey to Northamptonshire to meet Their Majesties and deliver the young prince safely to them. Ensure preparations are made," Alexander commanded. "We should be away for about three months."

I could not speak, I was so shocked that he wanted me to get up from my lying-in bed and go on such a long journey. It had only been six weeks since our daughter was born, and I was still in pain.

I'd heard him come into my bedroom and sit down at my bedside, then he pulled at my arm to ensure I was awake. I emerged from the covers and glanced at his face. I shuffled up the bed and ventured, "But what of our own little Charles?"

He gave me a withering look. "What of him?"

"He is only little and he needs his Mama. As does the baby."

"Don't be ridiculous, Grizel. Charles has Nurse to look after him and the baby has the wet nurse. Now get up and stop feeling sorry for yourself. We have much to prepare."

He had a look on his face that I had come to know and so I forced a smile; it was what he expected.

"That's more like it. Now, another thing. I shall expect you to wear the parure when we are in Their Majesties' company. So ensure your maid packs it; I have not seen you wear it for some time. Once you are up and dressed I shall come and select which gowns are suitable for the journey. You may need more made."

"There is hardly enough time for..."

"I shall tell you if you need more." He cut me off. "On the journey south, I shall prepare you for how to act at Court. The prince shall travel close beside us all the way and so, for once, you will attempt to look interested in him."

"But, Alexander, I have tried."

"No, you have not tried. You have been so obsessed with our own children that the royal child has been ignored by you. It is fortunate I have had time to tutor him myself."

"The baby has taken a lot out of me," I said feebly.

"She has a name. Will you ever call her by it?"

I swallowed. When my husband insisted our daughter take her name, I was shocked and can still hardly bear to say it. I prefer to spend time in the nursery with our little Charles, who is usually fit and healthy, unless my husband insists our son spends some time playing with the prince whose runny noses and chesty coughs seem to immediately transfer to my darling boy.

My husband stood. "Oh, and I need you to write to Aunt Marie Seton too. Tell her about our journey south and about the birth of little Lilias. She has written me three letters now and I simply do not have the time to write back to her. Tell her I intend to come over to France at some stage to see my wine merchants, and shall hope to pay her a visit, but for now, my energy is with the King and his family."

He smiled and headed for the door.

Dear Sister Marie,

My husband Alexander, your nephew, has asked me to write to you with the news from Fyvie Castle, for he regrets he has not had time to answer your kind letters. I hope this finds you in good health. Alexander says you have suffered from some aches and pains and I know from personal experience how debilitating that can be. I still have pains after the birth of our second child.

    Charles, our firstborn, is now two years old and a happier little boy you could not find. He is also, God be praised, healthy, with a good appetite, though he is sometimes prone to chills.

I cannot blame the prince in a letter to my husband's aunt, though I know it is only when he has been in the nursery to play with my son that my Charles becomes ill.

    He is now walking well and saying some words, though only Nurse and I can fully understand what those words might be. I think you will have heard that he has a playmate, the royal Prince Charles, who, though four years old, is shorter than our own boy. He came to us a weak and sickly child, but now can walk up and down every stair at Fyvie Castle. His speech has also improved a good deal, with my husband tutoring him daily. It is time, therefore, for him to leave us and return to his family in England.

Thank God. The sight of all those people fawning around him has been too much to bear. And then when I see him rushing over, with his disgusting, phlegm-covered nose, to hug my own dear boy, it breaks my heart. Keep your sickliness to yourself, I would cry inwardly.

    Alexander and I leave next week for Northamptonshire to meet the King and Queen and to hand over the royal child. It will be a moment of great joy for my husband, who has been so honoured to be given the responsibility of caring for the royal prince. We shall be away for three months, during which time I shall miss our son badly.

    I gave birth to a healthy girl six weeks ago and Alexander decided to name her Lilias. I know Lilias Seton was a friend of yours and so I am sure you will be delighted with this name. For one so little, she has powerful lungs and is both chubby and robust.

I cannot possibly write that I am simply unable to say her name, it is so painful for me. One night, when my husband was in a talkative and cheerful mood, I decided to ask him a question about something that had been troubling me.

"Alexander, after Catherine left today, it occurred to me that she must still be sad that her sister is no longer with her. I was wondering: I know she is buried in Fife, but I don't actually know how Lilias died."

He turned towards me and grabbed one of my wrists. "That is none of your business, Grizel. She died tragically young and left four children motherless. That is all you need to know." Then he stormed out, leaving me to rub my wrist to avoid the bruises that now regularly appeared.

The blossom has been wonderful at Fyvie all summer and has remained in bloom for longer than ever before, the gardeners say. The flowers give me great pleasure when I take a walk in the gardens with our son. I do so enjoy their scent outside, though I confess I find the aroma of any flowers inside, especially roses, rather overpowering.

I couldn't write that, when I used to see the green shape on those black moonless nights, hovering near where my parure's kept, there was always the smell of roses, and I have become so terrified, the maid now sleeps in my room every night.

I do hope this finds you well and I shall write again after our journey south with the royal prince.
Until then, I am your faithful niece,
Grizel Seton

Chapter 44

1604

Grizel

The news came as we were approaching Moulton, north of Northampton. I was exhausted and weary of the journey. We had just arrived at the viscount's house and I had gone straight to bed, leaving Alexander to deal with the servants and the little prince and our hosts. I had no energy at all; the past few days and indeed weeks had been so tiring. What I next remember is a loud slamming noise as the door flung open and my husband stood there, a candle in his hand. He came towards me and I saw his face was pale and he did not smile.

"Grizel, I have just had news from Fyvie." He sat down on the bed and took my hand. Dear God, what had happened?

"It is not good, I'm afraid. Indeed, it is deeply sad. Prepare yourself for what I am about to tell you." He eased himself up the bed beside me.

My heart raced as I braced myself for the news that our little daughter had died in her sleep. Many small babies did. I took a deep breath.

"Grizel, the letter informed me that Charles, our son, is dead."

"NO!" A great wail filled the room, followed by loud howls. I then threw myself at Alexander, hitting him with my fists. He grabbed onto me as my legs and arms thrashed and flailed.

"This is your fault! I said we must never leave him!" I flung myself back onto the bed and my chest heaved with sobs.

"Don't be foolish, Grizel. It was no one's fault."

"We left him and so she was able to get near, I said we must never leave him..."

He swept back the hair from my forehead. "What on earth are you talking about? You are raving now," he said leaning in close. "Desist!"

I wiped my tears with my sleeve then whimpered, "How did he die?"

Alexander took a deep breath. "The letter says Nurse had put him to sleep as usual and he had only a little cough, nothing serious. By the morning, he was dead. He must have died peacefully in his sleep." He glanced at me. "It happens you know, but don't worry, we will have another son."

"I don't want another son, I want Charles! Had we been there, he would not have died." I shouted. "I want to go home NOW!"

"Will you calm yourself, woman!" he hissed, grabbing my wrists tight. "Now listen very carefully. We will continue on to Northampton as planned. We will return Prince Charles to the King and Queen and attend Court with them for the week as has been arranged for some time. And then go home after that. Do you understand?" His face was so close to mine I could see the veins in his lined forehead bulging as he spoke.

I threw myself onto the bed and cried and cried. I heard him rise from the bed and head for the door. "I shall have your maid bring you some wine with something added to it to make you sleep. Then in the morning we will continue as normal. I hope that is understood."

I buried my head in the pillow, wishing I had the courage to suffocate myself, but I knew I did not. As I heard the door close to, I looked up towards the window where a shaft of moonlight had burst through the clouds. The light shone onto the necklace from my parure, which I had discarded on the table without even putting it away, I had been so exhausted. The emeralds gleamed a brilliant green.

Then I sat upright and gasped as the sudden realisation of what had happened at Fyvie struck me. Even though I'd agreed to give our baby daughter her name, an idea to placate her, I presumed, she had come in the night and taken our son. For this was the one and only thing she herself could not provide my husband with. She had taken my baby son for herself as if mocking me. It was her, the Green Lady, Lilias Seton.

Jeannie came into the room, set down a cup of wine into which she stirred some tincture, and gave it to me. She had tears in her eyes. Even though we did not get on at all, she too was a mother and so must be feeling my loss.

"Thank you," I managed to utter before I downed the wine and fell back onto the pillow, praying that if sleep did not take me, then death might.

Chapter 45

1604

Grizel

The next morning, I managed to stop crying long enough for Jeannie to complete my toilette. I was dressed in the new blue gown with the pearls sewn in around the neckline. I had had it made for my first day at Court and she had arranged my hair high off my crown, in the manner we heard the Queen favours. I thought it looked dreadful, even though my forehead is wonderfully smooth, but I was in no state to argue and my husband had approved the style when we had tested it before we left Fyvie. She had just left to fetch some more water when there was a knock at the door and Alexander entered. I immediately stopped snivelling and raised my chin. I could do this.

Then as he approached, I saw that he too had been crying. His eyes were red and sore-looking and it seemed as if he had not slept all night. He not only looked his age, he looked twenty years older. I opened my mouth to speak but thought better of it and so I waited.

"Grizel, the King has just sent a message. He heard our sad news and wishes to pass on his and the Queen's sincere condolences. He asked if you wished to delay your attendance at Court awhile. Obviously, I must go in any event to deliver the prince."

I was unsure whether this was a question or a statement and so I remained silent.

"I have just sent a message to His Majesty to say we would both attend Court today as planned but then, after three days, should that be acceptable to Their Majesties, we would return north to bury our son."

His head drooped and I waited for more. But there was nothing. He turned and headed for the door just as Jeannie was entering. She curtsied as he stepped past her, shoulders hunched like an old man.

"Will you wear these, My Lady?" Jeannie lifted the parure from its box.

"Yes, my husband would insist upon it, for my first encounter with the King and Queen." She began to put on my necklace and then the earrings.

I turned round and grabbed her hand. "But then, Jeannie, when we are back at Fyvie, I shall remove them from my jewellery drawer." I had been thinking about this as I sat in silence while she attended to my hair. "I will not wear them once we are back home. So if you cannot find them, do not worry, they will be safe."

I looked up at her. She was frowning.

"Why, My Lady?"

"Because they bring bad luck. Your previous Mistress wore them and she died. I have been wearing them and my darling son has just died." My voice caught but I swallowed and forced myself to continue. "They are a curse. After today, I shall keep them somewhere safe and yet out of sight, so you must not fret that they are missing."

"And if His Lordship asks me where they are?"

"Send him to me."

She bobbed and left the room and I looked in the glass before me. The emeralds and rubies glinted in the morning light. Usually, I would smile at my reflection, made even lovelier by the jewels, and feel blessed and happy. But today I saw only a young girl whose heart had just been broken.

Our first day at Court at the Earl's castle in Northampton passed quickly, thank God. Queen Anne had been charming and kind to me during our private audience, but once she had passed on her condolences, she talked more about herself and how she'd coped after the death of her two little ones, Princess Margaret and Prince Robert, than of my own darling Charles. She invited me to pray with her, which I supposed was an honour, but her Lutheran upbringing meant I felt no connection at all to her invocations. Even though we were all now Protestants at Fyvie, I still yearned for the familiarity of my Catholic childhood.

She was only thirty, a mere ten years older than me, and yet there was something mature and awe-inspiring about her. Perhaps it was her astonishingly ornate dress with all its lace and brocade and those elaborate jewels at her neck and in her hair. Her coiffure was so high, I wondered if she might bump her head against the ceiling. She also had a more fulsome figure than me, though she had had her last child some two years previously.

Or perhaps it was the fact that, when she sat beside the King and we conversed together, she did not appear to defer to him at all, even though she was only Queen Consort. It was almost as if she were his equal; this was so unlike the relationship between Alexander and me.

She did not wait for him to begin a conversation, nor did she always agree with him. When the King said how fine the weather had been and we all nodded and concurred, she said, "Well, in fact it was extremely cold this morning, if you recall. Or perhaps your rooms have more lusty fires than mine."

I glanced at Alexander who looked surprised, but the King simply shrugged and put his hand on my husband's arm, before drawing him away to a corner for a private talk. The Queen had been delighted of course to be reunited with her son and told us both how very grateful she was for our taking such good care of the prince, and we all had to watch as he walked then ran the full length of the Great Hall several times, but thankfully he was soon sent away to rest.

Then Queen Anne invited me to sit with her while she told me again about the two little ones she had lost. At least I had been able to forget momentarily about my own little Charles. But when I was about to leave, she drew near and whispered to me in her funny, clipped Danish accent, "What you need now is to be with child very soon. Ensure it happens."

And before I could even think of an answer, she swept away with her ladies-in-waiting.

At the masque later that day, I hardly saw either the King or the Queen amongst the crowds, though Alexander was of course almost always at the King's side. Soon after the Queen had retired, I told my husband I was going to bed and he said he would join me in our chamber later. He was merry and ruddy of complexion, obviously the royal wine was very much to his liking. If he had been full of sorrow a mere twenty-four hours before, he seemed to be covering his sadness well.

It took Jeannie ages to get me undressed and to pat down my hair. As I watched her in the mirror, I could see she kept snatching glances at me, presumably to see how I was faring. How very strange it felt to have some sort of reconciliation with my irascible maid over my darling son's death.

My shoulders began to shake as I thought once more of him and tears flowed down my face. She patted me on the shoulder and asked if there was anything else she could do, but I dismissed her and took to bed.

I must have been sound asleep when Alexander crashed into the room some hours later. His servant had obviously tried to undress him but not successfully, for he fell onto the bed with his shirt half off him. He began to kiss my neck and I swatted him away, but he persisted then soon ripped back the covers.

"No, Alexander, I am asleep!" I cried, but he persisted.

I ended up sobbing as he pulled off his breeches and flipped me over as if I were a piece of meat.

"Our baby has just died, I do not want this," I howled.

But he grasped my hands and flung them back above my head, then bent over me as I gasped for air under his claret and brandy breath.

"And I do want this," he hissed. "You will give me another son."

Chapter 46

1604

Grizel

Every long day of that tedious journey home, I hardly spoke. If addressed by one of our hosts, I was polite but said very little; silence suited my frame of mind better. When we were alone at night, Alexander admonished me for my reticence, but I said I had no desire to speak until we had buried our son, and that my life was no longer worth living.

"Do you not realise what a fortunate girl you are to have spent three days at Court with Their Majesties? You should be revelling in that, not sulking."

Sometimes I wondered if he had a soul.

When I said I was grieving, he became angry and reminded me, as he so often did, that I had a daughter waiting for her mother at home. I shrugged and said nothing. How could I possibly love a child who was named after the woman who had caused my son's death?

One wet, miserable day as we neared the Scottish border, he trotted up alongside my horse and I could see he was in good spirits. He said he wanted to cheer me up and had decided to tell me what he and the King had been discussing.

"As you know, just like me, His Majesty is a patron of the arts, a scholar who is keen on poetry and literature and architecture. Our conversation as ever was so wide and varied. I've always known he values my opinion and my counsel, but there is something else." He beamed. "I was only going to tell you after the burial, to give you some hope, but since you have been so sullen, I have decided to tell you now."

I feigned interest and turned towards him, water dripping off my nose as the rain pelted down and my horse's reins became more and more sodden.

"Grizel, I am about to be appointed Lord Chancellor of Scotland, which is such an honour." He beamed and I nodded, forcing a smile.

"That is truly wonderful news, Alexander. The King holds you in such high regard." This would surely mean he would be away not only in Edinburgh as usual for long spells, but presumably in London. Well, that would not bother me; I preferred my own company these days, though not at night.

"And," he said, patting his horse's wet mane, "there is more. This will affect you too."

I assumed my wifely smile. "What could that be, Alexander?"

"In a few months, I am to be made Earl of Dunfermline, in recognition of my committed and devoted guardianship of the young prince. Is that not wonderful?"

My first thought was, well, the guardianship was more onerous for me than for my husband. He was so often away either in Edinburgh or at the palace in Dunfermline, dealing with matters of state, while I was trying to keep the sickly prince with his runny nose and feeble cough away from my own darling boy.

But then he leant in and smiled. "You will be a Countess, Grizel. Won't that sit well with your family? And mine too – imagine my brother Robert's son's face when he hears. He thought he and his father were the only Setons to have the title Earl bestowed upon the family by His Majesty. You have to agree, Earl of Winton is not as distinguished as Earl of Dunfermline," he said, placing great emphasis on the city's name.

Ah, so this is what it's all about, his continuing resentment about not being the firstborn son and therefore unable to inherit the title Lord Seton, even though, in his opinion, he was more worthy than his now deceased elder brother Robert.

"That is good news indeed, Alexander."

"I believe I told you that my nephew is decidedly unbalanced and so he will surely bring his Earldom into disrepute anyway." He shook his head. "My poor brother would be turning in his grave."

It had been with great glee that Alexander had told me the gossip from Seton Palace a few months back: that his nephew, Robert Seton, second Earl Winton, had become mad on his wedding night, emptying the chamber pot all over his new bride. Poor Anna, she was even younger than I was to be wed. What an ordeal it must be, living with a madman. Though sometimes, when I see things at night, things I can never speak of, I wonder if I too am going mad.

"So, our son – when you produce our next child – shall in time also inherit the title of Earl of Dunfermline. It's such splendid news." He patted my horse's mane then kicked at his own horse's flank and set off ahead at a canter, leaving me to my thoughts and my misery. Even the prospect of being a Countess could not lift this black cloud.

1605

Many months later, I heaved my fat belly over from my bed to the dressing table and opened the drawer, just to remind myself that the parure was not there; anything to keep her away. I sat down with a thump on the chair and looked in the mirror. My face was pale and my skin dull and spotty. Please God, let this baby be a boy so I don't have to suffer the burden of pregnancy and the indignity and agony of childbirth ever again.

I peered at my eyes, which used to sparkle and shine. Now they did not even look blue, they were grey with fatigue. I'd just had another of my disturbed nights and even though Jeannie now sleeps on a mattress on the floor beside me, I still could not wake her up the minute I saw the Green Lady enter my room, for I was as usual frozen with terror. The shimmering emerald green shape floated in through the door and over to this table where I now sit, and here she hovered until I managed to yell for Jeannie to wake up.

As usual, she jumped up and rushed towards me.

"Is it the baby, My Lady? Is the baby coming?"

She lit the candle and I shook my head. I was trembling all over and I pointed towards the table where she had been. But of course, she was no longer there.

Jeannie took my hand. "Was it another nightmare, My Lady?"

I swallowed. "She was there again, Jeannie. The Green Lady, over there, waiting for me. Now I've hidden the parure, it's me she wants."

Jeannie laid the candle on the table and patted my arm. She spoke in a soft voice. "Do you want me to get some of the tincture?"

"Yes, but leave a candle burning. I don't want to be alone in the dark."

She sped out the door to the kitchen to find the elixir the physician had prescribed for me to sleep and I sat bolt upright, continually looking over to the table. She had been there, she was definitely still after my parure – or indeed after me. I took a deep breath and inhaled that familiar cloying, sickly aroma of roses that lingered in the air. Then I spoke out loud, to the shadowy room. "There, you see. I am not going mad, she has also left her scent."

I recalled the vision the night before as I gazed at my pale reflection. I sighed and lifted up the pearls that Jeannie would weave through my hair later, in readiness for my husband arriving home from London today. My husband the Earl; how he loves his new title. If someone had said to me before my marriage that I would be a Countess, I would have been overjoyed; but now it means nothing, for I am in a permanent state of trepidation. I jump at the slightest noise.

But my husband is enjoying his new status and indeed I must say he looks slightly less old and wrinkled; it has rejuvenated him. In his letters to me, he has repeated how pleasing it is to know that his son – the baby in my belly – would inherit the noble rank in due course. To him, it was all perfect. To me, there was a hurdle to be crossed first; and that involved me giving birth to a baby boy.

Chapter 47

1980

Maggie

I felt two hands close in around my neck. Even though I was warm under the blankets, I suddenly felt cold all over as those icy fingers clawed closer together. I tried to speak, to cry out "Stop – " but the hands continued to constrain my throat and I thought I was going to die. My hands flailed by my sides as I tried to move and shift those glacial fingers.

Then all of a sudden I broke free from the tight grip. I sat bolt upright in bed and gasped for air. It was pitch dark and my hand patted around on my bedside table to find my torch. I put it on and staggered over to the light switch. I was breathing heavily as I went back to bed and pulled the covers tight around me. What a horrible nightmare. It hadn't recurred for ages, months probably, and now here it was again, those memories surging back just when I thought they'd disappeared.

I slipped out of bed and went to the door; my hands were shaking as I turned the handle. I shone the torch down the narrow stairs as I headed for the bathroom. It was ridiculous but I'd actually contemplated getting a chamber pot to save me this dark, chilly trip down one flight of ancient steps in the middle of the night. I still didn't believe in ghosts and yet there was something unnerving about going down those centuries-old, narrow stairs in the pitch dark. A couple of nights before, the moonlight had shone through one of the narrow windows and it was somehow more unsettling as I was convinced I saw shadows on the stairs. I bolted upstairs and back to my bedroom.

I couldn't get back to sleep, so lay there trying to think of anything to take my mind off that harrowing weekend; but I could not. Len had picked me up from my halls of residence one Friday afternoon and taken me away to a romantic hotel in Aberdeenshire for the weekend. It was somewhere near Banchory, which I think is some considerable distance – to the south, I think – from Fyvie. On the first morning, we lay in bed with cups of tea and he began to ask me about friends at university. I was being deliberately vague but I'd let slip that I'd been at a Medics Ball. The minute I said the words, I knew it was stupid and I guessed what was coming.

"So who invited you?"

"Oh, no one, I just went with my friend Mary, you remember I told you she's doing medicine?" I tried to change the subject and said how excited I was about the delicious breakfast in bed we had ordered the night before.

But he continued. "What about that boy who was also doing medicine, you mentioned him yesterday – Rob, was it?"

My stomach tightened as I took a gulp of tea, then spluttered as it was far too hot.

"Oh, yes, Rob – well, he's Mary's friend so I was kind of making up numbers with the whole gang of them." I put down my cup and started to get out of bed, but he grabbed my arm, tight, and pulled me back. He gripped both my wrists and yanked me towards him so my face was only an inch away from his.

"Is he your boyfriend, Maggie?" His voice was very strange, almost unrecognisable.

"You're hurting me, Len," I said, trying to shake him off my wrists.

"Then tell me the truth," he hissed.

I'd just opened my mouth to say something when there was a loud knock on the door. I jumped off the bed and ran to open it. A teenager who'd served us in the restaurant the night before stood there, his trolley laden with silver cloches, an elegant coffee pot and dainty cups and saucers. He came in and began to set it all out on the table in the next room; Len had, as usual, booked the suite. I grabbed my dressing gown and put it on then stood chatting to the boy while he laid the table. He handed me the bill to sign just as Len came through from the bedroom, face like thunder. The waiter looked from him to me and his eyes widened.

I took the pen to sign but Len came over and snatched it away from me. "I'll sign for this. I am paying, after all."

The boy attempted to smile when Len handed him back the bill and I watched him go out, glancing to the left, into the bedroom. Oh God, he must have thought how weird I was, sleeping with a man so much older. Or worse, that I was being paid for my overnight services.

When I turned around to face Len, he looked even older, as if he had aged overnight. Normally all I could see was a handsome rugged face; that morning I saw a frown set in his deeply furrowed brow and a hard look about his eyes that I didn't like. I decided to say nothing and sat down at the table and began my breakfast, rubbing at my sore wrists when he wasn't looking.

The morning after my nightmare, I staggered over to the mirror and shook my head when I saw the bags under my eyes. What a terrible night. I must have got back to sleep eventually, but only for an hour or so till the alarm woke me. I stood under the shower for ages, trying to eliminate the memory of last night's dream. Soon, I was ready to face the day and headed downstairs to the kitchen, where I made myself a strong coffee before going to the entrance hall to begin the first of my three tours of the day.

I'd guided my eager visitors through the library and we all stood at the entrance to the cabin, so-called because a recent laird of

Fyvie had been in the Royal Navy. I pointed to the portrait on the wall inside the small room and told them it was of Grizel Seton, née Leslie, Alexander Seton's second wife.

"Grizel, Lady Fyvie, is dressed in an exquisite cornflower blue dress made of silk damask, with a narrow brocade of flowers around the neckline. As you can see, it's relatively simple in style for the era, given her status, but we mustn't forget how young she was at the time, still really only a girl."

"And how old was he when he married her?" boomed the stout woman who had been taking notes, which at first I'd found rather unsettling, but now found slightly irritating.

"Well, Grizel was just sixteen when she married and he must have been forty-six."

I looked round them all and every single one either shook their head or grimaced.

The woman's pencil scratched away and she raised a hand.

"Yes?"

"What's that necklace round her neck? It looks rather grand."

"I was just coming to that, actually," I said, fixing my smile. "The necklace is part of a set called a parure. This is a set of jewels intended to be worn either together or, as you can see here, separately. The necklace contains rubies, emeralds and pearls, all strung together with coils of gold. The gold was from the Leadhills estate in South Lanarkshire. In the sixteenth century, this area was called Crawford Muir, and that's where there was important gold mining. The gold from here was so valuable, it was used to refashion the Scottish crown for King James V, who was Mary, Queen of Scots' father."

A hand went up. Thankfully not from the persistent note-taker.

"All those pearls in the necklace – where would they have come from in those days? I thought they all come now from Japan and China."

Luckily, I'd read up on this. "Freshwater pearls came from Scottish rivers. They were extremely precious then, but not as rare as they are nowadays."

I looked over to the woman with the notebook whose hand had again shot up. The man beside her had been stooped until now, muffled in a scarf and a woolly hat, so I'd never noticed his face. But now, as he stood up straight and loosened the scarf, I gasped. He stared directly at me and for a moment I couldn't speak. Was it Len? An icy shiver ran down my spine. I turned my head, as if stifling a cough then looked back. The man was still watching me. His nose and his eyes were so similar to Len's, it was uncanny. But now his eyes were crinkling into a smile, his mouth was wide and full, kind somehow, unlike the menacing sneer I'd come to know in Len. I sighed with relief. "Excuse me," I said, clearing my throat.

I nodded to the note-taker.

"Is it true this parure has been lost for centuries?"

So she knew all about these jewels. That was clearly why she'd asked me about the necklace. She'd also been overly interested in all the Raeburn paintings, peering at them far too close. When I told her to "please be careful not to get too near", she ignored me and continued to inspect them at close range. I looked at her and a sudden thought occurred. I'd caught sight of one of her pages of notes and she'd sketched a diagram of one of the rooms' layout. Was she taking all those notes because she was part of a consortium of thieves, checking out Fyvie and how easy it might be to steal something?

"Well, the parure is certainly not on display here, but that's all anyone knows about it." I started to head back into the library but she continued, "Does the family who live here not have it then?"

Now she was more than a little annoying. "No," I said, turning towards the next room and ushering everyone out.

My tour continued without many more questions, but when

we arrived back in the entrance hall I checked to make sure she left with all the others and wasn't lurking around. I was standing at the door watching her on the grass gazing back up at the castle walls when Andrew arrived for the next tour. I beckoned him over and pointed at the woman, explaining my concerns.

"Oh," he said, shaking his head. "She's been before. Not on my tour, but Silvia said she was a bit of a pest, kept asking questions. At first, we reckoned she was a busy-body, but then I wondered if she was from a newspaper, you know, trying to find a story about the jewels."

"Should I tell Mr David?"

He shrugged. "He won't do anything."

We both looked outside where she was heading down towards the car park. "Anyway, if it's the jewels she's after, it's not likely she'll find anything. Even Mr David doesn't know where they are."

"Really? I presumed they were in one of the safes in the Charter Room."

"Not what he told me," Andrew said, before heading back inside in a haze of aftershave.

Chapter 48

1605

Grizel

I lifted my head from the pillow and sighed wearily. "Yes, what is it?"

Nurse had been instructed by my husband to bring the child to my bedroom to see me. "Bring her over here then." I tried to shuffle up the bed a little, my enormous belly impeding my every move. Nurse came over and helped haul me up with her strong arms.

"Thank you," I said and gazed over at the child. She really was not bonny. She had her father's pointed chin and unnaturally long ears. Her hair was ginger and so fine, she was almost bald. She staggered towards the bed like a tiny drunk.

"Isn't she doing well now with her walking, My Lady," said Nurse, beaming.

I reached down a hand and she took mine in her hot little fist. I looked at her miniature yellow gown and thought how it did not suit her colouring. I was about to ask Nurse where her woollen cap was when there was a noise at the door and Jeannie rushed in.

"Nurse, you're needed downstairs. Meggie the kitchen maid has slashed her hand badly and we're trying to stem the blood. Cook said to get you. Come now!"

Before I could shout to Jeannie to stay, both of them hurried out the door, leaving me alone with the child. She stood there, holding my hand and looking around.

I had no idea if she understood words, for clearly she couldn't yet speak. But I decided I ought to try, even though it meant I would have to utter her name.

"Lilias," I whispered. She continued to look all around and indeed, withdrew her hand from mine and began teetering away from the bed.

"Lilias, come back to Mama."

Dear God, she was heading for the door and presumably the stone stairs where she could tumble and fall. I'd heard talk that Alexander's first wife had dropped their infant daughter Margaret onto the Great Stairs and the impact on the stone precipitated the little one's death. I flung back the covers and swung my swollen legs out of bed.

"Lilias!" I was shouting now. Did she even know that was her name? I was just about to grab her when she stopped by the door and turned around, heading off at a wobble towards the dressing table by the window. I was already short of breath so I grabbed onto the wooden bedpost and leaned against the end of the bed. I watched her chubby fingers reach up and snatch a long string of pearls before she fell backwards, laughing. She landed on the floor with a thump, the pearls clutched tight between her fat little fingers.

"Lilias, are you all right?" I said as I watched her push herself up to a sitting position, legs outstretched. She beamed at me; perhaps she did in fact know her name. She then lifted the pearls in both hands and put them over her head. They slipped down around her shoulders and she pulled them up again so the strand looped once more around her throat. She pulled again and I could see the coils tighten around her neck as she drew them even tighter.

"No, Lilias, you'll hurt yourself. Take the pearls off!"

I pushed myself away from the bedpost and strode towards her. I bent down to scoop her up with two hands but as I lugged her heavy weight up onto my hip, I suddenly felt it. As I stood there, untangling the pearls from around her neck, her hot little body wriggling like a worm, I could feel the wet trickling down my legs.

"Jeannie!" I bawled towards the open door.

The little girl flinched, but I yelled again. "Jeannie. Come quickly, the baby's on its way!"

I lay in the dark with my eyes wide open, listening to Jeannie's soft snores from the mattress by the fireplace. I was still so exhausted and weary after yet again an endurance test of pain and then at the end of it all, the ignominy and anguish of giving birth to another girl. That had been about a fortnight ago, perhaps longer. I had lost track of time and simply wanted to sleep all day long while trying to shift the black gloom that hovered over me. I refused all the food they kept forcing me to eat; I knew I would never feel hungry again. And because I dozed all day, I was awake most of the night, twisting the covers between my fingers, round and round as I thought back to the birth.

The girl had been hale and hearty and the midwife said I had done well; for a girl, she was a big baby. I did not want a big baby girl; I wanted a baby boy of any size. Alexander muttered something about how at least she would be a sister for Lilias and that I was bound to have another son next. The very thought of that made me feel queasy. And when he said her name would be Jane, I simply shrugged and said, "Whatever you want, Alexander" then turned my head back to the pillow to continue weeping my pale, silent tears. I knew he was whispering to the servants about me, but I had no desire to hear. I was too wearied to even try to listen.

The room tonight was warm, even though I had asked Jeannie to open the window just before she went to sleep. I flung off the blanket and tilted my head to one side. There was not a breath of wind outside; it was a balmy summer's night and so the only noise came from Jeannie's regular snores. I began to pray for sleep to come. Perhaps if I thought of something joyful, it would happen, but I could think of nothing at all that made me glad, not one thing.

I must have dozed off, as the next thing I knew I was awakened by two icy cold hands clamping around my neck. I gasped and as I bent my head back, I smelt the roses. The hands were clawing at my neck as if trying to scratch something from me. And I realised it was her, the Green Lady, trying to wrench the necklace of my parure from around my throat.

I wrested free from her clutch for a moment, but then she was back and this time I could see her. The green haze shimmered above me as I thrashed my head around on the pillow. My hands flailed on the blanket and I began to feel more desperate. I tried to shout out but my voice didn't work. I would have to get up and waken Jeannie by kicking her. I flung myself out of bed and staggered over to the dressing table, thinking that she might be placated with my other jewels.

I patted frantically around on the table in the dark, trying to find the rest of my parure. Where were the earrings and the brooch? For still she clung to me, her icy cold hands closing in around me. My throat ached and her grip was so tight now, I could hardly breathe. I brought up my hands to try to wrestle hers away but could not. I tried to shout out but still my voice was silenced. As I thrashed around on the dressing table, I suddenly began to feel hot. The ice-cold grasp had gone.

I woke up in bed, sweating all over. I rubbed my neck and looked around and at first could see nothing until I noticed a shimmer of green on the window ledge. I had to go over there; I was now so hot that if I stayed inside this room, I would surely die. I needed to get some fresh air. I stumbled over the floor, guided by the haze of green, which seemed to be calling me, even though I could hear nothing.

I opened my mouth to try to speak but nothing came out. Perhaps I was still asleep. I climbed upon the chair by the dressing table and got up onto the window ledge where the green now seemed to be hovering, just outside. It must be so wonderfully cool out there and I was so hot. I had to follow; it was the only way to remove this heat from my body and to rid myself of her forever. She would not have my parure.

A sudden noise interrupted my thoughts and I swivelled around just as someone reached out to try to grab my hand, but I didn't want to be brought back in. I wanted to be outside, in the fresh air, floating down in the cool breeze, like the Green Lady. So just as Jeannie's fingers touched mine and a shrill scream rent the air, I breathed in the exquisite waft of roses then let myself go, and soon I felt free. And at last, I was cold.

Part Six

Chapter 49

1606

Marie Seton

Chère Tante Marie,

I do hope this finds you well. Here, the winter has taken a tight hold and we have been snowed in for some ten days now. Fortunately, with the recent renovations I have been undertaking, the castle is now well insulated, which means that inside, with our roaring fires, we are quite warm. We simply cannot travel anywhere. One of the grooms saddled up a horse yesterday but the poor beast could not even get out of the stables, the snow was up to his flank.

Yet I feel there is something welcome about heavy snow and it gives me more time to write letters. Since I last wrote to you about dear Lilias, so much has happened, both in matters of state and also here at Fyvie Castle. But these are poor excuses for my lack of communication, dear Aunt. Do please forgive me. I have always enjoyed receiving your news, though your last letter addressed to Grizel I had to read by myself. For once again, I must convey bad news.

Mon Dieu, what has happened now? I raised the letter a little towards the light, my eyes struggling to read his handwriting. I really must address my failing sight, but at sixty-five there was surely little that could be done. I moved my chair towards the window and continued.

Since Grizel was in correspondence with you, you will no doubt have been aware of the tragedy we suffered, losing our firstborn, our precious son Charles. We heard the news just as we arrived at Court to deliver Prince Charles to the King and Queen in Northampton, and I decided to curtail our stay there in order to start the long journey back north to Fyvie. We buried little Charles here in the small chapel at the end of the inner garden. You will recall this sanctuary is only for the family, not even distinguished guests.

So perhaps those rumours I'd heard that my nephew was now worshipping at the Protestant church in the village were untrue. Surely they must be, for even though Alexander is a confidant to the Protestant King, he must undoubtedly be adhering to his Catholic faith. I clasped my crucifix tight in my hand and read on.

So now I can visit his grave and pray. And as I contemplate, I consider how blessed I am to have had a son, if only for two precious years. I am convinced that I shall not only have one but more sons in the future. But on this matter, there is the other sad news to convey. I do not know if Grizel told you she was expecting her third child: a girl was born six months ago. The baby was and is hale and hearty . and resembles little Lilias who is now not only walking, but also speaking some words, though I understand nothing she says. The baby is called Jane, another Seton family name as you of course are aware.

Grizel suffered greatly, both in the final stages of her confinement and also during the long, gruelling labour. Not long after she delivered the baby, sadly she passed away. There had been too much blood loss and she was simply not strong enough. The tragedy has affected everyone here badly, for she was only twenty years old. She had, however, lived a wonderful life, having been able to meet the King and Queen and enjoy the privilege of assisting in the guardianship of the little Prince. She also died a Countess, for she will have no doubt told you that the King honoured me with elevation to the title of Earl of Dunfermline.

I shook my head. I was never keen on that girl, for I somehow felt she was instrumental in Lilias's death, but it vexed me that the poor thing died so young and, as so often happens, in childbirth. God rest her soul. But I could not hide a wry smile as I thought of my nephew now as an Earl. How he will be rubbing his hands in glee, since all he ever wanted was a noble rank; and of course a son. What was he to do now?

I must tell you that I am betrothed once more. Do you recall James, Lord Hay of Yester? His father visited Seton Palace on occasion when I was young and so perhaps you too met him and his family? His wife, Lady Margaret Kerr, is the daughter of the Earl of Lothian, so they are a very well-connected family. Their daughter, Margaret Hay, is fourteen now and therefore eligible to marry, and I am delighted that soon I shall take her for a bride. Her father and I have set the wedding date for early next year when she becomes fifteen.

Well, well. My nephew hardly waits till his wives are cold in their graves before marrying another. I think he must forget how old I am now for, though I do remember James Hay's father, he was only a lad when I saw him at Seton Palace, but I remember his grandfather William better. My brother George was always keen that Willie Hay and I should become betrothed, but I would have none of it, and then fortunately I was called to serve my Queen first in France and then in Scotland. He was not at all to my taste: I seem to recall a short stout man with pockmarked skin. But who could possibly have been to my taste in those days, I was only a child. And then when I eventually found love, it was all too late.

I hope this might be my last marriage for I am tired of forcing myself to become acquainted with the foibles and ways of young girls once more. She is younger than my two eldest daughters, both of whom I am in the process of marrying to eminent men. Anne will marry Viscount Fenton and Isobel is betrothed to the Earl of Lauderdale. My nuptials, however, shall come first. I am now nearly fifty-two, dear Aunt, can you imagine how difficult it is to engage with a spouse thirty-seven years younger than me?

Alexander, I find it much more difficult trying to imagine how a young girl aged fifteen must feel marrying a man so much older. I tried to recall how it felt to be that age and shuddered at the thought. For it was not only the fact of giving up everything – one's own family and home – to marry a man, any man, but when it entailed the union of two bodies, one so ancient and withered and one so fresh and young, I felt queasy. I trembled as the thought of the bedroom flashed through my head and I turned back to the letter in my hand.

I shall write again after the wedding and give you news then. Also, depending on how long His Majesty requires me at Court, my intention is to travel to France in the next couple of years, to see my wine merchants while I deal with matters on behalf of the King. I shall endeavour to visit you, dear Aunt, perhaps even with my new wife. Since my parents have now departed, you are my only relative of their generation and I am eager to see you before too long.

You mean, before I die? I presume you know I have no money or anything to leave, so there is no point hoping for anything at all in my will. Besides, I am not sure I could face meeting anyone who took Lilias's place. Yet, as I twisted my ruby ring around my thumb, it occurred to me that it could be an interesting encounter with my nephew, for at last I might come to understand a little of what happened on Loch Leven.

Until then chère tante, stay well.
Your loving nephew,
Alexander

There was so much news, I could hardly take it all in. Alexander was to marry for the third time, in the hope once more of having sons. Well, let's hope this new girl Margaret is able to fulfil her role and then he might actually pay more heed to his wife and not think only of himself. I should so love to visit Scotland again, but even though it was some time ago, I cannot forget how long it took me to recover from my traumatic last visit. So if Aberdeenshire is able to come to me, then so be it.

I put the letter away in my drawer and tightened the belt around my waist, preparing myself for Vespers. I forced my shoulders back and stood up tall. I might be old and arthritic, but I would not stoop. My Queen never did; they said not even at the end. And I, her loyal servant, never would.

Chapter 50

1980

Maggie

On the landing halfway up the Great Stair is the Douglas Room, and though it's small, I liked to try to cram in all the visitors as there was so much to see.

"Here on the heavy oak door you can see the carving of a crescent. This is part of the Seton crest, which we also saw in the Charter Room. Just like in that room, there's dark wood panelling all around. Over there is a seventeenth-century tapestry and here is a portrait of an unidentified young girl, dating from 1553."

I stood aside as they all edged towards it.

"She's clearly from a noble family, given her clothes and head covering – but also, only the nobility could afford to have portraits commissioned. And though we don't know who painted it, the style is similar to Flemish portraits of that time."

"Does it not say on the back who the girl is?"

I tried not to smile. Almost every tour, someone asked that question, as if no one had thought to turn the painting around.

"No, sadly not. There have been residents of Fyvie Castle over the years who insist it's the earliest known portrait of Mary Seton, whose nephew Alexander Seton carried out so much work at Fyvie Castle both outside and inside. The stairs we've just come up, the Great Stair, which is technically called a wheel stair, was the biggest in the country when Alexander Seton built it in the late sixteenth century. Mary Seton was one of Mary, Queen of Scots' four Marys, her ladies-in-waiting, also sometimes known by their French name, Marie. In 1553, she would have been twelve years old. When this painting is compared to later portraits of Mary

236

Seton, there are a lot of similarities, particularly in the colour of her hair and in her features."

I paused for questions. There was always someone asking something if I merely mentioned the words Mary, Queen of Scots, but today, nothing. So I turned and pointed to the painting along from the girl's portrait. "This is Margaret Hay, Alexander Seton's third wife. As you can see, she has auburn hair and dark brown eyes. She looks quite different from Grizel Leslie, his second wife, whose portrait we saw earlier, with her striking blue eyes."

"Why is she not wearing the necklace the other wife wore? You said it belonged to a set of Seton jewels," asked an elderly man who was wearing a thick overcoat even though it was an unusually warm day.

"I was coming to that," I said, turning back to point at the painting. "It's thought that, because of this high, intricate lace collar she's wearing, the necklace – which as you correctly say was part of the Seton parure – would have looked out of place. But also, it could be that by the time she married Alexander Seton, it was no longer in the family's hands."

"What, you mean it was lost?"

I shrugged. "It doesn't appear on any pictures after the portrait I showed you of Grizel downstairs in the little room off the library. Other than that, there's nothing more I can tell you about the jewels." I stopped there, thinking that I really must ask Mr David more about the parure; I was always fobbing the visitors off with that anodyne sentence.

I leant in towards them to relay the final piece of information about the Douglas room in a loud whisper. "There have been stories over the centuries that in this room, one of the laird's wives was starved to death. When we were in the Seton Bedroom, I told you about the Green Lady who's meant to haunt the castle. Well, some think it was Lilias Drummond, Alexander Seton's first wife, who was kept prisoner in this room, without any food, because she was unable to produce sons – therefore heirs – for her husband. She only had daughters."

I watched them all grimace then I smiled. "But this is incredibly unlikely. As I said, this room is at the top of the finest wheel stair in Scotland, so there was no way that Alexander Seton, who must've been proud of his staircase, would have kept his wife locked in here, to starve her to death. He'd have shown guests all the way up here; surely a dying woman wasn't locked in behind this door all the time. It was far too near the hubbub of the castle." I shrugged. "Who knows, perhaps he starved her somewhere else."

"Was it Lilias Drummond who ended up as the Green Lady? Has anyone seen the ghost at the castle?"

I shook my head. "Supposedly. But no one's seen her here in this room. There've been stories, though, of caretakers having to go up to the Seton Room at night when the burglar alarm's gone off. But when they investigate, all they find is something like an open window, which has been banging against the ledge and triggered the alarm. To my knowledge, nobody has actually seen a ghost."

I looked around. They wanted to believe in this ghost. I must ask Mr David more about his aunt's putative sighting.

"But who knows? All I can tell you is that I've certainly not seen her, and I've been sleeping at the castle for the past month."

"Is Mr David available later, Mrs MacPherson?"

"Why do you ask?"

Was this woman ever anything other than frosty? "I hoped to catch him at some stage today, there are some things I wanted to ask him."

"Nothing I can help you with?"

I shook my head. "No. Thank you, though."

She opened a big desk diary and scrolled down the page with her finger. "I think he should be free now, unless you have a tour?"

"Just finished my morning one. I've got an hour till the next one."

"Well, if you proceed to the Leith Tower, I shall phone Mr David and say you are on your way."

"Thanks," I said, bizarrely excited about seeing the only part of the castle I'd not been allowed in yet. The Leith Tower was for the family's private use only.

I walked into the billiard room then through the door to the stairs leading to the Leith Tower. I noticed that the wood on the doors wasn't as heavy and dark as in the other parts of the castle, and in fact this newer wing was much lighter and airier. I was about to knock on a door when I heard a voice behind me.

"Miss Hay. Please come into the kitchen."

I followed Mr David into a large Victorian kitchen, which was wonderfully warm. The Aga was obviously on all summer.

He gestured for me to sit down and proceeded to fill the kettle. "Tea?"

"Yes please."

I shuffled in the rickety wooden chair and looked around. There was a family photograph on the dresser and I peered closely to see a younger Mr David with another boy – possibly his cousin Charles – and a man and woman, presumably one of the boys' parents, all sitting around a piano in a grand room, not one I knew at Fyvie, although as I studied it I realised the view outside the window looked familiar. The man was dressed in plus fours and tweed jacket and the woman, in twinset, sensible skirt and brogues, reminded me a little of the Queen Mother. She was an attractive middle-aged woman with hair in a stylish perm and strings of pearls around her ample bosom. The two boys were dressed in matching long shorts and school blazers and looked thoroughly bored.

"Is this you and your cousin?"

He turned around from the open pedal bin where he was dangling a tea bag. "Yes, I used to spend exeats with Charles here at Fyvie."

I thought it might seem impertinent to ask more about the photo or his childhood, so I kept to safe ground. "What date is the kitchen from?"

"Around 1890. Of course, it's far too old-fashioned now, but since we seldom entertain, it suits me fine."

He put a mug of tea in front of me, lifted up a jug of milk that had clearly been sitting there for some time and sniffed it. Then he pushed it towards me and said, "Now, what did you want to speak to me about?"

"Well, there's a couple of things I keep being asked about by the visitors and I feel my answers aren't sufficient."

He smirked. "And you have more scruples than your fellow guides and refuse to invent things?"

I smiled. "First of all, the Green Lady. You said ages ago that your aunt was the only person you knew who'd seen her. Can you tell me some more about that please?"

He swung back on his char, not shifting his gaze from my face. "Remember I said my aunt was in the early stages of dementia, so we don't know if what she saw or said she saw was real."

I nodded.

"But for some reason, she'd decided to go along to the Seton Bedroom in the middle of the night. She said when she opened the door, she was aware there was, as she called it, a presence. She went to sit at the dressing table chair and looked in the mirror. She hadn't put the light on so the room was dark apart from some moonlight coming in through the window. Then she said she could see something green hovering behind her in the reflection and she was so scared, she didn't move, she simply watched the shimmering green drift over towards the window and linger for a moment before disappearing. She was convinced she also heard something."

"What?"

"Don't forget Aunt Ethel's mind was already fragile, but she insisted she heard three words being whispered."

I nodded. I could guess what was coming.

"'He killed me.' That was what she said she heard." Mr David shrugged. "Utter nonsense, but she told the same story to my cousin and my uncle before he died soon after."

"The same words that were heard on that radio programme."

"Oh, you know about that, do you? Shocking publicity, we all thought at the time, but then we realised that, in fact, that's what would draw in the crowds. So that helped persuade Charles he had to open some of the castle to the public. The thing is, Aunt Ethel's mind was fine at the time it had been broadcast, so she must have remembered the shock the presenter experienced hearing those words when they listened to the programme again."

I nodded. "Nothing else about that night?"

"Oh, yes, she'd gone to the window where the green figure had vanished and it was wide open. The caretaker always went round shutting and locking every window at night, but he'd obviously forgotten on that occasion."

I took a gulp of tea. It was one of those horrible smoky teas I'd tried with Len at some fancy place he took me for afternoon tea. I didn't like it then or now.

"Did she feel threatened?"

He shook his head. "She told us that, though she was scared at seeing something she was convinced was spectral, she felt the ghost was benign." He shrugged. "But as I say, this was clearly the start of her dementia." He looked at his watch. "Anything else?"

"Well, the other thing is about those jewels, the parure the Seton family owned in the sixteenth century."

His aloof, arrogant manner changed and he suddenly appeared rather cagey.

"What about it?"

"Visitors ask what happened to it, after they've seen the necklace on Grizel Seton's portrait. I tell them it was part of a parure that was in the Seton family, including earrings and a brooch, but then I don't know what happened to it after."

"Quite the Miss Marple, aren't you?" he sneered. "How did you find out about the parure? Only the necklace appears on the portrait."

"I've got lots of archive materials from my university lecturer, and research I'd already done on the Seton family at the time Alexander lived here."

"I see. Well, I'm sorry to disappoint you, but no one has any knowledge of what happened to it after that portrait of Grizel in the early 1600s."

"Really? So has no one's tried to find it?"

He sighed. "What do you think, Miss Hay?"

I loathed sarcasm anyway; coming from him, with his smug expression, I wanted to react, but was aware I needed to keep in with him.

"No historian or archivist has tried to trace it back?"

"No."

I glanced at his face, full of disdain, and ventured, "I thought it might be in the safe in the Charter Room."

"Do you actually think there are any valuables kept there? With all those people filing through that room every day?" He shook his head. "There is nothing there, I can assure you, and-" He stopped and tilted his head. There was a phone ringing somewhere nearby.

"Excuse me," he said, rushing for the door.

I waited till he was out of the room before tipping the horrible tea down the sink. Then I peered at the photograph once more. They were all dressed so formally, and apart from the mother, no one was smiling. Perhaps they were always that stiff; he certainly didn't dress with formality these days – big jumpers and corduroy trousers were his style now.

I glanced at my watch then realised I'd only ten minutes before my next tour. I went out to the hall and heard him talking loudly on the phone. I thought I'd better go and gesture a thank you to him, so I followed his voice and came to the door of the small study where he sat in a tall desk chair, his back to me, oblivious to my presence as he bellowed down the phone. I was about to leave when I noticed a large portrait on the wall behind him. It was of an elegant lady, in a long red gown, painted in the 1950s I would say, by the style of dress and the hairstyle. It was the woman in the photo next door, who was presumably the laird's mother, Mr David's aunt.

I let out a gasp when I saw what she was wearing round her neck. It was the Seton necklace.

Chapter 51

1609

Margaret

We sat at the breakfast table, the servants fussing around my husband as they were wont to do. It was a beautiful summer's day and yet as usual it was gloomy inside, with all the candles alight. I looked over at Alexander and realised that over the past two years since our wedding, it's always early in the morning, and no matter how dark or bright the light, that I notice how very old my husband is. In bed, thankfully, it is dark so I cannot see his saggy, lined flesh, but here I gaze at his wrinkles and deeply furrowed brow and silvery flecked ginger beard. Perhaps his appearance becomes better as the day wears on, but I notice the difference in our ages especially at our morning meal. I am now seventeen but he must be fifty-three or fifty-four? To be honest, I have no idea his precise age and don't really want to know.

He sipped his ale then looked towards me adoringly. I was never regarded as beautiful when I was growing up, for my mother sensibly never paid heed to appearances, even though of course we all had to dress in a manner befitting our status. And even now, as Countess of Dunfermline and Lady Fyvie, I seldom have the maid do anything to my hair other than comb it with my ivory comb. Not for me those high elaborate coiffures like all the ladies are wearing now, trying to emulate the Queen.

But my husband often tells me how alluring I am, which I find neither wonderful nor offensive, simply odd, since such words of praise are still unfamiliar to me. And even though I am now fatter than I was when expecting my first child, our darling little Charles, Alexander still seems to find my expanding belly attractive. He really is a strange old man, both arrogant and self-assured, and yet somehow dependent on me, his very much younger wife. He is becoming more needy emotionally; and in truth, he is also now less able in practical tasks, because of his failing sight. So I have begun to help him in some administrative matters that he says he simply does not have time to do, but I know it is actually because he is no longer as adept as he was in younger years, nor can he see as well for the finer details of letter writing. I intended to write to his aunt, Marie Seton, this week again too, to tell her the news of the next child due to be born at Fyvie Castle.

I looked up at Alexander as he cleared his throat.

"Margaret, my dear, I do not wish you to ride your horse today. Or indeed any day while you are expecting our second child."

I smiled. "Your concern is most welcome, dear husband. But I shall be fine, I always am. I have ridden since I could walk."

He frowned and his brows furrowed even more. "No, I have made a decision. I am not happy about this; indeed, I forbid it."

I tilted my head to one side, smiled at him once more and stood up. The servants rushed to pull back my chair.

"I shall see you later, Alexander. Let me know if you would like my assistance in the Charter Room with your correspondence. I shall be in the nursery this afternoon with little Charles, then hopefully I shall take the girls out to the gardens if the weather continues fine."

He mumbled some reply and turned back to his beer. I nodded graciously then proceeded downstairs and out through the pend to the courtyard.

There I called over to the stables. "Saddle my horse, Billie. I am going out riding."

The grooms used to try to suggest that my husband might not be happy if I rode while in my state, but they have given up now, since I simply shrug and tell them the physician prescribed fresh air and gentle exercise to keep me healthy. And what harm would a gentle trot do?

Billie helped me up onto the mare and I patted her soft neck, whispered in her ear then trotted out through the pend towards the west. Once I was out of view of the castle, I settled firmly into the saddle, bent my head low and tightened the reins. Then I sped off in the morning sun across the castle dale at full gallop.

"Here he is, My Lady, just woken up from his nap." Nurse handed me the snuggly bundle and I clasped my son towards me, inhaling the heady scent from his warm body.

"Thank you. I am happy to be here with him for a while. The girls are arriving soon but I can easily supervise him myself." I smiled. "It must be time for you to have your dinner?"

Nurse bowed. "Thank you, that would be most helpful, My Lady. Are you sure you will be fine with all the children? I won't be long."

I shrugged. "Yes, of course." I loved children. I used to enjoy playing with all my nieces and nephews at home and now I was able to have fun with the girls here, even though they were not mine.

Lilias's eldest two girls of course were now both married and living in splendour elsewhere in Scotland, much to my husband's delight. But the younger two, Margaret and Sophia, are very much part of my life here at Fyvie; they are both such a joy. Grizel's two little girls, Lilias and Jane, are coming on nicely too, though always rather more diffident. But they are fit and healthy, which is surely the most important.

As I made funny faces at my son and watched him crinkle up his face in glee, I wondered about my next child. It was only about four months till he or she was to be born. My husband of course wanted another boy, but I told him we already had a boy, so perhaps a sister would be lovely. He did not agree, but he was not the one to have to go through the pain of childbirth.

In fact, I had already decided that we would call a girl Grizel, as the more I heard about her, both from Anne and Isobel, and also from Jeannie my maid, the more I realised what a hard life she must have had. She very kindly allowed her first daughter to be named after Lilias, and so I shall call my first daughter Grizel.

Jeannie can be wonderfully indiscreet at times and recently told me that Grizel had been perhaps more than a little difficult as a Mistress at first, but then, as tragedy struck, when her son died as an infant, she became more and more queer, in a state of constant agitation. Jeannie believed she was unbalanced and deranged towards the end. Her life really was rather tragic.

Jeannie said she would tell me soon about Lilias and what they (the servants) thought happened to her; it sounded as if she too became demented. But there was so little time to chat with the servants, much as I enjoy doing that, with my role as Lord Fyvie's wife and mother to all these children. I also like to look after the poor in the village and have Cook send pies and broths to those living in the filthy hovels we pass on our way to church.

In addition, I have a project I am trying to persuade my husband upon. Fyvie Parish Kirk is old, dating from the twelfth century, the minister told me during our last visit. There are therefore many repairs that need funding. I have almost persuaded Alexander that we ought to become benefactors and I am already planning the commission of a large silver communion cup for the church, as a mark of our commitment, just like my own father did for Yester Kirk. My husband is slowly coming around to the idea, yet keeps trying to insist it should be less grand and elaborate than the one I have in mind. Slowly but surely, however, I am persuading him. He simply needs to believe it was his idea in the first place.

The door flung open and in rushed Margaret, the three other little girls behind. They all raced towards me to coo over their brother, baby Charles. Jeannie stood at the door and beamed. "You said you wanted to take the girls out to the garden, My Lady. Shall I stay here with the baby?"

"Thank you, Jeannie. Nurse shouldn't be long." I turned to the girls. "Who wants to go to the bowling lawn?"

They all jumped up and down with excitement.

"Let's go and ask Donald to set it up for us. Come along," I said, kissing little Charles and handing him over to Jeannie.

"Will they need bonnets on, My Lady?"

I looked out the tiny window. "No, it was mild when I was out earlier, I'm sure it will be even warmer now."

"Were you out on the horse, My Lady?" She frowned.

I shrugged. "What if I was, Jeannie?" I said, beaming. She shook her head and began to dandle Charles on her knee as I took two of the little girls' hands and headed for the door.

Chapter 52

1980

Maggie

A whole day of research stretched before me. It was my first day off in ages and I was looking forward to staying in my room to study. I'd had a long letter from my mum, so planned to walk into the village in the afternoon to post a letter back. But till then, it was time to get into the books.

I'd reached the stage where Margaret Hay had married Alexander Seton in 1607 and very quickly had a son named Charles and then a daughter named Grizel. I still thought it so weird that both second and third wives had agreed to name their first daughters after the last wife. Or perhaps they had no choice. Margaret Hay seemed to be active in helping the poor in the village and in renovating the old church where they worshipped. So those ruins where I'd seen the engraving MS in the old chapel to the south of Seton Tower were surely very old, before the family converted to Protestantism in the early 1600s. Unless they just decided to bury some family members here anyway; surely it couldn't be Mary Seton as she was presumably buried at her French convent. Perhaps it was Lilias's daughter Margaret who died as an infant.

I wanted to pop into the church in the village to see if there was anything about the Seton family there. I'd discovered that the Earl and Countess of Dunfermline had commissioned what has become the second oldest communion cup in Scotland for Fyvie Church and that it was still in use. Presumably this would not be on display as it was obviously so valuable, but perhaps I could call at the manse and ask the minister about it.

I was scribbling down notes on Margaret Hay and was surprised to find out she assisted her husband with administrative matters, which was unusual in those days. There was a knock at the door and I went to open it. There was Mrs MacPherson, holding a mug of coffee; well, this was unexpected.

"Good morning, Miss Hay. I was making coffee and thought you might appreciate a cup."

"Thank you," I muttered. "That's really kind of you."

She continued to stand there. I took the mug from her and smiled. It was not as if I could invite her in, my room was tiny.

"Mr David was telling me you were interested in the Seton parure."

"Yes. Do you know what happened to it?"

"No, no one does," she said, "but as you know, there's a secret chamber in the Charter Room and it's thought that it could be there."

"Not Lilias Drummond's bones then?"

She smirked. "That might be what Andrew and Silvia tell the visitors on their tours, but we know that can't be true, she's buried in Fife."

I nodded. Why on earth was she here telling me this?

She cleared her throat. "Mr David is away for a few days, but he left me instructions. He said that your questioning him about the parure made him wonder again if it is indeed in the secret chamber. He is obviously keen to find it, but of course there's the curse. You know all about that I presume?"

"Remind me. It's something that visitors ask about from time to time when we're in the Charter Room."

"Well, the curse states that should a laird of Fyvie attempt to open the chamber, he'll die and his wife become blind."

I grinned. "Oh that? Superstitious nonsense."

"You might not say that if you were one of those two lairds

whose early deaths occurred soon after attempting to open the secret chamber. Their wives then had eye problems, one going blind."

"It's medieval folklore, all superstition."

"Mr David is superstitious, as are his entire family. Even though he's not the laird – that's Mr Charles – he is wary. He believes his uncle tried to open it just a week before his fatal heart attack, though he never told the family he was going to attempt it. Mr David's aunt, though she didn't go blind, began to show the devastating effects of dementia soon after."

Where was this going?

"Mr David wonders if, while he is away, you could try to open the chamber and see what, if anything, is in there."

"Me?"

"Yes, since you've no ties to the family and your work here will be over in a couple of weeks."

This was so extraordinary, I had to smile. "So if I die, no one need know why?"

She tutted.

"I'm joking. Of course, I'll give it a try. All by myself?"

"He suggested Andrew is in the room with you in case you require any assistance, but he will not do the actual opening of the chamber."

I shrugged. "Yes, I'd love to. When?"

"Mr David is away until Sunday so perhaps Friday evening, after the last tour is finished?"

"Fine by me, I don't ever do much in the evenings," I laughed.

She nodded and turned to leave when a thought occurred to me.

"I presume Mr Charles's wife's okay, so there's no danger of anything happening to her?"

Mrs MacPherson's lips pursed. "As far as I know, she is in good health."

After she left, I chuckled. Whether or not this would be an amazing revelation or nothing of interest at all, I found it amusing that an entire family – one born into such privilege – held such irrational, superstitious beliefs. I couldn't wait to tell Mum – and indeed Dr Birkett. What on earth would she think of this?

I thought back to the portrait of Mr David's Aunt Ethel wearing the parure and wondered, perhaps, if he wasn't lying about it as I'd suspected, and he actually had no idea where it went after his aunt wore it for that portrait. Or perhaps this was all a strange ruse. Whatever was behind it, I had some challenge ahead of me.

Chapter 53

1610

Marie Seton

Chère Tante Marie,
I am sorry I have not written for a while, but only a few months
after our little Grizel was born — thank God, fit and healthy — I
realised I was expecting another child and have continued to feel rather
sick for the first few months. Only now, with some three months till my
delivery, do I feel more myself.

I presume my nephew will continue to want more children
until he has a second male heir. What a duty that poor girl has, to
keep producing babies for her ancient husband. I tried to consider
how old he must be by now. I am sixty-nine and so he must be fifty-four as I think I was fifteen when he was born. And this charming wife Margaret is still only just a girl. I sighed and stretched out
my arthritic fingers to try to ease the pain.

We'd both been keen to journey together to northern France for
him to see his wine merchants and deal with some Court matters in
Paris. He also wants to visit a bell foundry in Flanders as we intend to
commission a bell for Fyvie Church. My husband is about to be given
patronage of the church by the King; it belonged formerly to Arbroath
Abbey. Being patron is such an honour, we thought it would be a good
idea to install a special bell to mark this. Apparently, the foundry run
by Jan Burgherhuys in Ghent is the best in Europe.

So Alexander has, it seems, abandoned the Catholicism of his
birth and gone to the other side. I suppose it was inevitable, but it

still breaks my heart to think what his royal godmother's reaction would have been. It is interesting that Margaret often uses the word we when mentioning her husband, as if he is not reigning supreme in their household, as he clearly was with Lilias and Grizel.

> *The journey south from Ghent to Reims is then on the itinerary, so that your nephew can see his much-loved aunt after so many years. I too had hoped to meet you during the trip, but the arrival of this new baby soon means everything is postponed for me. Although these days Alexander likes me to be with him if possible, he is looking forward to visiting you in the next few months, even without his wife at his side. I shall send you details once his plans are in place. He continues to be busy as one of the King's closest advisors, and as well as visits to Edinburgh in his role as Lord Chancellor, he has to journey to London every few months. Though he would not admit it, I know he finds the travel all rather tiring.*

Even though he is much younger than me, I can empathise with his fatigue. I wiggled my toes a little, to try to alleviate the pain in my feet, while thinking once more that, though my body is gradually letting me down, at least God has given me an active mind. Rather like Job, I sometimes feel I must suffer so much, but then I recall one of the verses and feel His grace within. "Wisdom belongs to the aged and understanding to the old," as it is written in the Book of Job. I hope that, should I indeed get to see my nephew soon, I shall begin to somehow comprehend what happened all those years ago to his dear first wife, Lilias.

> *The children are wonderful. Lilias's four daughters continue to thrive, the eldest two married, as you know. Anne is expecting her first child and both she and Isobel visit us as often as they can, for they miss their little sisters. Margaret and Sophia are full of joy and*

mischief. Grizel's two daughters Lilias and Jane are quieter, though just as loving as their bigger sisters and thankfully all are in good health. As to my own two children: I often fondly call Charles the fat little tyrant, whose nurses and servants dote on him almost as much as his own family, his father in particular, of course. And my little Grizel is sweet and lively and, though she has only recently begun on solid food, eats with such gusto, it is as if she thinks there is about to be a famine in Aberdeenshire. Greed was never the Hay way; perhaps my husband was a greedy eater when he was young?

I grinned on reading this. He most certainly was a greedy child. I recall him at Livingstone's wedding eating so many oysters and so much mutton, I thought he would burst. But he has always been slim and so presumably does not suffer from the problems so many gentlemen of his age encounter if they have too much embonpoint. Even the King, who is years younger than Alexander, seems to suffer from gout. And I believe that His Majesty also has arthritis, even with all his physicians and their so-called cures to hand. I know from personal experience how painful this can be.

I am sorry this letter is so short, dear Aunt, but I promise to write again within a month, as soon as I have more details of Alexander's trip and when you might expect to see him. Until then, wishing you good health and love from all your family at Fyvie Castle.
Your friend, Margaret

I find it interesting that even though I have not met this girl, after all our regular correspondence I now count her as my friend, almost as I did Lilias. I must ensure that I remain as healthy as possible until my nephew's visit, for there will be much to discuss. I lifted up my right hand to the fading daylight and watched the light glint on the ruby ring that graced Lilias's fair finger for so many years.

Chapter 54

1610

Margaret

I sat at the desk in the Charter Room beside my husband and opposite the minister, the Reverend Robert Smith. Though normally this conversation would just be between the men, more and more these days Alexander liked me to be at his side, to write down anything that required notes and to ensure that he missed nothing. I had begun to wonder how he managed at Court, advising the King by himself, but presumably there were clerks to assist. Here at Fyvie, though we have many servants of every description, we have no clerk and my husband refuses to contemplate hiring one. He is a vain man and would never admit his eyesight was failing and his memory not as good as it was. So I play the dutiful wife to my Lord and Master in the company of others.

"Your Lordship," the minister said in his grave, earnest voice, "Might I know more about this communion cup you are so kindly commissioning for the church? Also, I have just heard from Jimmy Henderson the carpenter that the special laird's pew he's making is now, at long last, ready."

"Oh, that's good news on the pew," my husband said, pointing at my paper and quill to note that down, which I did with a humble bow. "We asked him to carve the Seton crest into the wood at both pew ends." He glanced at me. "And the date of my patronage, I believe?"

I nodded and smiled.

The minister beamed, wonder in his eyes. It was clear he thought my husband was as near to God as is possible for a human.

"As for the communion cup, I have already spoken to two

silversmiths, one in Aberdeen and one in Banff. Whichever I choose, the design will be the same. A simple solid silver goblet standing ten Scottish inches tall and..." He turned to look at me. "Did we decide on ten or twelve inches?" He was frowning.

I smiled. "If my memory serves me well, dear husband, you decided on twelve inches."

He nodded and proceeded to expound on his brilliant idea. "I shall present it to the church at a special service to celebrate my patronage."

"That is a good idea, Your Lordship. I look forward very much to seeing you and Your Ladyship and your growing family sitting on the family pew at the front." He glanced down at my belly then turned his head away, face flushed, as he realised this was not proper. "It will bring such," the minster looked up to the ceiling as if for inspiration in his choice of word, "such succour to the congregation who admire all you have done for Fyvie Church."

He began to stand up and I coughed. My husband looked at me and I mouthed the words, "the bell".

"Ah, yes, Mr Smith. There is also the matter of the bell. Do you recall I wrote to you about this?"

"Of course, Your Lordship, the bell. What joy that will spread throughout the land." He sat back down on his chair and beamed at Alexander.

"I travel to France and then Flanders in a month and shall visit the foundry of Jan Burgherhuys in Ghent about my commission. You have no doubt heard of his work?"

The minister looked rather flustered. "I can't say I have, Your Lordship, but anything on your recommendation I know will be magnificent."

"I would hope to have it ready to install in the belfry before the summer is over," Alexander announced, standing up. He had obviously had enough of this fawning man, though deferential company usually pleased him greatly.

The minister nodded in my direction, bowed at my husband and took his leave.

"Will you write up the notes for me, my love?" he said.

"Of course," I said, smiling. "The girls are all occupied at their studies or at play. I have no other duties this afternoon."

"Good. I shall see you at dinner."

I pushed myself off my chair, holding my fat belly.

He frowned. "How much longer do you have, Margaret, till the baby arrives? I pray it shall be another son."

"I should have another six weeks, but who knows. Remember little Grizel came early."

"Ah yes, but praise God she has always been healthy."

"And that is more important than its gender," I said, before turning and heading for the door.

We had almost finalised the details of Alexander's trip to France and Flanders. He was due to leave for Edinburgh and attend to some business there for a few days then sail from Leith. I intended to write to his aunt in Reims this afternoon and inform her of the dates she might expect his visit. I was wondering what I could send with him as a gift for her, but it was proving difficult, since nothing either frivolous or perishable was possible.

I wondered if there was perhaps something of Alexander's first wife Lilias's, since they were so close. There might be a shawl or even a breviary, though taking a prayer book to a nun was probably superfluous. Jeannie had told me all her possessions had been taken to the Preston Tower and so I asked her to accompany me there to open the chest of her belongings.

We went out the back door from my bedroom through what

my husband calls grandly the Seton Tower, and into the older Preston Tower.

"Be careful, My Lady," said Jeannie, taking my hand, as we came to the landing leading to the old narrow staircase. "These stairs are narrow and there's no handrail. My Master would never forgive me if you fell."

I took her hand and whispered, "Your Master will never know we have been up here, Jeannie."

She shook her head and smiled, guiding me up with a lighted candle. At the top of the stairs, she paused to catch her breath.

"Are you all right, Jeannie?"

"Yes, just a bit out of breath. I'm not as young as I once was."

"How old are you, if you don't mind me asking?"

"I think I'll be forty next year, but I never knew my mother, so I'm not really sure."

"Oh, I'm sorry." How terrible of me, I had never thought to ask about her childhood, I only ever ask about her children.

"The chest's in this room, My Lady." She ushered me into a gloomy room with wooden shutters keeping out the light. Jeannie went to open them up and light flooded in. There were stacks of paintings against the wall and a large trunk by the window.

I went over to the paintings and began to drag one out. Jeannie rushed to help me and we pulled out a portrait of a beautiful young woman wearing a green dress. I knew this was Lilias as I'd heard rumours about a Green Lady haunting the castle. Two of the kitchen maids had been summoned to my room to make up the fire one morning while Jeannie was away visiting her new grandchild, and while they thought I was sleeping I heard one whisper to the other that she must close the window, for that was where the Green Lady entered.

"And then where does she go?"

"She flies over to the dressing table to look for her jewels, the ones the Master gave to his second wife."

"Have you seen her?"

"No, only Lizzie saw her but then she was sent away when she talked about it and Cook overheard."

I opened one eye and saw the smaller maid looking all around as if she was about to see a ghost.

"So she only ever comes into this room?"

"Aye, but I don't think she haunts Lady Margaret. Only Lady Grizel, and you remember what happened to her..."

The door swung open and another maid from the kitchen entered with my breakfast tray and the conversation ended.

"Jeannie, I presume you've heard the idle talk of a ghost haunting Fyvie Castle?"

She nodded but did not look at me.

"Is she meant to wear a dress like this one?"

"Yes, My Lady. This is Lilias, the first Lady Fyvie. She loved that colour so much she had many dresses made in it. But His Lordship didn't like the colour." She glanced at me and I smiled, encouraging.

"She was a fine lady, everyone was so sad when she died."

I looked closely at the portrait. "What is this beautiful necklace she is wearing?"

"That's the necklace from the parure."

"What parure?"

"The one that was a gift from His Lordship's aunt, Marie Seton, to Lady Lilias, just before she left to become a nun and before Her Ladyship's wedding."

I peered closely at the gold chain entwined with snake links and set with rubies, pearls and emeralds.

I stood back and gazed at it, then a thought occurred. "Is Grizel's portrait here too?"

She shrugged and we pulled out the next painting together.

This was also a young girl, with striking blue eyes and a cornflour blue dress that matched their colour. She had a rather aloof gaze. I stepped forward and saw the same necklace around her throat. "So Grizel wore the necklace from the parure too?"

Jeannie nodded and pulled a dust cover off a chair at her side. "Sit down, My Lady, and I will tell you everything I know."

I sat down and stared at both paintings as Jeannie pulled a stool from under the window and perched herself on it.

Chapter 55

1980

Maggie

I looked up to the belfry above the clock at the entrance to Fyvie Church. There were two bells there and I knew that Alexander Seton had gifted one of them in 1610, the other was from 200 years later. Of course, much of the church had been rebuilt in the early 1800s, but the Flanders bell, as it was called, was still in use. I was about to open the church door, but it was ajar, so I pushed it open and walked in.

There was a ladder leaning against the wall at the entrance and I heard a voice.

"Careful you don't knock me over, lass. Hang on, I'm just coming down."

An elderly man, wearing a tattered tweed jacket and a bonnet, climbed slowly down the steps.

"Sorry, I didn't mean to disturb you. Please carry on."

"It's fine, I'm just finished."

I looked up to a tiny cupboard above the entrance, between the two doors. "Is that where the electric meter is?"

He laughed. "No, I've been winding the clock. The clock weights are in that wee cabinet up there and once a week I put myself in mortal danger to climb this shoogly ladder to keep the time right."

"Oh. What do the weights do?"

"They keep the clock going, but they gradually lower on the unwinding cable, so I've to wind it back up again. Every single week I have to do that, imperil my life on behalf of the congregation."

He was chuckling.

"Are you the minister?"

"No, just the lowly beadle. I'm the one who keeps things ticking over." He winked. "Literally."

I smiled at him. He was the first person I'd spoken to outside the castle since I arrived six weeks ago.

"Are you here to see the window?"

"Window?"

"Yes, the Tiffany window. Come and I'll show you."

I followed him down the aisle and we stood at the front of the church with the organ pipes and the pulpit to our left. He pointed at the stunning stained-glass window behind the communion table.

"Best time of day to look at it is first thing in the morning as it faces east and you can see the sun behind it. Made by Tiffany of New York, it's a memorial to the laird's son."

"It's beautiful," I said, staring at the saintly figure depicted, resplendent in armour and with his wings extended behind him.

"He died in the Boer War in 1900. Percy Forbes-Leith was his name, he was only nineteen, such a shame." He glanced at me. "At least when I was in Libya for three years in the war, I was in my late twenties; I'd seen a bit of life."

He shrugged. "I've got to lock up now, anything else you want to see?"

"I was reading about a communion cup that Alexander Seton had given to the church in the early seventeenth century."

"Yes, we still use that," he said, ambling back down the aisle towards the door.

"Is it here? Could I see it?" I couldn't help sounding excited, which was pathetic. I really must get out of my history books more.

He beckoned for me to follow him and we stood at the foot of the ladder. "Remember I said that's where the clock weights are?

Well, at the top of that small cupboard is a hatch and up there is a wee hidey hole. You can only access it from the Lairds' Loft. That's where it was always kept."

My eyes opened wide.

"Obviously not now, lass, it's far too precious. It's in the vaults of the bank and whenever we have communion the minister or the session clerk goes there to get it out for the Sunday service. Then it's kept at the manse all weekend till the bank reopens on the Monday. The last minister said he never left the manse all weekend when it was Communion, he was so scared of being burgled. It's the second oldest cup like that in Scotland. Worth a fair bob or two."

"Priceless, I imagine. So when's it likely to be out of the bank again?"

"Communion's a week on Sunday, come along if you're free. You're from the castle aren't you?"

"How did you know?"

"Fyvie's a small village, everyone knows everybody's business." He shook my hand. "I'm Bert Blair, by the way."

"Maggie Hay," I said, smiling.

"How're you finding everyone at the castle?"

"Well..."

"Never been the friendliest bunch since Mr David took over as factor. Mr Charles, the laird, and Mrs Arabella are splendid people though; he's a gentleman in the true sense of the word." He drew closer, conspiratorial. "There's folk around here say Mr David wants someone to open the secret chamber so his cousin'll die and he'll inherit." He raised an eyebrow.

"What?"

"All daft rumours, of course, but you know the family believes in a curse?"

I nodded and was about to tell him what I'd been asked to do but thought better of it. "Is Mrs Arabella the laird's wife?"

"Yes, Mr Charles's wife, they live in Italy somewhere now. But she pops into Fyvie now and again. I'm sure my wife said she was around at the moment, maybe not."

"I've certainly not met her yet. What's she like, then?" Bert Blair obviously enjoyed a gossip.

"Sweet as anything, kind, like the laird – not at all stuffy like Mr David. She got on really well with her mother-in-law, Ethel, too. She was heartbroken when she died, poor soul, her dementia was bad at the end."

He looked at his watch. "I've got to go. Unless I'm home by one, my soup'll be cold. And my wife's broth is a thing of beauty, bulging with kale and peas and barley." Bert smiled then ushered me out.

As I walked through the entrance gates and along the path towards the castle, I thought back to the first time I'd walked here, dragging my heavy bags along. At least I wouldn't have to lug those back by hand. Mum had written to say she was coming to collect me with Auntie Liz on my last day. And though it would be nice to see my aunt, it was Mum I really missed. But Mum of course didn't drive.

I'd just spent six weeks almost on my own, apart from the occasional chats with Silvia and Andrew – and talking at rather than with the visitors. But I'd never felt either lonely or solitary. I knew that was because at last I felt safe; I wasn't always looking over my shoulder. Len was now at the other side of the world and I need never fear his grip again. I shivered as I remembered that weekend, when I'd tried to break up with him just before we were leaving on the Sunday morning. When I told him I wanted to enjoy life at university and felt I couldn't, given our relationship, he stood perfectly still for a second. And then he hit me. The slap was so hard, I fell backwards against the chair and collapsed into it, hands up at my face, cowering into the comfort of the cushion.

He raised his hand again and through my fingers I saw his eyes blaze with anger. But he turned and strode to the door, slamming it shut. I went to the bathroom and gazed at the livid red mark on one side of my face. I ran the tap and scooped up handfuls of cold water to try to cool down the heat. I looked up again and knew it was going to bruise. Just then, I wanted out, at once.

I rammed all my clothes into my bag and ran downstairs where I saw Len laughing and chatting to the receptionist as he paid our bill. They both looked around at me and he smiled, as if everything was normal.

"I was just saying to – Sandra, isn't it? – what a lovely stay we've had."

He turned back to sign the bill and I glanced at Sandra who was giving me a strange look. My face must have looked as dreadful as it felt. It was now throbbing.

I went to sit at the door while Len ran up to get his things. I tried to position myself so that my sore cheek was away from her, but out of the corner of my eye I saw her leave her desk and come towards me.

"Are you all right?" she said, leaning over.

Just as I was about to reply, Len bounded down the stairs.

"Right, let's drive!" he announced, far too cheerily.

I stood up and walked steadily after him, knowing that Sandra would be watching. But I couldn't look around.

After a journey in complete silence, we arrived at the campus in Dundee. I leant round to get my bag from the back seat and he grabbed my wrist. I froze and looked up at him.

"Don't think I am letting this go. I'll be in touch again very soon," he hissed, his menacing look boring into me.

I leapt out of the car and dragged my bag along towards my halls of residence, not daring to look as I heard the car drive away behind me.

Before I reached my halls, I passed the entrance to the library where someone was emerging. My first thought was, the library's shut on a Sunday. My second thought was to try to hide my cheek. But it was too late. It was Dr Birkett and of course she came across to speak to me; but then she saw my face. Her look of horror and sympathy made me break down and that was the start of the end. Though I told her she absolutely must not phone my parents – certainly not my dad – she waited till the next morning when Dad was at work, and spoke to Mum. Then Dr Birkett came to see me in my room in halls on the Monday afternoon and told me. I was livid, but she said it was the only solution.

When both my parents came to take me home that evening for a week, Dad said nothing in the car, not a word. Once I was home, I stayed in bed all week, with hot water bottles and soups as if I was an invalid. But I could see the hurt in Mum's face. Dad never came to see me at all.

The morning before I was due to go back to Dundee, Mum came into my room and handed me a mug of tea. "You know, Allison used to sometimes have bruises on her wrists. I asked her once about them and she said she'd been lifting furniture while she was spring cleaning. It sounded odd at the time, but I'd never thought to query her."

I nodded and patted my cheek. "It's getting better, isn't it?" I tried to smile.

She nodded then turned to look out of the window. "Dad's going out to the pub with Len after work."

"What?" I was horrified.

"It's fine, he's got a plan. You won't be bothered by that man ever again, sweetheart." She swept my hair off my forehead and planted a kiss, just like she used to do when I was a child. I was still her child; how on earth could I have hurt her so much?

Fyvie Loch was now on my right and so I wandered down to the edge and sat on the grass. I took a deep breath and looked over towards the boathouse where a swan was gliding over the water. I felt so safe here, calm, not only with this beautiful view but knowing he could and would never reach me again.

I watched as the swan landed then began to paddle over the loch towards me, and as it approached I thought of the car journey back to Dundee with Dad after my week at home. Dad continued to look straight ahead at the road as he told me that Len had decided it would be a good idea, now he was a widower, to move to New Zealand to be near his son who worked on a sheep farm on South Island. His house was going on the market and he would be leaving in the next few weeks. He'd be getting a job over there; tennis coaches were needed everywhere.

I couldn't look at Dad and I couldn't ask him what he had said to Len. But of course Mum told me sometime later that Dad had threatened to expose him as a sexual predator and rapist to his childhood friend who happened to be Chief Constable of Lothian and Borders Police, unless he left the country as soon as possible. That was over a year ago, but Dad had not really forgiven me. He still left the room when I entered and refused to eat at the same time as Mum and I did. Mum keeps saying, "He'll come round, it just takes time."

The swan was now directly in front of me, in the water. I know they're meant to be scary, but I didn't want to move. I just stared at its beauty, took a deep breath and thought how lucky I was to be free from harm. I watched as the swan lifted its head high, began to flap its wings, paddled with its feet then lowered the long neck and set off into the air, skimming the water at first and then gliding high. I now understood where the expression "free as a bird" came from. I walked back up to the path and soon came upon the view of Fyvie Castle which, even after all these weeks, took my breath away.

Chapter 56

Margaret

"Tell me more about this parure, Jeannie. Why has my husband never mentioned it to me? Is it lost?"

"My Lady, the jewels are not missing, though His Lordship thinks they are. He believes that after poor Lady Grizel died, they were somehow taken away by the Green Lady and—"

"Dear Lord, my husband does not believe in ghosts, surely?"

The maid shrugged. "They've always been a superstitious lot, the Setons. Not Lady Lilias, but His Lordship is and Lady Grizel certainly was, God rest her soul."

There was something about Jeannie's expression that bothered me. "Jeannie, how did Grizel actually die?"

She sat up straight on her stool and clasped her hands together on her lap. "What did His Lordship say happened to her?"

What a strange question. "Well, everyone knew she died in childbirth, soon after delivering little Jane. Was this not true?"

"My Lady, ever since her little boy died, she was not the same. She was nervous, fidgety, always anxious about everything – and it got worse. So much so, she never left her bed after Jane was born and became convinced the Green Lady was coming to get her."

How could anyone believe in this nonsense?

"I slept every night in her room – your bedroom, My Lady, the Seton Bedroom. But the night she died, I woke up too late." She paused. "She'd obviously convinced herself again that the Green Lady was in the room and she'd followed her to the dressing table – she always ended up there – and when I woke up, she'd already climbed up onto the window sill."

She sighed.

"What? She fell out the window? But my room's on the second floor, no one could have survived that."

"She didn't fall. She jumped out, she wanted free of the Green Lady and of her life, which had no meaning."

I sat back on my chair and shook my head. "Poor, poor Grizel." I looked over to her portrait and saw an innocent pretty girl with her whole life ahead of her and then, this.

"So what happened to the parure?"

"Not long after the little boy had died, she asked me to swear to keep a secret. The secret was that she'd hidden the parure, trying to keep it away from the Green Lady. She became more and more, well, unbalanced, and I was worried about her. So one day, shortly before she was due to give birth to Jane, I asked her if she still had the parure and if so, should I perhaps move it somewhere else, so that she wouldn't feel in danger of it being taken."

"What did she say?"

"She agreed and told me she'd hidden it in a secret chamber in the corner of the Charter Room, which she had a key for. She was rambling a little, as she often was at that stage, but then she suddenly stopped speaking, stood perfectly still and whispered to me, 'Of course, Jeannie, I've just realised the Green Lady is not happy her parure is in His Lordship's Charter Room. She hated him and we must do all we can to please her. We must bring it up here.'"

"She scrambled around in her drawers, found a key and gave it to me. 'Go now, Jeannie, go downstairs to the Charter Room and open the door over by the window. My husband does not know I have a key to this secret chamber. It was my priest who told me about the hiding place.'"

"You might not know that Grizel had continued to worship in the Catholic faith for a while after she was married, My Lady, even though His Lordship had banned it. So then she told me to go and fetch the parure and that we would hide it again, up in her room."

This was all hard to take in, but Jeannie continued.

"When I got it back up to her bedroom, she had a strange, disturbed look about her and she pointed over to the dressing table. 'We are going to hide it behind there, then she can easily take it. I don't want it now, it brings bad luck.'"

"I followed her over to the dressing table and she asked me to drag it out from the wall then sit on the floor in the space where the table had been. As she instructed me, I reached towards a wooden panel that jutted slightly out of line from the others at the base. I prised my fingers underneath and eased it towards me, sliding it upwards. A small crack revealed a larger hole and I pulled out the small panel and laid it on the floor. I bent down and, on her instruction, pushed my hand inside. I was terrified there'd be a rat or a big spider. But there was nothing, just a tiny secret cavity in the wall. When I asked how she knew this was here, hidden in the panelling, she told me she'd dropped an earring down there a few months before and, with no maid to hand, had scrabbled down there to find it and the panel came loose. She'd never thought anything more about it since the parure was safely downstairs in the Charter Room."

"And presumably that was the new place she hid the parure?"

Jeannie nodded.

"But where is it now?"

"I presume it's still there."

"What? No one has thought to ask about this fine piece given by Queen Mary to Marie Seton and then to her good friend Lilias? Not even my husband?"

"His Lordship was in such a state after she died – not just because she died, but the manner of it – that he never asked. I was sworn to secrecy about how she died. Donald and I are the only ones who know the truth as it was Donald, poor man, who had to go and bring her body back up from the ground below and into her bed where I had to make her look as if she'd just died in her sleep." She grimaced. "It was horrible."

I took her hand. "Jeannie, my husband should not have asked you to do this."

"It was the shame, My Lady. He was burdened with guilt and shame. And it meant she could have a decent Christian burial in the family vault."

I nodded. "I see."

"I've never tried to open that panel again since. I've no idea if the parure is still there."

I got to my feet. "Then let us go now."

I sat on the stool as Jeannie shifted back the heavy dressing table. I felt guilty she was doing this, at her age, but with my fat belly I knew I couldn't help her. She sat on the floor and I looked down at the wainscoting as she pushed her fingers in and shifted a lower panel.

"Ow," she said, and sucked her fingertips.

"I hope you haven't got a splinter?"

"It's fine, My Lady," she said, removing the small panel and then reaching her other hand inside. I saw a smile spread across her face and knew she had found it. She withdrew her hand, which was holding a dusty black velvet case. She blew off the dust and handed it to me.

I unclasped the hook, opened the lid and let out a gasp. I lifted up the most beautiful necklace I had ever seen and as it caught the light, the rubies, emeralds and pearls glinted and the gold gleamed and shimmered. I replaced it in the box and brushed my fingers along the earrings and the brooch. I let out a long breath.

"Jeannie, I must ask you to continue to keep this a secret, you must not tell a soul. You understand why, don't you?"

She nodded. "My Lady, you can trust me. You know that." She lifted up the panel. "Shall I replace it for now?"

"Yes, please, I shall take some time to contemplate what I am to do with this stunning parure. His Lordship is in Banff seeing the silversmith today and won't be back until late. I will have made my decision by then." I raised my eyes from the beautiful jewels on my lap to my maid.

"Thank you, Jeannie. You know you shall be rewarded."

"It's fine, My Lady. It's an honour to work for you." And she pressed the panel back into position, got to her feet and slid the dressing table back in front of it.

"Will that be all?"

"Yes, thank you," I said, and she left the room and me to my thoughts. Should I break up the parure and give, say the necklace, to one of Lilias's daughters; and give another part – the earrings? – to young Lilias, Grizel's daughter? Though what about my own darling Grizel, named after the tragic second wife of her father?

What should I do with it? I took the parure over to the chair at the window and sat down, holding up each piece to the light as I turned over the possibilities in my mind. None of them involved telling my husband about this extraordinary find.

Chapter 57

1980

Maggie

I sat in the library waiting for Andrew to join me for our assignment in the Charter Room. The more I'd thought about it, the more I realised how odd it was, not only that they'd asked me to do this, but that the family were all superstitious. In this day and age? Of course, we can all get a little spooked in the dark and maybe if I'd heard a voice whispering "He killed me" in the middle of a radio programme or in a dark room, I'd be a bit scared, but I wasn't now. It was five o'clock and still light for several more hours so surely I wasn't likely to find anything scary, even if I could open the so-called secret chamber. I'd been thinking about Bert Blair joking that Mr David wanted his cousin dead so he could inherit. But I decided I'd not mention that to Andrew; it didn't seem right somehow.

I'd just come up from the staff dining room where the post is laid out and I was disappointed there wasn't a letter for me from Dr Birkett. I'd written to her a couple of weeks ago asking if her friend Elspeth who was curator of Renaissance and Early Modern History at the National Museum could help. She'd mentioned how valuable her expertise had proved for some other students' research. So I asked if anyone knew the whereabouts of the parure that had been given by Mary, Queen of Scots to Marie Seton and then to Lilias, Lady Fyvie. The last time it was seen in public had been on Grizel Seton's neck.

I'd been keen to hear from her before this strange commission in the Charter Room as I was hoping she'd say that it was still being worn by a certain aristocratic family who'd inherited it over the years. But there was nothing in today's post. Dr Birkett was a kind person – strict as a tutor, she stood no nonsense, but she had each of her students' best interests at heart.

"Shall we go then?" Andrew stood in the doorway, a large hold-all in his hands. I got up and pointed at the bag.

"What on earth have you got in there? You thinking we might find a body or something?" I grinned.

"Not 'we', Maggie. 'You'. You're the one opening up the chamber and going in. I shall be staying in the safety of the Charter Room."

"For God's sake, Andrew, you don't believe all that superstitious stuff, do you?"

"Not really, otherwise I wouldn't have agreed to assist. But rather you than me going down there."

"Why?"

"If what Mr David says is true, his uncle died soon after attempting to open it. And his aunt went mad."

"Dementia affects a lot of old people, she didn't go mad because of that."

"She wasn't that old. His uncle was seventy when he died, but his aunt was only in her sixties." He shrugged.

We pushed open the heavy wooden door and Andrew placed his bag on the flagstone floor. "Have you got a torch?"

I brandished my mum's little torch as I headed for the far corner. "So we know it's this side of the window?"

"Yes, pull that section of panelling open," he said, sitting on a chair, pointing, as if he was the gaffer overseeing work on a building site.

"What sort of tools have you got in that bag, then?"

"I've got screwdrivers and chisels in various sizes, a hook pick and a bolt cutter."

He opened the bag and pushed it across the floor towards me.

"How on earth have you got all this?"

"They're not mine, they belong to the caretaker."

"Old Sandy?"

"Yes. He refuses to have anything to do with this as he's been with the family for decades and thinks the curse is real too."

I shook my head. "Honestly, it's just ridiculous."

I turned round and pulled out the panelling nearest the window. It folded back on itself to reveal a small wooden door, set deep in the old stone.

"There's a door handle. What are the chances of this actually opening first time?"

"Slim," Andrew muttered, coming to stand behind me.

I tried to turn it, but it wouldn't budge in either direction. "There's a keyhole here. Presume no one's thought to try a key?"

"Sandy gave me this massive bunch of keys, so you can try all of them, Maggie. If not, you'll have to try the lock pick."

He handed me a heavy ring of ancient looking iron keys and one by one, I tried to insert each in the lock. After trying about ten, I took one smaller one and it at least fitted in the hole.

"Oh, this might be it," I said, crouching down. "Can you take it off this massive ring? It's all too awkward."

Andrew grabbed a pair of pliers from the bag and removed it from the ring.

I held my breath as I pushed the key in and turned. I heard a slight click and leant in as I continued to turn. "Yes!" I said. "It's opening."

Andrew stood behind me holding the rest of the keys. I swatted him away with my hand. "Move out of the way, Andrew. You're blocking the light." I was also feeling rather nauseous when he stood too close, with the overwhelming smell of his aftershave.

As the small door creaked inwards, a dark void appeared. I took the torch out of my pocket and shone it inside, but was able to see very little.

I could hear Andrew raking in his bag and he prodded me in the back and held out a head torch. "Put that on," he said, flicking its switch.

"You've thought of everything, Andrew!"

I secured it around my forehead and looked inside again. There were some stone steps, but unlike the stone in the Great Stair these didn't look worn down by centuries of treading feet. It was obvious people had seldom come in here. I stood on the first step, then took a deep breath. There was something musty and stale in the air. Hopefully this was just the lack of fresh air over the years, not anything dead, I thought, as I crouched down and stepped down onto the second stair. The ceiling above was low, so I had to stoop as I climbed down the next two steps and then onto a floor.

"Think I'm in the chamber, Andrew," I hissed.

There was silence.

"Andrew!" I shouted, this time a tiny panic in my voice as I realised that if the door closed, I could easily be shut in here forever, sealed in like a mummy.

"Sorry, I was trying to find another torch in the bag."

I had never been so glad to detect the whiff of Old Spice in the air. He laid a large hand torch on the top step. I reached up for it, banging my head on the ceiling, and shone it around. This was a small chamber, where someone could hide or be hidden. Was it one of those priest holes where a Catholic priest had to hide? I looked all around, now I could see better in the gloom. There was nothing there, just cold, stone emptiness. I reached out to my sides and touched the walls, which were icy cold, then I touched the wall in front and found that it was warm.

"Andrew, what's beneath this?"

"The little sitting room beside the butler's pantry."

"This wall's warm. How's that possible?"

"Must be the chimney down there. Though I've certainly never seen the fire lit. Anything else down there?"

"Not a thing." I shone my torch behind me to the stairs. "Oh no, hang on, there's some kind of small chest here. I'll see if I can hand it up to you."

"I'm not opening it."

I sighed. "I'll come up and do it. There's nothing else to see down here."

I hunched down as I climbed up the steps then sat on the floor in front of the old box. "Let me guess, that'll be locked too," I said, peering at the tiny lock. But then when I held both sides of the dark wooden lid and lifted, it opened. I looked inside and picked up a yellowed piece of parchment. I turned it over and peered at the ancient script.

"Does that say Banff?"

Andrew looked down at the old paper. "Looks like it – and here I think it says William Reid, Silversmith."

"What d'you think used to be in here, then? It's too big a box for a necklace, so it can't be that. Oh, when I was at the church I heard there was a really precious silver communion cup. This could be its box?"

"Yes, but why is it not kept in the box?"

"True. Well, anyway, at least there's no skeleton down here."

"Nor rats," said Andrew, wincing.

"Just an empty old box. Should I put it back?"

"Nothing else in there then?"

I thrust my hand into the dark wooden box and felt something smooth and soft. I pulled out a small black velvet bag with ancient drawstrings, which I pulled open. I slid two fingers in and felt something hard.

"There's something in here," I said, pulling out a ring, which I held up to the light.

"Let's have a look," Andrew said, pulling my hand towards him.

"That looks really old. Is that a ruby, d'you reckon?"

"I think so." I lifted it to the light and stared at it. "Well, this certainly isn't anything to do with the parure as that's a necklace, earrings and brooch. So I wonder where on earth this ring fits in."

Andrew shrugged. "You going to put the box back?"

I frowned. "Think so. It seems as if it's nothing to do with the ring, which I'll give to Mr David when he comes back."

Andrew nodded and I went down the steps and replaced the box where I'd found it, then came back up.

"Well, that wasn't what we'd expected."

Andrew shook his head. "No, but it's still quite a find. The ring looks really old."

"True, I wonder if it's a family heirloom that had been forgotten about." I smiled. "At least I wasn't struck dead when I opened the chamber."

"I wouldn't speak too soon. We don't know if the curse is still to work." Andrew raised an eyebrow.

"Don't be ridiculous. Right, hand me that key again, I'll lock the door."

As I turned the key slowly in the lock, all of a sudden a feeling of sadness came over me, a crushing sense of melancholy. It was as if by opening the chamber, I had unleashed some heartache from the past.

Chapter 58

1610

Marie Seton

I hobbled along the corridor from my room towards the refectory where my nephew was waiting. How many years was it since we had met? Could it possibly be twenty-five? *Mon Dieu*, it must be. I had not seen him since I spent those wonderful few months at Fyvie Castle before I left with his father for France, where I have been ever since, apart from that awful trip to Loch Leven nearly a decade ago.

He would now see a very old woman with arthritic knees and hands, and hair that was almost white all over. Thankfully as nuns, we must cover our heads. I chuckled as I thought how vain that seemed, but when he saw me last, I had just given up as lady-in-waiting to my Queen and so still had all the finery – the dresses and jewels and hair entwined with pearls – suitable for Court.

I slowed down as I neared the entrance to the refectory. I had not planned what to say to him about Loch Leven; I would per-haps just let him explain. I opened the door and saw a gentleman sitting at the far end, his back to me. I saw a high ruff collar at his neck and a fine cloak trimmed with fur trailing on the floor. His hair, always so brown and thick, was grey and thin. I came to stand in front of him and he jumped to his feet. His face crinkled into a smile as he grasped my hands with his two and kissed them both. I sat down slowly in the chair opposite him and looked at his face. His features remained sharp and his beard, though flecked with grey, was still the colour of a fox, but he looked like an old man, which of course he was.

"*Tante* Marie, how are you?"

"Well, thank you, dear nephew. Or should I say, as good as my ageing bones allow. It's good to see you after so many years."

I would let him lead the conversation; let's see where it took him.

"You have received news over the years from my wives, I know, so you are aware I now have one son and seven daughters, all thank God in good health. They certainly bring joy and laughter to Fyvie Castle."

"God blesses us in so many ways."

"Yes. Margaret, my wife, is due to be delivered of another child any day now. I await the news of a second son eagerly."

"Or an eighth daughter?"

"Of course, but I should like another son."

"Children are a gift, given by God's grace; not by your predilection."

He smiled. "I have come to accept this over the years."

I asked him then to tell me about the children and about Margaret his wife who is surely as delightful as she seems in her letters to me. Then after some time, he snapped his fingers at the servant who had been standing all the while in the far corner. "Bring me the gifts."

The man rushed across, a large woollen bag and wooden box in his arms. He laid these down before his master, bowed low then retreated to his position.

"I have brought some wines from my Paris wine merchant. I am going to see a new wine producer during my stay here in Reims – Pierre Gosset, recommended to me by my friends at the French Court. When I come again, before my return to Scotland, I shall bring you some."

I nodded.

"And here is a mutton ham from Fyvie, I think you used to enjoy that."

I beamed. He had obviously put some thought into selecting gifts for his only remaining aunt. "Sadly, I could not bring you any oysters, which I know you also liked. They would not have lasted the journey."

He handed me another package, wrapped in woollen cloth. "There is a special gift in here from Margaret for you, and a letter, which she says is to be opened in the solitude of your room."

I took it from him, thanked him then waited until he'd ended his monologue about his journey and the courts in both England and France, then I stretched my right hand towards him and he took it in his. "Do you remember this ring, Alexander?"

He stared down at my ruby ring, the only vestige of luxury the Abbess permits me to wear.

"Was it your mother's, Aunt?"

I shook my head and let him continue looking at it. I watched his face as realisation dawned. His eyes grew large and his cheeks flushed a little. "Well, it resembles the ring my wife Lilias used to wear, but it cannot be."

He looked up at me, fear in his eyes.

I retracted my hand and waited. He did not break the silence, so I did. "How did Lilias die, Alexander?"

He swallowed. "She died of a terrible wasting illness, she could not eat and so..."

"So she starved to death?"

He shook his head. "There was nothing we could do."

I lifted my hand once more. "How do you think I acquired this ring, the ring given to me by your royal godmother and which I then gifted to your wife Lilias?"

He was flustered. He tugged his rusty beard and bit his lip. "I cannot say."

"Then I shall tell you. I went to Loch Leven Castle and saw dear, sweet Lilias just before she died. She perished from lack of nourishment. I also think that she died of a broken heart, for you abandoned her, didn't you?"

He dropped to his knees and laid his head in my lap.

"It was not like that, I can assure you. It was not meant to happen like that," he muttered, snivelling like a child. He wiped his face and looked up at me. "I had instructed the caretaker to look after her. I had written down my commands, to feed her three times a day and give her water and keep her warm with a fire. But..."

He was whimpering like a baby now.

"Then how was it that she died the most awful death, deprived of any food at all – and obviously kept a prisoner in that filthy room?"

"Please let me explain."

"I look forward to it greatly."

He sat back on his chair. "The day she sailed over to the island, I was meant to join her with my orders for the caretaker..."

"Kenneth."

"Yes. But then there was suddenly an urgent request for me to attend the palace at Dunfermline from the shores of the loch and so I sent one of the servants over to the castle with her bags and with my instructions – and most importantly, with the money I had agreed to pay that wretch Kenneth." He sighed.

"I ended up spending over a week with the King who desperately needed me, then I had to go south at once to Seton Palace as you remember my mother was gravely ill at that time, even though she somehow survived another two years. To my shame, I did not visit Lilias as I had planned. I was going to explain to her that we would separate and I would marry Grizel..."

"Why? So that you could have a male child?"

He nodded.

"And I was going to explain that I had to keep her locked up for a while, just until Grizel and I were married, then she could return to Aberdeenshire and live nearby to see her children again. But the servant I had sent over was a swindler, he took the money I had sent for Kenneth and so that wretch did nothing to look after her."

"Why did he neither send a letter to you asking for his wages nor obey your instructions?"

"I had no idea he was illiterate. He presumed I just wanted her to be given water, for that was about the only word he could recognise."

"Did she have nothing in her own bags she could have given him as payment?"

He took a deep breath. "I am ashamed to say, I had gone through her bags and removed the jewellery I knew she had packed in there."

I shook my head.

"I regret everything about that time, Aunt, truly I do: planning the trip to Loch Leven, entrusting my wife to a swindler and then to an illiterate brute. I have tried to make amends ever since, by giving much to the church, by helping the poor nearby, but—"

I raised my hand. "Stop. Have you asked God's forgiveness?"

"I have, almost daily, and I pray for Lilias's soul every single day."

"I see." I lifted Margaret's gift from my lap and stood up. "I shall consider what you have just told me, Alexander, and will see you again in a few days."

He got to his feet, his face a mess of tears.

"Thank you, dear Aunt Marie. May God bless you."

"May God bless those who truly repent," I said, sweeping past him as I headed straight for the chapel.

Maggie

I was at the top of the Great Stairs, showing the visitors the small statue of Mary Seton, telling them about Mary, Queen of Scots' lady-in-waiting's connection to Fyvie Castle, when a hand shot up.

"Did she die here at the castle?"

"No, she was a nun in Reims in northern France from about 1585 and I believe she's buried there."

"So she just abandoned the Queen to her fate? She was executed two years later, wasn't she, in 1587."

I nodded. "To my knowledge, Mary Seton had to leave Mary, Queen of Scots for health reasons. She went to the Queen's aunt's convent."

"Mary of Guise?"

"Yes, her sister Renee de Guise was abbess of the St Pierre Abbey in Reims from the age of twenty-four till she died just before her eightieth birthday. Eighty in those days was an amazing age."

Everyone else nodded and looked happy with the facts, but just as I was about to usher them back down the stairs, the woman raised her hand again. "So did Mary Seton not come back to Scotland at all till she died?"

Thankfully I'd been reading up on Alexander Seton's aunt.

"She died in 1615, so she had thirty years in the convent. To the best of my knowledge, she never returned to Scotland." I shuffled on the step and pointed down the stairs. The others began to move down but this woman came to stand in front of me. "But what about her necklace? How did it get back to Scotland?"

"What necklace?"

"The one you showed us on those two Lady Fyvies' portraits."

"Oh, but that was gifted to the first Lady Fyvie, so Mary Seton must have given it to her nephew and wife shortly before she left for France."

"Quite something, giving away a gift from someone who was not only the Queen but also her best friend, wasn't it?"

What was this woman's point?

"I suppose so, but it must have happened. Mary Seton died a pauper, so it wasn't as if she had the necklace hidden away somewhere at the convent." I began to edge past her, hoping she would give up. "Right, let's go and follow the others down."

"So where's the necklace now?" She called after me.

I turned around and lifted both hands. "No one knows."

I'd just said goodbye to all the visitors, trying as usual to insist that I didn't require any tips. I turned around and saw an elegant woman in a black dress and pearls standing there.

I smiled and she came forward, hand outstretched.

"Hello," she said, "I'm Arabella. You must be Maggie."

At last, a firm handshake and warmth in a voice.

"Hi, I was just seeing off my afternoon tour."

"David hates the visitors, has he told you? But there's no choice, the castle can't keep running without extra income. I've just been telling him about my friend Jane down in the Borders working on plans to open her castle up for weddings. Far more money in one weekend than an entire summer of castle tours."

"What does your husband think about that?"

She laughed. "Not much, as you can imagine, but Charles leaves most of the running to his cousin." She looked at her watch. "D'you want to come along and have a cup of tea?"

With yet another evening alone ahead of me, this sounded like a rather pleasant offer. "Yes please," I said, following her towards the Leith Tower.

"Have you enjoyed your stay at Fyvie?"

"Yes, it's been great, I've got loads of studying done. Which was really the main purpose of working here. And I've learnt a great deal doing the tours."

"From Andrew?" She raised an eyebrow.

"Some things, but also from my own research."

"Excellent," she said opening the door to the Leith Tower. I followed her into the kitchen where she put the kettle on the Aga.

"The fire's on next door in the drawing room," she said, pointing out into the corridor. "Go and sit in there, the seats are far more comfy than these rickety old things. Milk and sugar?"

"Just milk please," I said.

On the way, I couldn't help peeking into the study and looking once more at the portrait of Mr Charles's mother, noticing again the necklace at her throat.

I was sitting in a comfortable armchair by the fire when she arrived holding a tray with two mugs. She handed me one and sat down. "David said you opened the secret chamber."

"Yes, they asked me to do it. That was three days ago, I've not died yet."

She grinned. "Honestly, the superstitious nonsense in this family. I mean, in this day and age to believe in some ancient curse. Ridiculous."

"And you've seen the ruby ring?"

She nodded. "It's amazing, so beautiful. David's taken it to the family jewellers in Aberdeen to try to ascertain its age, then we can maybe find out whose ring it was."

"Who knows, it could've belonged to Mary, Queen of Scots." I smiled.

"I was thinking that too, but of course she never visited Fyvie."

I took a sip of tea. Thankfully it was normal tea, not the smoky variety Mr David had made.

"David told me it was in an old box?"

"Yes, a large wooden box the communion cup from the church must've been stored in at some stage. Maybe the tiny cupboard at the church where it was stored was too small for the box. It's really quite big."

Arabella nodded. "Yes, the cup's kept in the bank vaults now."

"Bert the beadle was telling me all about it."

"Oh Bert, he's such a sweetheart. Have you seen him wind the clock?"

I nodded.

"You'd think it was Big Ben," she said, "the importance he puts on it, bless him."

"Have the family always been superstitious?"

"Yes, well, certainly for as long as I've known them, and we've been married twenty years." She sipped her tea. "Charles's father died not long after he tried to open the door to the chamber you managed to get into. Somehow he couldn't get the right key. Mind you, he was never the most patient man. They all thought his death was caused by the curse, and then when Charles's dear mother Ethel got bad dementia, they blamed that."

"I heard she saw the Green Lady."

"So she told all of us, and that she'd heard the ghost pronounce some spooky words." She shook her head. "Poor soul, she was already quite doddery by then. She used to wander around the castle in the middle of the night, in the pitch black."

I had finished my tea and was about to leave when a thought occurred.

"Could I ask you something, please?"

"Of course."

"The portrait of Mr Charles's mother in the study."

"What about it?"

"She's wearing the famous necklace from the parure, the one both Lilias and Grizel, the Ladies of Fyvie, wear in their portraits. We show the paintings to the visitors in the tour."

Her eyes widened. "Did David show you Charles's mother's picture?"

"No, but I went into the study to thank him for tea and he was on the phone. I couldn't miss it."

She smiled. "That's why David's convinced the parure is somewhere here at Fyvie. But it's not. Charles and I don't think it's been since – well, since those two laird's ladies wore it, centuries ago."

"What? But how come his mother was wearing it in the portrait?"

"She wasn't." Arabella was smirking.

"I don't understand."

"His Ma and I had such a good relationship, she was a darling, but her husband never took her seriously; he thought she was frivolous, silly. She was certainly neither of those things. She was a good woman."

"But what about the painting?"

"Because her husband – just like David nowadays – was keen to find the parure so they could sell it for a small fortune to save the castle from having to open to the public, she asked the artist to paint it on her neck. He happened to be a friend of her sister Beth's and she asked him to study the necklace on those two early portraits and then add it to her own portrait, almost as an act of defiance. And he did. When her husband saw the painting, he was so furious with her he refused to hang it, but Charles hung it after his father's death. Though I never told my husband the truth, he guessed what happened, but we certainly never told David, who's still convinced that she'd hidden the parure when she became struck with dementia, poor love."

I sat back in my chair. "Wow. Mr David still believes that, even after it wasn't found in the Charter Room?"

She shrugged. "He still reckons it's somewhere else in the castle. At the end of the visitors' season, he told me he intends to check every loose wooden panel in the whole place." She laughed. "Madness!"

I looked at the clock. "Sorry, I've been here too long, I'd better go. Thank you so much for tea – and for telling me all this."

"A pleasure. Hope to see you before I go."

"Will you be here long?"

"Only another couple of days. Italy's already calling to me."

"Thanks again."

"You're welcome. I'm just delighted you've not died of the curse!" She burst out laughing.

Chapter 60

1610

Marie Seton

I sat in the chapel for quite some time after I'd met my nephew, attempting to make sense of what he said had actually happened. I tried to convince myself that what he had told me was true, that it had all been some terrible accident, a miscommunication, but none of it seemed plausible. I forced myself onto my sore knees and prayed for guidance, for God to show me the truth.

Then I hobbled along to my room, shut the door and laid the bundle on my bed. I wanted to enjoy this moment. Until Alexander had brought all those presents for me, I had not received a gift from anyone for so many years. Indeed, I hadn't had any visitors. I struggled speaking English again, but my nephew understood me even when I reverted to French.

I untied the package from its heavy woollen cloths, thinking the material would keep my knees warm when I sat outside in the cloisters. There was a letter in Margaret's beautiful hand, but first I was keen to open the present; I felt as excited as a child. I removed the fine cloth around a black box and as soon as I saw it, I gasped, for I knew what it was. Before I even lifted the lid, I smiled, then I opened it and gazed inside.

The necklace was just as beautiful as ever, the rubies sparkled in the light when I raised it up to the window. I held up the earrings I'd always adored and marvelled at how the pearls gleamed and the emeralds shone. And the brooch, how could I have forgotten how stunning this was; look at the detail, the craftsmanship of the intricate gold work. I felt my emotions rise and I tried to control them but soon I was weeping as I remembered the day the Queen gave them to me, the joy I had wearing them and then of course the delight I felt giving them to dear Lilias.

I have no idea how long I wept, but when I was able to stop, I put the parure back in the box, but kept the lid open so I could see the jewels as I began to read the letter.

> *Chère Tante Marie,*
>
> *I hope this finds you in good health.*
>
> *This parure belongs to you and to no one else and so I hope you will accept it. My maid Jeannie told me that Grizel's life was perhaps not as happy as it might have been and she had hidden it.*
>
> *No one knew where it was for several years, but Jeannie located it for me. I knew it must be returned to you, for though it has been on loan to the Ladies of Fyvie for some years, it is yours. And I hope that you have joy, perhaps if not wearing it, simply by enjoying the sight and the touch of it and the memories it will evoke.*
>
> *I do not have very long until my third baby is due and so I shall write again once he or she is born. Indeed, by the time you read this letter, I might already be mother to three little ones.*
>
> *Your dear friend,*
>
> *Margaret*

"Thank you, dear Aunt, for agreeing to see me again. I was not sure you would want to receive me after my last visit. Will you believe me if I tell you I have done little else but pray for forgiveness since we met? I have not even gone to see Monsieur Gosset yet, that is for tomorrow."

"When shall you leave for Scotland?"

"In three days' time."

"I see."

"I have news from home, that should bring you joy."

"What is that, Alexander?"

"Margaret was delivered of our third child, a baby girl." He smiled. "Praise be to God, the baby is hale and hearty."

"Praise God indeed." I looked directly at him. He looked exhausted, as if he had not slept in a while. Perhaps he was indeed contrite.

"I have decided that the child shall be named after her dear great aunt." He cleared his throat. "Her name shall be Marie Seton and my only hope is that she grows up to be as kind and devoted and faithful as you, dear Aunt."

His voice was cracking and I found myself feeling rather emotional too. "This is wonderful, dear nephew. But what of your wife? She might not be happy with your choice of name."

He smiled. "Even before I received the news of her safe delivery, I had decided a baby girl would be called after you. Then in the letter from Fyvie was a note to say that Margaret wanted the baby to be called Marie. It was meant to be; this child is our special gift."

I felt a tear run down my cheek and as I wiped it, I felt my nephew's hand on mine. "Thank you, dear Aunt."

I nodded and with that I felt, if not forgiveness, but somehow understanding, as if my nephew and I had come to some sort of accord. The gift of his child was his apology, his petition to me and to God for forgiveness.

He rose from his chair. "I can call back in two days' time if you like, dear Aunt, to say farewell?"

I stood very still for a moment as I considered this, for this would be the very last time I ever saw him before I died; I knew that. "Yes, thank you. Perhaps I shall have time to write a letter for you to take back to your wife."

"That is kind. And I shall deliver it to her with pleasure."

Chapter 61

1610

Margaret

I was sitting up in bed, gazing at the new baby in my arms, when the door swung open. Jeannie jumped to her feet and pulled a chair across to the bed. She gestured to me that she should take the baby but I shook my head.

"Margaret, here I am," Alexander said, sweeping in. "I thought the child would be in the nursery, but I see she is up here with you. Is that advisable?"

"Of course, dear husband. Nurse has the other little ones to tend to in the nursery. And I find that I am quite capable." I pointed to the chair for him to sit but he came towards me and bent down to kiss my forehead. Then he stared at the baby and stroked her downy cheek. "She has the Seton colouring. I am pleased we decided on the name Marie."

"I am delighted. Marie Seton will grow to be a wonderful woman, I can tell," I said, kissing her perfect little fingers. "Tell me about the trip. I hope your meeting with your merchants went well. And your visit to the bell foundry in Flanders? How is Aunt Marie?"

He told me at length about his time away, ending up by describing how Marie looked well, considering her age.

"How old is she?"

"Sixty-five, I believe. She is frailer than before, of course, but still sprightly of mind."

Little Marie began to cry and so I called Jeannie over. "It's time for her to feed. Please take her to the wet nurse."

She scooped up the warm bundle from my arms and I smiled.

"Was Aunt Marie pleased when you told her this little one was to be named after her?"

He nodded and took my hand. "It made her very happy. I believe it brought her joy that will comfort her in her final years."

He reached down to the floor where he had deposited a package.

"This is from her. She said to open it and to read the letter when you are on your own. There's something in there that she possibly doesn't want anyone else to see – probably some crucifix you'll have to dispose of before the minister sees it," he said, chuckling.

I smiled and took the package in my hands.

"Do you mind if I go downstairs, Margaret dear? I'm sure there is plenty to be done in the Charter Room."

"I dealt with as much as I could before the baby arrived, Alexander. There shouldn't be too much work for you."

"Thank you, my dear. What would I do without you?" he said as he rose and headed for the door. He turned and smiled. "You have done well."

"What, even though I delivered another girl?"

"That matters not," he said, shutting the door quietly behind him.

I turned down to the package in my lap and unravelled the fine cloth. There was a letter on top, so I opened this and began to read.

Chère Margaret,

My nephew's visit brought me both joy and sorrow. The sadness came as I realised how very old I am and how perhaps I shall not have much longer on this earth. He and I spoke of many things, and by the end I sensed we understood each other a little better. I feel that as he too is now heading towards old age, he deserves atonement for his past sins. And I shall continue to pray that God will, in his grace, forgive him.

The gift that you gave me was too kind. I appreciate it so very much. The Queen gave it to me in 1575. It was the most splendid thing I had ever been given and it still is very precious to me.

But I now pass the parure on to you, dear Margaret. Lilias wore it for many years and I believe Grizel must have done too. It is for you now to wear and to remember me by.

Thank you for naming your new baby girl after me. I am both honoured and touched and to my dying day, though I shall never meet her, little Marie Seton shall be precious to me.

With all of God's blessing,
Marie

I lifted the lid on the black velvet box and marvelled once more at the beauty of the parure, given by a Queen to her friend; and now entrusted to me. I sat there for some time, contemplating what to do with it. I wondered whether, if I told my husband about it, he would want me to wear it, though his wishes were not always executed exactly as he might desire.

Later that afternoon, when Jeannie came back into the bedroom with little Marie, I was still gazing down at the open box.

She handed the warm bundle to me and I nuzzled in to kiss the perfect little cheek.

Jeannie gasped and pointed to the parure.

"My Lady, I thought you said it had gone back to its rightful owner."

"And now it is back at Fyvie and it shall go to its rightful owner when she is old enough to wear it." I picked up an earring and held it up above the sleeping baby. "But until Marie comes of age, we shall keep it hidden once more, over there where we found it. If you could please pull out the dressing table and hide it away."

Jeannie frowned. "Are you sure, My Lady? What if, God forbid, something happens to you and..."

I smiled. "After you have done this, I want you to fetch me a quill and some ink. I shall write my own will declaring that, should I die before my daughter Marie comes of age, then the parure can be retrieved from its hiding place in my room. I shall explain exactly where it is. I shall put this decree alongside my husband's in the Charter Room, for as you know, I now deal with such affairs for him."

I shut the case and handed it to her. "And Jeannie, do not worry. I intend to live many years yet. I know I shall see my daughter wear it when she comes of age and I will tell her about her great aunt Marie, whose gift came from the Queen herself."

Chapter 62

1980

Maggie

There was a knock at my door just as I'd started to pack my bags.

"Come in."

Mrs MacPherson stood there with a letter in her hand. "I thought I'd bring this to you, Miss Hay. Is it tomorrow afternoon you leave?"

I nodded. "Yes, but I thought I'd start packing today." I took the letter, presuming it would be from Mum, confirming the time for the pick-up, but it was Dr Birkett's handwriting. Just when I'd almost given up hope of hearing from her.

"Thanks. See you later," I said as she closed the door and I went to the desk to open the letter.

Hi Maggie, hope you're doing okay and that you've managed to do lots of work as well as have a well-deserved break. Here's the information you were after about that parure. Elspeth managed to find out some things I think you'll find fascinating. I made a copy of her letter and enclose it here. Look forward to seeing you at start of term.

Jenny

Jenny? She'd never called herself that. It was always Dr Birkett to her students.

I unfolded the enclosed photocopy and began to read.

The Seton Parure
A gift from Mary, Queen of Scots to her friend and lady-in-waiting

Mary/Marie Seton in 1575, this set of necklace, earrings and brooch was then gifted to the wives of her nephew Alexander Seton, Lord Fyvie, later Earl of Dunfermline, in 1585 on the occasion of his marriage to Lilias Drummond.

It remained in the Seton family and was bequeathed in particular to Marie Seton, born in 1610, daughter of Alexander Seton and his third wife, Margaret Hay. Marie Seton then married into the Hay family by her marriage to John Hay, eighth Earl of Yester, nephew of Marie Seton's mother.

Marie Seton had no children and so the parure remained at the Hay family seat, which was Yester Castle and is now Yester House in the Borders. Nothing was heard of it until the early 1890s when William Hay, the eleventh Marquess of Tweedale, discovered the parure hidden at the back of a safe in the muniments room of Yester House.

It was then sold at auction at Christie's in February 1894 to Algernon Borthwick, Baron Glenesk, who gave it to his only daughter, Lilias. She became Countess Bathurst and as such, presented it to Queen Mary on the occasion of King George's Silver Jubilee in May 1935. It has remained with the royal family ever since.

Here at the National Museum, we are already in talks with the Royal Household, advising them, as they begin to set up the Royal Collection Trust. The plan is that Holyrood Palace will display pieces in the royal family's collection with a particular Scottish interest. It is therefore highly likely that, in the not too distant future, the parure will be on display at Holyrood Palace.

I stopped and let out a long breath. This was unbelievable. Margaret Hay's daughter, who was named after Mary Seton, was given the parure and it left Fyvie Castle with her for the Borders. Then it was hidden away again for many years till it was discovered then sold at auction to this Baron whose only daughter was called – I could hardly believe it – Lilias. And this Lilias presented it to the Queen who was called Mary.

I smiled. The parure had indeed come full circle. There was even a chance I might be able to see it once this collection was set up. I hadn't felt happier in ages. I folded the letter away and continued my packing, for once looking forward to where my life was going next.

I sat outside the entrance on the gravel, waiting for Mum and Auntie Liz to arrive. My bags were still inside, as I wanted to be here to greet them. Hopefully they'd have time to come inside for a quick tour of the castle. All last night I'd been thinking of the parure and how those who truly appreciated it seemed to have been called Mary, Marie or Lilias. I was just considering how incredible it was that I might be able to see it for myself at Holyrood Palace when I heard a car on the drive. I got to my feet and looked down the slope towards the road.

It wasn't Auntie Liz's car, I was sure hers was red. This was black. It must be a visitor, not realising the castle was closed on Mondays. I continued to stare at it as it got nearer and then, with a sudden lurch, I realised it was Dad's car. I watched as he parked it on the gravel and Mum got out and waved. I waved back but stood still, unsure what to do. Mum rushed straight over and gave me a hug then stood beside me as we both watched Dad shut the door and lock the car.

He came towards me and I saw that he was smiling. As he reached out both arms, I could feel tears begin to prick my eyes. He took me into his arms and I began to sob.

"Dad," I stuttered, "I'm so sorry."

"There's nothing to be sorry about, sweetheart. In fact, I'm the one who should apologise."

He stood back and looked at me, smiled, then handed me his handkerchief.

"Now, let's get you home."

Epilogue

1615

Dear Alexander Seton,

You have already received the sad news that your aunt Marie Seton died last month. She had no personal effects apart from the enclosed. On her death bed, she asked me to send it to you as a reminder of her. She said it would mean a great deal to you. She died a much-loved sister here at the convent St Pierre de Reims and has been laid to rest in our chapel, alongside the tomb of Marie de Guise, the mother of Marie Seton's friend Queen Mary of Scots. I hope that, should you ever travel to France again, you might be able to pay your respects.

With God's blessings,
Marguerite Kirkaldi
Abbesse, St Pierre de Reims

Alexander Seton's hands were trembling as he opened the small velvet bag that had been enclosed with the letter. He was used to having his wife Margaret at his side for administrative matters these days, since his sight was failing him and, he had to admit, his judgement was sometimes found lacking. But she was away visiting the new young minister in the village. As his fingers grasped the object inside the bag and he realised what it was, he was glad she was not with him.

He withdrew a ring and held it up to the light where it sparkled and shone with a glint of red. It was the ruby ring that his godmother Queen Mary had given to his aunt Marie Seton. She in turn had gifted it to his first wife, Lilias, who died with it on her hand. He grimaced with pain at the memory of her time at Loch Leven, as he turned the ring between his fingers. His aunt had taken the ring from his dead wife's hand and now he held it in his. His eyes widened as he began to understand what this meant. Why would his aunt want him to have this ring, which was surely cursed? She had seen through his excuses, he knew that; she was clever, she had the Seton insight.

Even though it was many years ago, he couldn't forget the look of fear and bewilderment on Lilias's face as she was rowed away from him on the shore of Loch Leven. Soon after, he'd gone over to the castle with her bags, having, to his shame, riffled through them. And when Kenneth asked him not once but twice to clarify his duties – "So she's not to get any food, Your Lordship?" "Nothing to eat at all?" – even that callous brute had looked baffled. But when he thrust his money at the man, the keeper simply shrugged, grabbed her bag and trudged off towards the tower.

Alexander bowed his head and sighed when he thought of the day Kenneth sent word to him that she'd died and that he'd taken her body to Dalgety Bay where he was awaiting instructions. Fortunately, he was at Court in Dunfermline and so was able to travel at once to set everything in motion. The burial at the family vault took place the following day, the minister having been furnished with the news that a terrible and sudden illness had befallen his beloved wife as they travelled through Fife.

He sat completely still for a while then, once his mind was made up, he pushed the ring back into the bag, opened the drawer in front of him and took out a key. He headed for the corner of the room where he pulled out the panelling beside the window. It folded back on itself to reveal a small wooden door, set deep in the stone. He pushed the key into the lock and turned the doorknob. He grabbed a candle from the table and crouched low, before descending the stone steps into the dark, damp chamber.

Here he patted around until he found the wooden box, which he opened, checking it was still empty. His wife Margaret had suggested the new silver communion cup be stored at the church, but the box was still here. He placed the ring inside and shut the lid then tucked it back in the corner. He returned to the Charter Room, locked the door and shifted the wooden panelling back into place.

He had just replaced the candle holder on the table when an intense pain stabbed him in his heart. He clutched his chest with two hands and staggered towards the seat where he slumped down. The sharp pain began to ease and soon it became an excruciating ache, yet his breath was still shallow. He continued sitting there as his breath returned to normal and his heart beat less fast. He suddenly felt an overwhelming fatigue and shut his eyes.

Some time later, the door opened and Margaret, Lady Fyvie, entered, the broad smile on her face illuminated by the candle in her hand. She tiptoed towards her husband, placed a hand on his brow and he awoke with a start.

"Come, Alexander," she said, in her soothing voice, "it's late. It is time for your medication."

He stared at her with bleary eyes and stretched out his hand to her to help him up. "The curse, Margaret, I cannot fight the curse much longer."

She patted his arm and walked him slowly to the door, a young woman helping an old man as he shuffled off into the night.

The End

Author's Notes

The Green Lady is a work of fiction, but it is based on historical fact. When I began looking into Fyvie Castle's history, I was struck by the possibility for so many different stories. Over the centuries, there were occurrences that today seem astounding. But perhaps the one fact that drew me in most of all was that Alexander Seton, created Lord Fyvie in 1597, allegedly starved his first wife to death for failing to produce a male heir.

The more I discovered about the man, the more fascinated I became, and my research took me not only north to Aberdeenshire but also to the National Library of Scotland and then to Holyrood Palace, where I saw the parure, given by Alexander's godmother Mary, Queen of Scots to his aunt, Mary Seton. By this stage, I was hooked and the story began to take shape.

I decided to change some dates and events to ensure the tale ran smoothly. But the main historical facts, such as when Mary, Queen of Scots died, when her son James assumed the crown of both England and Scotland, and also the names and backgrounds of Alexander's wives were unchanged. Meanwhile, some events – the location of Loch Leven Castle for Lilias's imprisonment, for example – are invented for practical reasons that suited the narrative.

I wanted to give the women a voice, something they did not have in the sixteenth and seventeenth centuries, when men ruled absolutely over their wives and children. In so doing, I hoped to portray their lives, which were so often tragic and subservient, as perhaps a little more hopeful. With the freedom that fiction enables, I have written a story set in history, but not based exclusively on fact.

Here I have noted what actually happened in my characters' lives.

Alexander Seton was born in 1555. His father, George Seton, was Mary (Marie) Seton's half-brother. He was Mary, Queen of Scots' godson and became Prior of Pluscarden in 1565 then Lord President of the Court of Session in 1593, Provost of Edinburgh in 1598 and Lord Chancellor of Scotland in 1604. He bought Fyvie Castle from Andrew Meldrum of Drumoak in 1596 and was created Lord Fyvie in 1597. Of his sophisticated outer and inner renovations, the only remaining interior manifestation of his work in the castle is the Great Stair, the finest wheel-stair in Scotland, built in the late 1590s.

He was created Earl of Dunfermline in 1605 by King James I/VI, in acknowledgement of his custody of Prince Charles who later became King Charles I. The prince lived mainly at Dunfermline Palace during this guardianship.

The second oldest communion cup in Scotland belongs to Fyvie Parish Church and was gifted by Alexander Seton in 1618. Alexander Seton died in 1622.

His first wife was **Lilias Drummond,** born between 1571 and 1574. They married before 1592 and she produced five daughters, one of whom (Margaret) died in infancy. Lilias died in 1601, some accounts say of a broken heart, others that her husband starved her to death so that he could marry his second wife, Grizel, with whom he had fallen in love.

Grizel Leslie was born between 1575 and 1585 and she married Alexander in 1601 and gave birth to a son, Charles, who died in infancy. Her first daughter was called Lilias and she died unmarried. Grizel then had a third child, a daughter, Jean. Grizel died young, of unknown causes, in 1606.

His third wife, **Margaret Hay**, was born around 1592, and she married Alexander in 1607. She had a son, Charles, who became second Earl of Dunfermline after his father's death. Her first daughter was called Grizel and she too died unmarried. She had a second daughter, Mary, who died young, and a fourth child, recorded as "unidentified". After her husband's death, Margaret married the first Earl of Callendar and lived until 1659.

Mary Seton was born c.1541, into one of Scotland's grandest families. Along with Mary Beaton, Mary Livingstone and Mary Fleming, she accompanied Mary, Queen of Scots to France in 1548. They then all returned to Scotland in 1561 after the death of the Queen's French husband, Francis II of France.

Mary Seton was the only one of the Queen's Four Marys or ladies-in-waiting never to marry. She was a skilled hairdresser, having learnt the art in France. She was tall and so wore in the Queen's clothes as she too was tall. After the Queen's imprisonment by her cousin Elizabeth I, Mary Seton stayed by her side for fifteen years, before retiring to the convent in Reims, France, run by the Queen's aunt Renee de Guise. It was there she died in 1615.

The Parure

The parure that I first saw during my research and that partly inspired the story is now part of the Royal Collection Trust (RCT) and is on display at Holyrood Palace. It consists of a necklace, earrings and a brooch – each of gold with translucent blue and green enamel scrollwork set with pearls, emeralds and rubies. According to the RCT, the oldest piece in the parure dates from the sixteenth century and the information in the display cabinet states the parure was "c.1575 with later alterations ... a gift from Mary, Queen of Scots to her attendant, Mary Seton. A devoted companion and friend of Mary, Queen of Scots, Mary Seton shared many years of her exile."

It is also known as the Seton or the Eglinton parure. The necklace used to be longer: it was a "cotiere" – a long chain worn by women and caught up in the breast. But Mary Seton's descendant Alexander, sixth Earl of Eglinton (died 1661) removed four of the snake links and four S ornaments from the chain on his succession to earldom in 1612 and these (which now form the shorter necklace, plus earrings and brooch) eventually passed to his descendant Archibald William, thirteenth Earl of Eglinton (1812–1861).

The parure remained in possession of the Eglinton family until it was sold by the three daughters of the thirteenth Earl at Christie's in 1894. It was bought by the newspaper proprietor Algernon Borthwick, first Baron Glenesk (1830–1908), whose daughter, Lilias, Countess Bathurst (1871–1965) then presented the parure to Queen Mary on the occasion of King George V's Silver Jubilee in May 1935.

The remaining sixteen snake links and sixteen white S ornaments, set with rubies and pearls – the longer necklace – were passed to the Hon. Elizabeth Seton when she married William Hay of Drummelzier in 1694. This necklace has been on long-term loan to the National Museum of Scotland since 2001.

I admit I was both delighted and amazed at the incredible coincidence of discovering that the parure was handed back to a Queen called Mary by a noblewoman called Lilias, so many years later. I like to think this was karma.

The BBC Radio Recording

On 28 February 2004, a live transmission of BBC Radio 4's Excess Baggage went out from Leap Castle, supposedly one of the most haunted castles in Ireland. Some twenty minutes into the transmission, while the wonderful Sandi Toksvig, the presenter, was talking to the guests, listeners reported hearing a ghostly whisper, that was interpreted as either the words "'Lie down" or "You liar" or "I died". The unsettling, spooky words caused many listeners to write in.

This incident affected me personally as on that Saturday morning in 2004, I parked my car at Ocean Terminal, Leith but could not get out until the programme finished as I too had heard the words and waited for an explanation at the end of the broadcast. Neither the presenter, the guests nor the crew were aware of the ghostly whisperings until they played the recording back later.

Like some others, I clearly heard the words "I died" and the hairs stood up on the back of my neck. Explanations to listeners later were that it was white noise or possibly EVP (Electronic Voice Phenomena). There was a 1971 paper on EVP that suggested that the personality of the person survives the death of the physical body. Whatever you think about that – and I am the world's greatest sceptic – I can still recall so many years later the tingling chill that I experienced on hearing those ghostly words.

I wondered therefore if, since Fyvie Castle too is meant to be haunted, Lilias did in fact come back to haunt those who had wronged her, as the Green Lady. And even if they did not "see" her, they either felt her presence or became victims of her curse.

Acknowledgements

~ Thanks to MaryAn Charnley and Anne Dow for reading drafts of *The Green Lady* and commenting so wisely.

~ Also thank you Cathy Tingle for your assiduous reading, insightful comments and for re-introducing me to the vocative comma. And to linguist Celia Greig for confirmation of my rather rusty French.

~ Thanks to Dr Mary Duckworth for medical knowledge, to Maureen Kelly and Dr Annie Gray for their expertise on food throughout Scottish history and to Sheila Jardine for her inestimable knowledge on all things jewellery.

~ Thanks to the National Trust for Scotland and in particular to Susan Ord, Visitor Services Supervisor at Fyvie Castle, for so kindly showing me around the castle, socially distanced, during the few weeks permitted in 2020.

~ Thank you Alison Jaffrey, Carole Eddie and Audrey Clark at Fyvie Church for insider knowledge of your beautiful church.

~ I am grateful to Dr Anna Groundwater, Principal Curator of Renaissance and Early Modern History at the National Museum of Scotland for invaluable information on the parure, part of which is on display at NMS and part at Holyrood Palace.

~ As ever, thanks to the National Library of Scotland for allowing me many days of poring over books.

~ Finally, thank you Sara Hunt at Saraband for continuing to support my fascination with the history of Scotland's women.

Bibliography

Coventry, Martin: *Haunted Castles and Houses of Scotland* (Goblinshead, 2004).

Doran, Susan: *Mary Queen of Scots: An Illustrated Life* (British Library, 2007).

Fenton, Alexander: *The Food of the Scots* (John Donald, 2007).

Fraser, Antonia: *Mary, Queen of Scots* (Weidenfeld & Nicholson, 1969).

Goodare, Julian: *State and Society in Early Modern Scotland* (Oxford University Press, 1999).

Gordon, Catherine J B: *A Legend of Fyvie Castle* (British Library, 2011).

Guy, J A: *My Heart Is My Own: The Life of Mary, Queen of Scots* (HarperCollins, 2004).

Hartley, Christopher: *Fyvie Castle* (National Trust for Scotland, 1996).

Marshall, Rosalind K: *Queen Mary's Women: female relatives, servants, friends and enemies of Mary, Queen of Scots* (John Donald, 2006).

Slade, H Gordon: *Fyvie Castle, Aberdeenshire, Scotland* (University of Aberdeen Special Collections, 1971-2001).

Wormald, Jenny: *Court, Kirk and Community: Scotland 1470–1625* (Edinburgh University Press, 2018).

More historical novels by Sue Lawrence

If you have enjoyed *The Green Lady*, you can read the author's other novels describing women of Scotland's past, whether real or fictional characters. Together, by weaving fact and fiction, they paint a picture of a fascinating past during which women were subjected to almost unimaginable injustices and hardships.

EDINBURGH 1732: It's the funeral of Rachel, the healthy, still-young wife of Lord Grange. Yet Rachel is alive and has been kidnapped by the man who falsified her death: her husband. Banished to a remote island exile, to a life of hardship, she can never be found. Gripping and dramatic, this story has been retold from the woman's own perspective.

When Rona and Craig buy a house in Edinburgh's Newhaven district, they plan to set it up as care home. But something isn't right. Back in the 1890s, young Jessie is sent to the Poorhouse and begins to discover secrets with dangerous future consequences. This is a captivating and eerie historical mystery set in Victorian Edinburgh and the twentieth century.